ALSO BY VALERIE TAYLOR

What's Not Said

What's Not True

PRAISE FOR THE *WHAT'S NOT* SERIES

FOR *WHAT'S NOT SAID* (BOOK ONE)

2021 Firebird Book Awards Winner: Romantic Comedy, Contemporary Novel, Chick Lit, and Marriage
2021 CIBA Chatelaine Book Awards First Place, Best in Category: Romance Fiction
2021 Literary Titan Book Awards Silver Winner
2021 Best Book Awards Finalist in Fiction: Literary and Women's Fiction
2021 American Fiction Awards Finalist in Women's Fiction
2021 International Book Awards Finalist in Fiction: Women's Fiction
2020 Canadian Book Club Awards Finalist in Fiction

"Taylor's dialogue is snappy and contemporary . . . A witty and often amusing marriage drama."
—Kirkus Reviews

"In this dramatic tale of love, lust, and lies, author Valerie Taylor crafts an entertaining and gripping story. . . . a shocking novel full of secrets, twists, and turns, but it also has elements of pure humor and deep love. If I had to pick one word to describe *What's Not Said*, it would be the word 'captivating.'"
—Readers' Favorite

"*What's Not Said* is highly recommended for women who look for not just stories of marital relationships, but the unexpected revelations that revolve around life purpose and the immortality of love."
—Midwest Book Reviews

"Overall, this was a wickedly fun read, and entirely engaging in its soap-opera-esque style of storytelling."
—Reedsy

"Taylor's debut is a mystery, a romance, and a tale about chance and coincidence. It's a book about secrets and lies and the elusive dream of a fairytale ending."
—BookTrib

FOR *WHAT'S NOT TRUE* (BOOK TWO)

"Valerie Taylor's prose is crystalline . . . she does not waste words, rather using them to create a tense nerve-shredder that offers full entertainment to readers. *What's Not True* is compelling, real, and utterly enjoyable."
—Readers' Favorite 5-star review

"*What's Not True* is an engaging story of love, honesty, tangled family relationships, jealousy, and ambition. . . . As a beach read and satisfying stand-alone sequel to *What's Not Said* . . . *What's Not True* expands upon many themes while staying true to the course of charting Kassie's emotional and romantic growth."
—Midwest Book Review

"This was a dramatic, comedic telenovela of a women's fiction about infidelity and fickle hearts . . . Overall, this was an enjoyable read, with spicy characters and drama galore."
—Reedsy

"*What's Not True* is a heartwarming story that would make a great beach read, filled with plot twists and interesting characters. This captivating and romantic story is anything but predictable."
—Literary Titan 5-Star review

What's Not Lost

What's Not Lost

A Novel

Valerie Taylor

Edited by Sara Walker
Cover design by Tabitha Lahr
Book design by Danna Mathias Steele

Published 2022

ISBN: 979-8-9865995-0-2 (paperback)
ISBN: 979-8-9865995-1-9 (ebook)

Library of Congress Control Number: 2022913096

For information, contact:
Aspetuck Publishing
159 High HL
Shelton, CT 06484

Printed in the United States of America

Dedicated to all those who dare to dream.

What do we live for, if it is not to make life less difficult for each other?

— George Eliot

To dare is to lose one's footing momentarily. Not to dare is to lose oneself.

— Søren Kierkegaard

Chapters

Prologue

Black is not my favorite color. My mom should've warned everyone not to wear black yesterday when they came to the house. I much prefer blues and grays. Sometimes yellow works, but then that would clash with my handsome orangish-and-white mane.

Though the sun blazes high in the pale-blue sky on this Wednesday in late July, I'm a cool cat living in Newton, a suburb of Boston, with Kassie O'Callaghan—my mom. I'm home alone, again, as usual. But I'm staying out of trouble as I'm on a reconnaissance mission.

Won't you come along with me?

My favorite plaything is missing. One day, my mom tossed him across the room saying, "Go get Puss!" Was Puss a new kitty about to crash my pad? Nope. Puss is a navy-blue-and-silver toy with eight paws, twice as many as I have, and smells minty and crinkles when I punch or chew him. I love him so much I could just lick him for hours.

So far in my search for Puss, I've stretched my white mitts under each piece of furniture in the dozen rooms in this house, and I've come up empty-pawed.

Seems we're both lost.

I think I'll skulk into a room where humans sometimes sit and talk or, in my mom's case, curl up with something she calls a "book." I love cozying up to her when she does that. She calls this the "family room." Not sure why? I spend many of my afternoons in here spying critters running freely outside, wishing they were my playmates. But, alas, I'm an indoor kitty. So Puss is the next best thing.

But where is he?

How about this chair I sometimes nap in? It doesn't smell citrusy like Mom, and it moves up and down when a human sits in it. Eureka! Not Puss, but paydirt, sort of. I found two furry gray toys with long tails. One by one, I whack them onto the floor. *I'll hide them later.*

All this search and rescue is making me hungry. *Time for lunch.* As she always does before she leaves the house and goes who knows where, my mom left me something to eat in the room where clothes arrive so stinky they make my whiskers twitch and depart smelling like something I'd love to roll around in before taking one of my ten required daily naps.

Hmm. There's a closet here, especially for my toys. Why didn't I check this out first? Every Friday, a female human who doesn't live here gathers my toys and tosses them in a wicker basket on the floor of the closet. When my mom opens the door, I scurry in either to rescue my toys or hide those I don't want anyone to touch. I think it's a game. Not sure any human would agree.

I'll poke at the door first with my right paw. It shimmies but doesn't open. Let me try the other paw. Nothing. Maybe if I raise my haunches and slam into it? *Whack!* Still the door won't open. My cute white button nose alone can't decipher if Puss is in there. I'll have to wait until Mom gets home and ask her to open it for me.

I worship Kassie. She's my human. She tells her play pals she chose me from the other kitties at the orphanage, but the truth is, I picked her. I was surprised, though, to discover when she brought me to this house that I'd be sharing her with another human. She calls him Mike when he's home and Bastard when he's not.

Mike Bastard (MB, for short) seems to ignore me unless Kassie isn't around, and I meow at him until he gets the message it's chow time. Over the years, MB and I have learned to coexist. I never chew his socks or pee where I shouldn't. As much as kittenly possible, I try to avoid him when Kassie isn't here. Once in a while, we exchange sounds, and then I slip away and curl up in friendlier and cozier places.

Okay, now I'm frustrated. So let's check out the room where humans eat whatever they eat, which couldn't be as lip-smacking good as the meal I just devoured.

With my full belly, the bay-window shelf looks inviting. I'll look for Puss later, perhaps whenever Kassie shows up again. I'm not worried. She'll help me find him!

I think I'll swat this curtain aside so I can curl up and bask in the warmth of the early afternoon sun before it disappears and shows up again in the backyard. Just what the kitty doctor would order, if asked. Especially given the horrifying morning I just had.

Wasn't yesterday distressing enough? Who were all those humans in black? I had a hard time decoding one from another, except for the few I identified through my highly tuned olfactory skills. Thinking I'd at least know MB, I searched for his voice among all the murmurs, but I couldn't hear him at all. Maybe he doesn't like black either.

And even though he wasn't here, for some reason Kassie called him just Mike.

Oh well, it's time for a mini-mani-pedi. Mini because I only have rear claws. Chewing is a nervous habit I picked up years ago in the orphanage I lived at before Kassie adopted me.

As I bathe my magnificent coat, I think about the humans in black who were here yesterday and hope they have one of those sticky thingamabobs like the one I've seen Kassie roll along her clothes each day.

My fur sheds like a blizzard, which I kind of like, because then I'm never forgotten.

I love rubbing Kassie's calves, walking in a circle on her lap, sniffing her pillowcase. I adore claiming her chaise lounge as mine even after she moved it from that big room with the bed that's toasty and sways when I prance across it to the room with a smaller bed that's cold and stiff.

Across the back of the chaise lounge, Kassie keeps something she calls her mother's "multicolored afghan," which makes my highly advanced brain just about explode out my cute little ears I love to have scratched. The only afghan I ever knew was a hound who shared air, space, and attention with me at the place where I lived before those humans dumped me off at the orphanage. They called the hound Bruno, which kind of fit because he was way bigger than me.

Dumber than dog shit, though, and white, not multicolored.

Perhaps those humans kept Bruno because he didn't shed as much as I did. I wonder if they would've kept me if they'd known about the sticky roller thingy.

Nevertheless, the multicolored afghan seems to follow me everywhere. One day about a year ago, I looked all over the house for Kassie. Up the stairs, down the stairs, in the showers. When I curled up in my cozy bed in the kitchen to wait, the shiny things that hummed, sizzled, beeped, and swished helped me nod off for a good snooze. Surely she'd show up when it was feeding time.

But Kassie went missing for a while. I waited, but she didn't come home. Living with MB was not how I dreamed of spending the rest of my cat years, but I tried to accept this new living arrangement. Just shows I'm as adaptable as I am loose-limbed.

One night Annie showed up at the house. I recognized her as a playmate of Kassie's. She's a pretty human, but not as pretty or fruity-smelling as my mom.

Suddenly, I heard Annie and MB mention my name, so I scurried up the stairs to the chaise lounge, thinking I'd be safe there. Before I could say "I have claws and I'm not afraid to use them," MB wrapped me in a fluffy white towel and shoved me in the same cage Kassie had brought me home in from the orphanage. Fearing MB was taking me back there, I yowled until my throat got sore and I direly needed water.

Annie placed me next to her in a bigger cage that moved. She talked to me softly and sang about an octopus that wanted to wrap its arms around me and eat me. Though I liked listening to her voice because she reminded me of Kassie, I knew what she sang was a lie. Puss would never eat me. Thinking of that now makes me miss Puss even more.

Before I knew what was happening, the multicolored afghan and I flew into the air, landing in Kassie's arms. I was in kitty heaven and forgave her for leaving me with MB.

We ate and slept at Annie's for a while. I kind of liked it there. After a few sunrises and sunsets, another human showed up for dinner one night. He smelled yummy, like the French toast Kassie often made on Sunday mornings. Kassie must have thought so too, because she kept sniffing his neck and licking his lips.

A week or so ago, Kassie rolled up the multicolored afghan, and we moved out of Annie's and back into this house. I expected MB to welcome us home, but he was replaced with the French toast guy—my new competition. I heard her call him Christopher.

How about that? She named him after me!

Topher, July 2018

The Mourning After

"You're not gonna wear your father's boxers, are you?"

"He's not my father, remember?"

"Of course I do. Habit."

For the last year, six words—*an affair with my husband's son*—had rocked her world. Now she needed to replace that endless looping tape with five incomprehensible words:

My fiancé's ex-girlfriend is pregnant.

In either case, Kassie was the odd man—odd woman—out. And in both cases, she was the *step*mom. Always the bridesmaid, never the bride, as the saying goes.

Swoosh. Kassie lifted one eyelid, rolled over, and touched something peculiar, unfamiliar. Not the warm skin she expected, but smooth silk. Not the sheets. Not her nightgown—it lay draped across the foot of the waterbed. Then a vision from the night before hit her: Chris rummaging through Mike's armoire, pulling out a pair of emerald-green silk boxer shorts, and snapping off the price tag.

He'd chastised her for referring to Mike as his father. She rolled her eyes, asking for forgiveness. She'd need more than six hours to process the results of the paternity test that confirmed the husband she just buried was not her fiancé's father.

"God knows where he got them. Not from me," she said under her breath.

"Maybe Karen," Chris said, stepping into the boxers and sliding them over his well-toned swimmer's bottom.

Kassie ignored his remark. The last thing she wanted to do was to get into a kerfuffle about his mother just before slipping into bed. However, if there was ever a reason to make waves, his wearing boxer shorts to bed would be as good a cause as any. In all their time together, that night was the first time he'd worn anything to bed. He always slept au naturel with her. She shrugged it off. There's a first time for everything.

They spooned without talking much before she dozed off. No sex that night. It was unusual for them not to get it on, to skip a night, now that they were back together after their year apart.

Kassie chalked it up to exhaustion, to the events of the day. The entire day—Mike's funeral, the reception at the house, the revelation that Charlie Gaines was Chris's real father, and oh, the unexpected guest.

Swoosh. She moaned. At that blissful moment between sleep and wakefulness when morning's reality exposes itself, she recognized the source of the sound. A toilet, flushing. But Chris snoozed beside her. Who then?

Ah, right. Lexi. Lovely, lusty, leggy Lexi. Chris's "friend" from San Francisco who'd become a funeral crasher when she knocked on the door Tuesday evening after Mike's burial.

Surprise! No one had shouted it, but Kassie supposed the few close friends who'd lingered to help clean up following the repast must have said it to themselves. How could they not? Kassie did.

Was it just a week ago Chris announced Lexi, the woman he shagged apparently once too often while he and Kassie were on a "break," planned to visit them in Boston?

"Why would Lexi want to visit us?" Kassie had asked. "Seems odd, don't you think?"

Chris shrugged her off, saying it never occurred to him to ask.

"You're such a guy."

"Well, there is that."

Then all hell broke loose. The hospital called. Mike was dead. A heart attack. Chris called Lexi and left her a message, so he said. *Don't come.* Too much going on. He and Kassie had just returned from Paris and, with Mike dying, he'd be busy managing affairs at Ricci and Son. Her visit could wait, would have to wait. They'd love to see her when life calmed down.

Calmed down? How much time would Kassie and Chris need to calm down and sort through what was true and what was not? For the better part of a year, Kassie reeled with the idea of Chris being her husband's long-lost son. She was beside herself with joy at the results of the paternity test. Now it was Chris's turn to come to grips with his true parentage. Once it was revealed yesterday that Mike couldn't be Chris's father, Karen admitted she'd two-timed Mike when they were in college with none other than Charlie. In a flash, Chris discovered his real father was Charlie Gaines, the man who'd adopted him at birth.

Now, with a whole new origin story for Chris and Kassie to absorb, the last thing they needed was one more family drama. So, when Lexi showed up on her doorstep, Kassie assumed she either hadn't gotten Chris's message or ignored it. It didn't take a PhD in women's health to realize Lexi's visit couldn't wait much longer. Time was of the essence. Lexi looked as though she only had a few more months before her condition would prevent her from flying coast to coast.

Kassie must've lost her mind. Was it the breaking news that Chris was going to be a father, or too much pinot grigio, that caused her to offer Lexi the spare bedroom for the night? She'd be more comfortable there than at a hotel.

"Oh no, I can't impose. I don't want to interfere," Lexi said, rubbing her palm across her middle. When she slipped Chris the key to her rental car so he could fetch her luggage out of the back seat, Kassie bit her lip, second-guessing her spur-of-the-moment hospitality.

"One night can't hurt, right?" Chris galloped out the door, just as Lexi asked.

Now wide-eyed, Kassie couldn't fall back asleep with a wash of daylight peeking through the edge of the curtains and bouncing off the wall. *Get up. You've got a houseguest.*

She untwisted her ankles from the sheets and wiggled her body out of the waterbed, trying not to wake up Chris. He should get some rest, even if she couldn't. Leaning over the brass headboard, she touched the dreamcatcher for good luck. She snatched underwear out of her bureau and slipped on the oversized T-shirt that hung on the bathroom doorknob.

Topher, who moved when Kassie moved, jumped off the bed after a lengthy stretch and a good morning mewl. *Time for breakfast!* He followed her downstairs, close on her heels. She clung to the handrail and let him pass. Once at the bottom, he romped his way to the kitchen.

Kassie expected to see Lexi at the table, waiting for Kassie to wait on her, like Chris seemed to do. Of course she would. Rarely did they have overnight guests, especially not pregnant ones. And her mother had brought Kassie up to be mannerly, a fine lady: a hostess with the mostest.

But her mostly reliable intuition failed. No Lexi.

Kassie carried an arrangement of seafoam-blue-and-cream hydrangeas from the oak kitchen table to the dining room, away from Chris and his allergies. Picking through a bowl of bananas, apples, and oranges sitting on the counter, she tossed the fruit that had seen better days. She moved two oblong Tupperware containers of baked goods from the counter near the stove to the table.

She peered into the stainless steel side-by-side refrigerator. Each shelf and drawer bulged to near overcapacity. There were plenty of leftovers from the post-funeral spread to feed the three of them. Or was it four, if she counted the baby? She could whip up something Lexi could handle, no matter what her food restrictions might be.

Topher pawed her left leg, sending Kassie his typical *Feed me first* message.

After she tried to wipe fingerprints off the refrigerator, she filled Topher's food and water bowls, and in lockstep with him, she carried them to the mudroom off the kitchen.

"What's that stench?" Kassie lugged four black trash bags out to the garage. She made a mental note to crown Chris the Titan of Trash, especially since she'd be heading to Paris in five weeks and wouldn't be around to do that chore herself.

How extraordinary, she thought as she sat at the kitchen table with her hands wrapped around a cup of English Breakfast tea too hot to even sip. For all the years she wanted a baby with Mike, the day after she lowered him into the ground, there was a woman upstairs with a child growing in her belly. Chris's child. Her fiancé's child. That would make her an honest-to-goodness stepmother—a moniker she shed for less than an hour yesterday, after agonizing

for the last year that she'd had an affair with her husband's son for
more than five.

Good grief! Here we go again.

Kassie found a small lined pad in the built-in kitchen desk.
Water gurgling through the pipes in the walls from upstairs meant
someone was up, showering. Better get a move on.

She drew three narrow columns and labeled them *Paris, R&S,
Lexi*. When she did this exercise before Mike's funeral on Tuesday,
there were only two columns—the first two, which were solved
yesterday after her final farewell to him. Or so she thought.

The plan had four components. Kassie would take the temporary nine-month assignment as acting managing director for the
Paris office of Calibri Marketing Group. Chris would co-manage
Ricci and Son with Bill Mahoney, Mike's long-time loyal colleague.
Within a year, she'd return to Boston and marry Chris. She'd resign
from Calibri and take the helm of Ricci and Son, the company she
inherited. Just as Mike had stipulated in his will.

Her phone announced a text from Annie. **U still going to
Paris?**

Kassie shook her head and flipped her phone facedown on
the placemat. Leave it to her best friend to ask the burning question. She'd get back to Annie later when she had an answer. At that
moment, she hadn't a clue.

All she knew was in a bedroom above slept a woman who
had the power to sabotage her long-held dream of achieving professional success and personal happiness on her own terms, not
someone else's. What choices did she have to make it so?

In the Paris column, she drew a heart, as in she really loved
this option. If she turned down the opportunity of a lifetime, she'd
have to resign from her job at Calibri now. No doubt about it. She
could still take the mantle at Mike's company and transform it into
her image, not his. Yet, she'd earned the Paris assignment on her

own merits; the other, Mike bestowed on her so he could die with a clear conscience—payback for the emotional pain he'd caused her throughout their thirty-year marriage. Even in death, Mike held the upper hand.

In the Ricci and Son column, she wrote *Yes*, not because she'd choose that role first, but because it was inevitable. Unless something unexpected happened, at some point she'd take the reins and lead the firm until she retired some fifteen years down the road.

Kassie drew a triangle in the third column. No one had foreseen Lexi, this pregnant fly in the ointment, not even Kassie with all her psychic powers. How would this sticky situation change her plans, their plans? It wasn't just Lexi's predicament, it was Chris's. And if it was his dilemma, it was Kassie's as well.

If Lexi's due date was January, as she claimed, Kassie would be in Paris then and still not married to Chris. More than likely, he'd take paternity leave to be with Lexi in San Francisco, at least for a time. With Kassie in Paris and Chris away from the office, would Bill be able to manage Ricci and Son alone? What's more, would Kassie and Chris's relationship endure or succumb to the strain?

"Good morning, sunshine." Chris kissed the top of her head, giving her ponytail a tug. "You have that faraway look. Paris, perhaps?"

"Funny you should say that. We need to talk, don't you think?"

A door closed above them. Their eyes met.

"Later." Chris tilted his head, indicating Lexi would soon join them. *Bing. Bang. Boom.*

"What the—?" Chris dashed toward the front hallway, Kassie close behind. Topher scurried past them in the opposite direction, his ears flattened, his orange fuzzy tail straight up.

Lexi lay splayed at the foot of the stairs, her body on the ceramic tile, cushioned by her left arm. Her legs crisscrossed, resting on the bottom step.

"Oh my God, Lexi, don't move!" Chris shouted. He knelt and placed one hand on her shoulder, shoving her messenger bag and sandals aside with the other. "What happened? Did you trip over the cat?"

Tears streaked down Lexi's face. "I'm not sure. It happened so fast," she moaned.

Chris glared at Kassie. "Don't just stand there, KO. Call 911."

"Her leg?" Kassie murmured, taking a step back toward the kitchen.

Trembling, Chris whispered, "The baby."

2

The Cat's Meow

Tumbling ass over teakettle down the center hallway stairs of Kassie O'Callaghan's gingerbread house in a Boston suburb that Wednesday morning wasn't how Alexandra Moore intended to get what she'd traveled three thousand miles for. She wanted Christopher Gaines. Full stop. Not his sympathy.

When she crashed in a heap on the cold tile floor, she was shocked, embarrassed, and in excruciating pain, in that order. Pain emanated throughout her body, especially her left leg. In a flash, she feared she'd need a new game plan, assuming she didn't miscarry.

"What happened?" Chris shouted.

Blaming it on the damn cat would be as good a pretext as any. Who names a cat after their secret lover, anyway?

"Topher. Cute, eh? Short for Christopher," he'd told Lexi six years ago when his ridiculous affair with a married woman who lived on the other side of the country quickly morphed from a one-night stand in Venice, Italy, to a regularly scheduled meetup around the good old USA.

Seriously? Lexi got it on the first note. She didn't need an expanded definition. No reason to rub it in that her relationship with him was convenience-based, simply FWB.

"Friends with benefits," she'd say, sobbing all alone the mornings after their weekly Thursday-night trysts, long before Kassie arrived and went to the head of the class.

A year ago, Lexi had shifted into high gear after Chris discovered Kassie was his stepmother, of all things, and he and Kassie had called it quits. Lexi schemed to make him forget Kassie and focus his full attention on her, even long distance. If it worked for Kassie and him, Lexi would make sure it worked for her.

Slowly but surely, she sensed he was coming around. Especially when he agreed to a week's vacation on the romantic Greek islands this past spring.

"Let's do it before it gets so hot there you could fry bacon on a rock alongside the road," he'd said.

Good idea. If she was going to sweat, Chris would be the cause, not the result of mercury rising.

All the online travel sites featured Santorini as one of the loveliest destinations in the world for lovers. Santorini, the one pictured on all the calendars—white buildings, blue domes on top of deep-brown cliffs overlooking the sparkling-blue Aegean Sea.

Obviously, those travel writers didn't know Chris. If they did, they would have warned her he may have been on the same island and in the same bed as she, but his mind was on a completely different continent.

From the time they stepped off the ferry, and the taxi whisked them up the switchbacks to their bungalow resort in Santorini, Chris blabbered on and on and on about how Kassie would love it there. This was not in Lexi's plan. After they checked in and found an empty table in a not-too-crowded café with a view to die for, Lexi discovered courage in a glass of Greek wine.

"Chris, can I ask a favor?" She reached for his hand and looked squarely into his baby blues.

"Of course, anything."

"No more about Kassie, okay? She gave you up. I never did."

"Right. You have my undivided attention. I won't mention Kassie again."

Of course, he kept his promise, which was just like him. But for the rest of the week, Lexi wished she could read the notes he scribbled in his little red pocket notebook every place they visited and dined. Had he suddenly taken up travel writing as a sideline?

Then there was the incident when he bought a chain with a silver Meander pendant hanging on it. Was it really for his mother as he claimed? Maybe so, as it symbolized unity and eternity. Why buy only one? After all, didn't he have two mothers? Karen Copperman, his birth mother, and Sarah Gaines, the woman who'd adopted him and raised him into the man he was. Or did he have three mothers, if you included Kassie?

Lexi decided not to press him on that topic. If nothing else, doing so avoided a potential explosion like the volcano they were visiting on their last full day in paradise.

"I'm thinking I should move to Boston. Time to take us to the next level, wouldn't you agree?" Lexi put it all out there following their customary afternoon delight.

At first, Chris said nothing. Rather, he left her sitting among the rumpled bed sheets and walked out onto their veranda, overlooking the magnificent deep-blue waters dotted with too many cruise ships to count. When he removed his phone from his pocket, Lexi expected him to take a picture. From inside, she couldn't tell if he was scrolling through his messages or his camera roll. She watched him study the phone, place it on his heart, and then put it in his pocket.

Moments later, he returned and sat next to her. He held her hand and gazed not into her eyes but at the floor. "I'm so sorry,

Lexi, so deeply sorry if I led you on. I thought we had an under-standing. This trip and you are terrific, but a mistake."

"A mistake? A rather expensive mistake, wouldn't you say?" Lexi stood to face him, to be taller than he, if that were possible.

"Let me explain. I care about you, Lexi. Just not the way you want. An ongoing *thing* isn't in the cards. I'll always care, you know that."

"Fine. Go back to your cougar stepmother, if she'll have you. She's probably replaced you with another sweet young boytoy by now."

That stung. She regretted it as soon as the words flew out of her mouth as she headed for the bathroom. She slammed the door and glared at the woman in the mirror. Why was she pushing Chris toward Kassie when she wanted him for herself?

They spent the rest of the afternoon saying goodbye to Greece separately and apart, cooling down. They joined back-up for the last dinner of their trip, and after two bottles from a Greek winery named Gataki—the most exquisite wine she'd ever swirled—they shed their clothes before reaching their bungalow and had unbelievable sex on the chaise lounge alongside their private pool. Could "makeup sex" heal the rift she'd created? Time would tell.

On the flight back to the States, they said nothing about the little chat they'd had or their last roll in the hay. As she started for the gate for her connecting flight from Boston to San Francisco, Chris clutched her arm, hugged her, and thanked her for pointing out the obvious about Kassie. He'd think about it and be in touch.

As usual, Chris was a man of his word. A week later, he called, announcing he decided to give it one more college try with Kassie. He'd learned from her best friend, Annie, that the two of them were planning a trip to Venice in July. So he and Annie cooked up a little surprise for Kassie. As she fought back tears, the only thing Lexi could bring herself to say besides "Fuck you" was, "Not

Venice, Chris. Paris." Venice held too much history, too much glue between Kassie and him, and Lexi still ached to break that bond. Paris might do that. She knew from her online research, Paris in July was not the romantic haven Americans believed. Too hot, too crowded.

She'd all but given up on Chris until one morning back home in San Francisco, Mother Nature took her own vacation.

Lexi knew Topher had nothing to do with her fall. Standing at the top of the stairs, she spotted him curled up in a rather large orange-and-white ball on a plush beige cat bed near the front door. A stream of morning sun sliced across his back, his white paw protecting his eyes. He had no designs on her, nor she on him. Perhaps, until now.

As she left the bedroom that morning, breakfast was on her mind. At least she hoped to nibble on something and keep it down. There should be leftover bread from yesterday's spread. Nerves had consumed her the day before—flying in from San Francisco, barging in after a funeral, breaking the news in front of Chris's fiancée that he was going to be a father. Not much nourishment traveled through her or to her baby on Tuesday. And the ongoing nausea in the middle of the night didn't help much either. Whoever invented the term *morning sickness* must have been a man.

Toast with a smidge of grape jelly. That'd be the ticket. Too early in the day for a baked potato. Later, maybe. Lexi was sure once Kassie saw the dark bags under her eyes, she'd bake bread for toast if there wasn't a fresh loaf in the cupboard. Ms. Hospitality 2018 opened her home to her the night before. Breakfast came along with the bed, didn't it?

She carried her sandals and her phone in her right hand and slipped her half-opened messenger bag over her left shoulder as she began her descent to the first floor. She thought she'd made it down at least three stairs when hot sweat swelled from her core up to her face. Chris's voice in the distance faded. The stairway swayed. Her legs wobbled. The entryway chandelier dimmed from view.

Lexi was down for the count.

And then. There he was. Those dazzling blue eyes. Standing— no leaning—over her. "Don't move," Chris said. "Lexi, don't move." He'd said her name. Despite being sprawled on the floor helpless, she hungered for his calm, comforting voice.

Dazed, confused, and hurting like hell, when he asked if Topher had tripped her up, she pooh-poohed that idea. Above her, Chris and Kassie exchanged sound bites. "Her leg. The baby." And that warning again, "Don't move," this time from Kassie, wearing a white cotton oversized T-shirt with Venice spelled out in sparkling silver sequins. Talk about adding insult to injury.

Lexi gulped and did as she was told, for once. She was in no position to argue. The initial shock of the impact with the tile floor must have worn off, as the stabbing pain in her left leg sharpened.

Kassie disappeared, leaving Lexi alone with Chris for the first time since she arrived the evening before. As he lowered himself to the floor in a lotus position, she inhaled his familiar tart apple smell. Whereas some fragrances made her retch, his did not then and never would. He gently lifted her head onto his thigh and brushed her ash-blond hair away from her eyes. He touched two fingers to his lips and then her forehead. "Help will be here soon."

Kassie returned. "Take this," she said, bending down to hand something to Chris. Lexi glimpsed a gondola and an Eiffel Tower pendant swinging from the chain around Kassie's neck. Had he not given her the Meander pendant after all?

"How's she doing?" Kassie asked as Chris placed a cool, damp cloth on Lexi's head and wiped the tears off her cheeks with his fingers.

Sirens blared to an abrupt halt in front of the house. Chris sat still. "Get the door, KO, now."

KO. Why did he call her that? Her initials, of course. He'd never given Lexi a pet name. LM didn't quite roll off the tongue, and neither did AM. He could've thought of something, clever as he was. She'd have to work on that. Maybe if she came up with a nickname for him? Daddy? Pappy? Old Man?

Did forty-four make him an old man? Probably not. She'd think of something and try it on for size with him when the time was right.

Chris stayed on the floor with Lexi as Kassie flew out the door. Lexi picked up certain words among the murmurs. "Fell … leg … no, we didn't move her."

The front door swung open as Kassie accompanied two emergency professionals. Paramedics, Lexi figured. Chris started to scooch back but was ordered not to move. He stayed in place, touched her shoulder and said, "Just breathe. I'm here. I've got you."

But he didn't have her, not for long anyway. Two more EMT-type chaps walked in wearing navy shorts and white Izod-type shirts, bringing in the July heat and humidity with them. They filled the hallway, spilling into both the dining and living rooms. They looked at each other, their eyes widening and shoulders shrugging.

"Excuse me, folks," one Izod said. "If you don't mind me asking? We were here a couple of weeks ago. Right, guys?" He glanced at the others for confirmation. "But it was for a fellow who had a heart attack. Right, guys?"

"Chris and I were in Paris last time you were here. We're engaged." Kassie held up her left hand. "Don't know where *she* was." She pointed at Lexi. "That last guy you saved? He's dead. He was my husband. We buried him yesterday. Lovely funeral. You should've been there." Kassie rocked from one foot to the other.

"Sorry to hear that, ma'am."

Kassie kept right on going. "Thank you. Just so you know, Lexi isn't having a heart attack. At least I don't think she is. I'm not a doctor. But she *is* pregnant. So, there is that. He's the father, which makes me the *stepmother*. Not wicked, mind you."

Lexi glowered at Chris, begging him to jump in and tell Kassie to put a sock in it. Did she always make things about her? He pursed his lips, and his eyes bulged, seeming to search for a safety zone, but he remained silent.

"I see. At least I think I see," said the fellow with a clipboard. "Well, can anyone tell me what happened here?" He looked at Chris and then at Lexi.

All heads lowered toward Lexi. "I fell over the cat."

3

Twin Peaks

Before Chris had a chance to ask one of the EMTs if she thought the baby would be okay, they stabilized Lexi's leg, lifted her onto the stretcher, and wheeled her out the door to the ambulance.

"My bag," she bellowed just before they closed and latched the rear doors. Kassie was one step ahead. She shoved the contents that had scattered across the hallway, including Lexi's phone, into her bag and headed for the driveway.

"I'll take that. I'm going with her," Chris said.

"You can't. They won't let you. That much I know. My mother, remember?"

"Follow us," said one of the first responders as he grabbed Lexi's bag, climbed into the driver's seat, and started the engine. "Boston Clinic. Emergency room." And off they went, lights flashing, siren silent.

"Oh fuck! Her car's blocking mine." Chris shook his head and bent over, his hands clutching his knees. "I put the key back in her bag last night."

Kassie rushed into the house and returned faster than Wonder Woman with her car key. "Here, take mine. I'll meet you there. I need to get dressed."

"Right. Thanks. I don't think she'll sue, do you?" Chris snatched the key and checked his pockets for his wallet and phone.

"Sue? Sue who? Me? Why?"

"Topher. She tripped over Topher. You heard her."

"Not sure she can. We'll cross that bridge—"

"What if she loses the baby?" Chris ran his fingers through his hair. "She'd sue then. You would …"

"You're getting ahead of yourself, aren't you?" Kassie touched her finger to the corner of her right eye.

Chris saw Kassie's eyes glassing up. "I'm sorry, babe. Lexi's pregnancy must bring back memories, huh?"

"Ya think? You better get going. Boston Clinic. Can you believe? Here we thought we were done with that place."

He pulled her close, hugged her tight. He was gone.

This wasn't his first trip to Boston Clinic. Chris visited Mike when they returned from Paris and then he accompanied Kassie when the hospital summoned her to take care of Mike's personal belongings the morning he died. She was his legal next of kin, after all, even though everyone thought Chris was his son at the time.

In an unexpected turn of events, the paternity test he'd taken the day Mike passed away proved Michael Ricci was not his biological father. When Chris announced the results to the mourners at the house after the funeral, his world turned upside down.

As it turned out, his real father was Charles Gaines, the man who adopted him at birth and raised him with his wife, Sarah. Evidently, his birth mother, Karen Copperman, prowled around during her college days, having shacked up with both Mike and

Charlie on more than one occasion. Not at the same time, of course, but close enough for her not to know which of the guys had gotten her pregnant.

Since Charlie was already engaged to Sarah—Karen's sorority sister—she opted to pin fatherhood on Mike, for whom she claimed undying love. But since Mike wasn't Jewish, Karen's parents put the kibosh on any long-term deal between them. Lucky for her, Sarah offered to adopt baby Chris, all the while suspecting that her soon-to-be husband could in fact be the baby's father.

Apparently, Karen and Charlie believed no one needed to know the truth about the affair they had in college *until* the truth needed to be known. Apparently, *until* was yesterday.

Chris wasn't surprised Kassie literally jumped for joy, relieved she hadn't actually had a five-year bicoastal affair with her husband's son. Being unfaithful was one thing, being in love with her husband's son was quite another. Loathing the very idea, Kassie insisted, despite Chris's protestations, they split up when the connection was discovered the year before.

Now with the results of the paternity test yesterday confirming that Mike was not Chris's father, the symbolic cross Kassie carried for the past year disappeared for good. Suddenly, Chris was just another guy whose connection to Mike was distant and innocent.

While the results of the test freed Kassie from her nightmare, Chris faced his own dilemma. He needed to redraw his family tree, grow accustomed to who was who, and figure out who he was. Reprogramming his lineage should've been quick and easy. After all, to him Charlie was *Dad* for over forty years, long before he ever heard the name Michael Ricci.

Yet that drama was only half of what threw Chris's world into disarray that day. Lexi's uninvited arrival on Kassie's doorstep was not only ill-timed but also rudely orchestrated.

A baby? What the hell? Must've happened while they were in Greece. Throughout their on-again, off-again affair over the years, Chris assumed Lexi took birth control pills. Getting someone pregnant was something he worried about when he was a teenager, not as an adult. Then again, they'd never talked about it. Not very adult behavior, he admitted late last night as he and Kassie got ready for bed.

"Why is it that men only think with their dicks?" Kassie asked.

"We were away, and you weren't in the picture. What do you expect?"

"I expect this will be complicated. Don't worry, it's nothing we can't handle."

"It's just a baby," Chris whispered as they'd drifted off to sleep.

Chris parked Kassie's car in the hospital garage and rushed into the lobby, not taking the time to find out where the emergency wing was located. Lining up behind three people ahead of him at the main lobby desk, he shifted from one foot to the other, looking more like he had to find the men's room than the emergency room. And then he was saved.

"Hey, Chris, what are you doing here?"

He turned to his left as he felt a slight touch on his arm. "Oh Cecilia, great! Someone who knows their way around! Where's the ER?"

"You okay? Are you sick?"

"Not me. Lexi. She fell down the stairs and the ambulance brought her here."

"Come with me," Cecilia said, grabbing his hand and hustling him down the double-wide hallway. "Who the hell is Lexi?"

"Alexandra Moore. An ex of mine, from San Francisco." Chris rushed to keep up with her.

"*An* ex? How many exes do you have? San Fran? What's she doing here?"

"Right. You left before she arrived and dropped a bomb last night." Chris ignored part one of her question.

"What bomb?"

"She's pregnant. And it's mine."

The elevator doors opened, and Cecilia and Chris joined a group of visitors and hospital staff.

"Holy guacamole." Cecilia tilted her head toward the right as they stepped out of the elevator.

"You probably didn't hear that Mike wasn't my father."

Cecilia halted her quick strides. "Wait. You found out you knocked up someone named Lexi *and* that Mike isn't your father after I left the house yesterday? Damn it, I missed all the fun."

"Not so much fun."

Cecilia picked up the pace again, leading and weaving their way past meal carts and stretchers, some empty, some occupied.

"You say she fell? Is this baby of yours hurt? Falls can be ghastly. Deadly, you know."

"Really, you think, deadly? Oh God, I hope not. Her leg looks bad."

"Well, you're in the number one hospital in the city for orthopedists. We've got the best and the brightest."

"You think?"

"I know so." Cecilia halted and faced Chris. "Did you know, in the U.S. six million people break a bone each and every year? A good deal of them right here in the Boston metropolitan area. Wrists, ankles, collarbones, and legs. Many from falls, I suspect."

"I'm sure you're right." Chris raised his eyes and lifted his arms as if to say "Can we get a move on?"

Cecilia wasn't finished. "A lot of sports injuries," she continued. "Especially football, professional and otherwise. Wasn't someone at the house yesterday talking about their son breaking their arm playing lacrosse?"

"That was Bill. His son Leo. This past spring. He hopes to play this fall in college. Not sure about that. You two should meet." Chris panted.

"What's her name again?" Cecilia asked Chris as they arrived at the ER desk. She exchanged words with a fellow in scrubs, and she grabbed Chris's hand again. "This way."

As she pulled back the curtain, Cecilia asked Chris in full voice, "Where's Kassie? Shouldn't she be here?"

Lexi sat up in the bed, one leg under the covers, the other wrapped to a board.

"Oh Chris! Thank goodness you're here. Who's this?"

Chris introduced Cecilia to Lexi as a young lady whom Mike thought so highly of that he included her in his will. "Cecilia will join Ricci and Son as an intern whenever she's ready."

He introduced Lexi to Cecilia as a friend, an ex-colleague from San Francisco.

"And the father of my baby," Lexi said, just as the privacy curtain screeched open.

"Well, good morning, Cecilia," Dr. Alexander said. "I see you've met my new patient, Alexandra."

"Why, yes, Dr. Alexander, just now. Wait just a minute. What a coincidence! Dr. Alexander and Alexandra. I just love when that happens! Don't you?" Cecilia said to the doctor.

"Alexandra is the Greek goddess who comes to save warriors," the doctor said.

"Isn't that your job?" Chris attempted to swing the conversation back to the crisis at hand.

"Saving? No one needs saving here. Alexandra's leg needs repair. Dr. Sawyer will be here soon to discuss the best course of action under the circumstances. But no reason to worry. We're going to fix her up. I predict Alexandra will spend three to five days in the hospital and then the rest of her pregnancy at home."

Chris shot Lexi a little grin in support, not yet grasping the impact of this news.

Dr. Alexander turned to take his leave and hesitated. "And in case you all are wondering? Who wouldn't be? The uterus is a wonderful thing. See those monitors over there? The twins look just fine. So far."

Chris stepped back and grasped the curtain.

"Don't say a word of this to Kassie or anyone," Chris said to Cecilia, wagging his finger, ignoring the smile on Lexi's face.

"Who me? It's not my secret to tell," Cecilia said, backing out of the cubicle. "Nice meeting you, Alexandra. Looks like you've got some saving to do after all."

4

Moneybags

Some would say Karen Copperman had a one-track mind. She'd say she was just taking care of business. Her business.

Karen's first thought when she opened her eyes that Wednesday morning after Michael Ricci's funeral was not how much she missed him or even Charlie Gaines. After all, she was still Chris's mother no matter who his biological father was. Confirming that it was Charlie who impregnated her years ago, however, did make her tingle inside, especially because he was the last man she'd had sex with right there in that very bed just over a week ago.

She rolled onto her stomach and stretched out her arms, recalling Charlie flipping her into a similar position. Closing her eyes, she reveled in the memory of his weight upon her, his slow, deliberate moves.

Enough already. Enough fantasizing.

She had a real-world problem to solve. Since Mike died believing Chris was his son, surely he left something sizable in his will for him. Something beyond a small percentage of Ricci and Son, which only had value if there was a profit-sharing plan to accompany that bequeath or, perhaps, if they sold the company.

Job one was to find out what was in that will for Chris and do whatever she needed to do to get in his good graces.

As if Charlie read her mind, her phone pinged, announcing an incoming text message.

You up?

Barely. You?

Karen chuckled at the double meaning of her response.

She counted. On ten, Charlie called.

"Good morning, Daddy-o. A booty call so early in the day?"

"Sorry to disappoint you, Karen. Just checking in on the mother of my son. I fell asleep last night thinking about what our lives would've been like had we known I was the one who knocked you up. Have you given any thought to that?"

Karen slid to an upright position, propping two pillows behind her and getting control of her wits. Charlie failed to be her meal ticket when she got pregnant in college, but maybe he could make up for that now. After all, he was a lawyer.

"What are you saying? Would you have left Sarah and all her money at the altar and made an honest woman out of me?"

"Ha! You're assuming Sarah would have agreed to be my blushing bride if the truth of our affair had become common knowledge. She is a prideful woman, you know."

"Prideful and rich."

"There is that. Perhaps you'll come into some funds yourself with Mike's passing?"

Karen realized she hadn't the chance to tell Charlie about the menial stipend Mike had left her.

"I'm not really sure what Mike left me," Karen said, crossing her fingers and toes. She recalled Kassie explained clearly that Mike wanted Karen to continue to work at Ricci and Son. In addition, she'd receive a thousand dollars a month for five years, equivalent to what Mike had sent her after her husband's death in a skiing accident years before.

Charlie asked, "When will the will be read?"

"The will be *read* ..." Karen repeated, staring at the ceiling light. "I don't know when. How could I find out?"

Charlie explained that if she was in the will, as she probably was, the executor should invite her to the reading.

"Who do you think the executor is? Kassie? Fat chance she'd invite me, if that's the case."

"Usually not the spouse, and since they were getting a divorce, it's highly unlikely Kassie is the executor."

"How can I find out?"

"Our son, my dear. Ask Chris."

"Right. Gotta go."

"Wait a minute. We're heading back to Chicago tomorrow. We're having dinner with Chris and Kassie tonight. Want to join us?"

"You're kidding."

"I'm not. Could be an innocent, non-prying opportunity for you to find out what's going on with the will. And I'd love to see you."

Karen let out a deep sigh. "Okay, count me in. But don't tell them I'm coming."

"I'll text you the details."

"Great. I know just what I'll wear."

"Really? Panties are optional."

Disconnecting the call, she swung the sheets aside and jumped out of bed. What had seemed a mountain of a problem suddenly dissipated into a molehill.

She threw on capri jeans and a black T-shirt, donned her flip-flops, and jaunted across the street to the deli for coffee and a muffin. Now that she'd be spending more time at her apartment in Charlestown rather than at Mike's, she'd have to stock the pantry and buy some small appliances like, God forbid, a coffeemaker. Much to her chagrin, Karen figured she'd need to locate the closest Bed, Bath, & Beyond sooner rather than later.

As she paid for her breakfast with Mike's credit card, she realized how critical dinner that evening would be for her to get more money of her own. Convinced, of course, that once Kassie got a load of the next Visa bill, she'd cut her off for sure. She knew she'd do it to Kassie if the situation were reversed.

Sipping her caramel macchiato, Karen stared out the window of her living room. The boats in Boston Harbor already started their day. So too had Karen, shifting her mind into drive as she contemplated a strategy for dinner. She licked her fingers, rescuing the few crumbs left on the waxed paper wrapper of the blueberry muffin she didn't even remember eating. Recalibrating her relationship with Chris and Kassie from now on had to be her number one priority. What could she do to swing the scales to her advantage?

She thought about Charlie and the advice he could give her beyond the will, which seemed like little to nothing. Besides, he could be her FWB, couldn't he? As Chris's real father, he'd have logical reasons to visit Boston without Sarah if he really wanted to. Don't fathers and sons do things together? Even as adults?

Karen shook her head, doubting Charlie would be interested in an ongoing fling with her now that their relationship was public knowledge. And Charlie had his own priorities. His marriage was based on a mutual understanding. He was in it for the security; Sarah was in it for appearances, needing to look good among her artsy-fartsy philanthropes. Charlie was Sarah's trophy husband, and she wouldn't give him up for all the tea in the harbor.

Chewing her lip in an unusual moment of self-reflection, Karen realized she, too, almost had a trophy husband. But Michael

Ricci bit the dust before making that happen. That would have been the least he could've done after she'd given him one of her kidneys. She wondered if a day would go by that she wouldn't second-guess that decision; the lack of return on that investment would haunt her forever.

All she had left to show for what might have been was the necklace from Guy's and Dolly's Galleria of Jewels. She'd wear it to dinner that night, and when someone asked her about it, which they most certainly would, she could launch into a story about the day Michael Ricci had, indeed, asked her to be his wife.

Tossing the coffee cup and waxed paper into the trash can under the sink, Karen ambled to the hallway between the kitchen and living room, her eyes scanning the open area for the bag Guy and Dolly had given her at the funeral reception the day before. Not there. She canvassed the bedroom, then the bathroom, and the walk-in-closet, picking up the pace as she checked each room.

She grabbed her keys and hustled out to the parking garage, assuming with great confidence that it would be on the floor of the passenger seat. But she returned empty-handed and void of any idea where the bag and the evidence of Mike's commitment and love for her were hiding.

Slumping onto the couch, Karen buried her face in a throw pil- low, recreating in her mind what she'd done with the necklace. She knew she had it after the funeral when she was sitting in Kassie's office at the house while she was told at least she had a job at Ricci and Son going forward and a monthly stipend over a five-year period. At least between the two sums, she probably wouldn't have to move, although the apartment in Charlestown was quite expensive for a receptionist's salary. *Damn it. This was supposed to be temporary.*

She also recalled holding the bag, twisting it ever so slightly between her hands, as Chris revealed he wasn't Mike's biological son, and she and Charlie admitted they'd hooked up in college.

It was when Kassie summarily dismissed Sarah, Charlie, and her from Kassie's office so she and Chris could yuck it up that Karen must have put the bag on a table in the family room before picking up her purse to skedaddle out of there.

Crap. In order to make an emphatic statement about Mike's commitment to her, Karen had to retrieve the necklace. *I better not have lost it.*

Pacing the apartment, room to room and around again, Karen did the one thing she didn't want to do. She called the woman who had the necklace and held the key to her achieving a charmed life even without Michael Ricci.

5

Barefooted

After Chris left her standing barefooted in her T-shirt in an overgrown patch of grass at the top of her blacktop driveway, Kassie dug her toes in the dirt to stifle the flow of tears. Once they started, she feared they might never stop. Why was she acting this way? So not her. Usually, she let her alter ego express her inner emotions, for better or worse. That morning Bad Kassie was in hiding, leaving her id to fend for herself.

Was watching Chris back down the drive faster than a toddler with new Hot Wheels on his way to Lexi the source of her pending waterworks? Had the reality of Lexi's pregnancy finally set in? Was the green-eyed monster rearing its nasty head? Was she scared Lexi's fall would cause her to miscarry? Maybe a bit of each or all of the above. Or was it something else?

She tiptoed through the lawn back to the house, avoiding the flagstone path roasting in the late-July heat. She intended to take a quick shower and join Chris at the hospital. But when she grabbed her phone to take with her upstairs, she remembered the earlier message from Annie.

U still going to Paris?

Heading for her bedroom, Kassie swallowed her pesky tears. She didn't want to appear weak, out of control, if she could help it. Curling up on the carpet in a lotus position with her back propped against the waterbed frame, she reached out and touched her best friend forever.

Kassie's self-control didn't last long. As soon as Annie answered with "What took you so long?" the blubbering began.

"You'll never believe what happened," Kassie wailed, "… the hospital."

"You're in the hospital?"

"No, Annie, not me." Kassie sobbed, releasing all the pent-up emotion of the last week.

"Snap out of it, girlfriend. I can't help you if I can't understand what you're saying."

As if Annie had reached through the phone and slapped her face, Kassie straightened up and recounted the morning's events.

"So, you don't know if you're still going to Paris?"

"That's what you got from all that?"

"Well … are you going?"

"Of course, I'm going. Why wouldn't I?" Kassie waited for a supportive response that never came. She proceeded with a mix of defiance and doubt.

"Shouldn't I? Give me one good reason why I shouldn't."

"Well, I don't know. Maybe because the man you're planning to marry is having a baby with another woman."

"You think that should stop me from a commitment I've made?"

"Maybe you might want to stick around to protect your best interests?"

"Twenty-four hours ago, furthering my career and planning a wedding were my best interests. Chris's mistake shouldn't prevent me from doing what I want to do, need to do. His failure to protect his own best interests should not force me to alter my plans."

There was silence.

"Should it?"

Crickets.

"Come on, Annie. You're on my side, aren't you?"

"Always, sweetie. But after the dust settles, and you're on the other side of this hospital situation, I imagine you and your beau will need to sit down and figure this thing out."

Kassie chewed her thumbnail, shook her head, sighed, and felt her eyes watering, again.

"I thought I had this all figured out. Yesterday. I was happy. As happy as one can be after a funeral. Now this."

Ding-dong. Ding-dong.

"Shit. Someone's at the door. Call you later."

Kassie hotfooted it downstairs, one hand on the handrail, the other on her phone, ensuring she didn't follow in Lexi's footsteps.

"Guess it's Grand Central Station here this morning," she said out loud as she shooed Topher toward the living room and swung open the door without asking "Who's there?"

Three young men whose muscles rivaled Sylvester Stallone's, wearing tattered jeans, mud-crusted work boots, cheap sunglasses, and gray T-shirts with Carl's Landscaping in green lettering across their chests, stood with their mouths open, gawking.

"Good morning, Mrs. Ricci."

"Oh, it's you, Jimmy." She recognized the crew chief. She always wondered if the Boss on his cap signified his position or if it was a fashion statement.

"Call me, Kassie, please, I'm not Mrs. Ricci anymore. Mr. Ricci died earlier this week. You're a day late. We buried him yesterday. At a cemetery. Not in the backyard."

"Yes, so we heard. Sorry for your loss," Jimmy said. "Sorry. Sorry," Jimmy's crew—one fellow wearing a Red Sox cap and holding both a shovel and a rake, the other with a camouflage hat backwards carrying small garden tools in each hand—echoed Jimmy's condolences.

"Thank you," Kassie said, realizing her attempt at humor had fallen flat.

"You been to Venice?" the Red Sox fan asked.

She tugged at the front of the T-shirt and then the back, causing the front to shift up. She crossed her legs at the ankles. "What can I do for you?" Kassie reached for the door, hoping the conversation was near its end.

"Just wanted to make sure you wanted us to continue our landscaping services, with Mr. Ricci gone and all," Jimmy said.

Kassie laughed and waved her hand toward the front lawn. "Of course. Carry on! Do what you normally do."

"Will you be selling the house?" the fellow with the Red Sox hat, full of questions, asked.

Kassie snorted. "I think it's way too soon to make those kind of big decisions. I'll need some time."

Her cellphone buzzed. She excused herself and closed the door, expecting the call was from Chris, though it wasn't his ringtone. Hesitating, she answered anyway.

"Good morning, Kassie. It's Karen."

"Oh, hi."

"Can I speak to Chris? I tried his phone, but he didn't answer." As usual, Karen didn't give Kassie a chance to respond.

"Never mind. You'll do. You at home? I'm on my way over."

"Karen, I am, but don't. I won't be here."

"That's okay. Chris will be home, right?"

"No, he's at Boston Clinic," Kassie said, grimacing as soon as the words slipped out. She'd gone and done it: opened a dam she'd have to find a way to plug.

Karen launched into the normal questions someone would ask, starting with "I'm his mother, damn it—now don't you hold back on me."

Since Karen had left the funeral "after-party" after admitting Charlie was Chris's biological father, she missed meeting lovely Lexi from San Francisco in person, and thus was unaware that she would have a grandchild within five months, give or take.

Nevertheless, Kassie doubted she was the appropriate person to break the news. So she said, "Chris's friend Lexi arrived last night, stayed over, and took a tumble down the stairs just a bit ago. In an overabundance of caution, we encouraged her to go to the hospital. Just to make sure she's okay. Since she has no family here, Chris followed the ambulance. Give her moral support, and all." *Immoral support.* Kassie rolled her eyes, grateful Karen couldn't see her thoughts.

"When do you think you'll be home? I need to swing by."

"I don't know, Karen. Later. Why come to the house? I thought you got all that was yours yesterday."

6

Parent Trap

Despite being in the ER with Lexi, Chris felt as alone as a batter waiting for the pitcher to deliver in the bottom of the ninth of the final game of a World Series tied 4 to 4, bases loaded, two men out.

With his heart pounding and the consistent hums and beeps of the multiple monitors hooked up to Lexi, Chris's ears confirmed this was real, not part of a dream sequence gone bad.

He was about to say something, anything, but nothing came out, though his wide-open jaw would have allowed for words to emerge if only he could find them. His tongue wasn't tied. His thoughts were mangled.

Get a grip.

"Twins." Lexi grinned. Her eyes sparkled. "No wonder I'm so big and sick 24/7." She patted her midsection.

"Honestly now. Didn't you know?"

"Honestly, Chris. No," she said, sounding a bit too flirtatious.

Chris half listened while Lexi rambled on about how she purposely scheduled her next doctor's appointment for the following week.

"I wanted you to know I'm—we're—pregnant before she did the ultrasound. I thought you'd want to fly back with me to San Francisco to meet the doctor and see the first pictures at the same time I did."

"That's not gonna happen, Lexi. Not now. You heard Dr. Alexander. You're in here for a few days. And then … "

"You sound mad. Are you angry, Chris? And why are you sweating?"

He slumped onto a chair at the foot of her bed, leaned over, and raked his hands through his hair. Mad? Confused. Panicked? Perhaps. Angry? Not yet, anyway. Sweating? Damn right he was. Time. He needed time to sort things out. He looked at his phone. Where the hell was Kassie when he needed her?

Fatherhood was not on his agenda, short or long term. Marrying a woman in her fifties, who had accepted the reality she'd never have children, meant he'd given up on any dream of ever being called Dad.

In the few hours since he'd learned he was going to be a father, he plotted a scenario in his mind whereby Lexi would live on the West Coast and raise the child, while he and Kassie lived happily ever after on the East. Chris imagined flying west for quarterly visits during the child's early years, and then, at an appropriate age, the kid could fly to Boston for school vacations and summer breaks. Isn't that what airplanes and flight attendants were for? He'd seen youngsters escorted on and off planes, given wing pins, and special meals. Maybe even a visit to the cockpit. *Oh, but that was before 9/11.*

Mulling it over in his mind overnight, Chris was determined not to abandon Lexi, not to let her have a baby on her own and raise it without him in the picture, even if the view was long distance. More than anything, he was adamant his child would know their real father. And if some guy happened along and swept Lexi off her feet and she married, he'd jump through every legal hoop to ensure no one adopted his offspring.

Twins blew up his scenario. Without a doubt, one baby made his life complicated. Two babies would be life-changing to the extreme. Not just for Lexi but for him—and for Kassie.

"Funny, isn't it?" Lexi broke his train of thought.

"What?"

"Dr. Alexander calling me a Greek goddess," she giggled and sighed as she admired her pristine manicure. "If I only had the power, I'd take us back to Santorini …"

"And do what? Practice birth control?"

"A little harsh, Chris, don't you think? Especially for you. As I recall, you always said you wanted a family and regretted the reality that as long as you were with Kassie, that would never happen."

"Are you saying you got pregnant on purpose? *As I recall,* when we were in Greece, you suggested moving here. Was this your grand plan all along?"

"A trap? You think this is a trap? Last I checked, I have no control over how many children I can bear at one time."

"How many children are you having, Lexi?" Chris spun in his chair, confirming the voice he heard came from Kassie, who stood there with her hands on her hips.

"Chris, go ahead—you tell her. It's your good news as much as it's mine."

He jumped up and ushered Kassie out to the hallway, hoping to control her reaction, as not one but two orderlies wheeling stretchers sped by them. Chaos seemed to be every which way he turned.

"Thank God you're here." He held Kassie's hands in his and cupped them close to his chest. "I do have good news and bad news." Once he uttered those words, he wasn't sure which news was which.

Kassie pulled away from Chris's grip and headed back to Lexi. He followed close behind as she said, "Just tell me. I'm a big girl. Lexi doesn't seem too distressed, so I guess I can assume she hasn't lost the baby."

"Babies," Lexi said, in a gotcha sort of way

"What?"

"Twins," Chris said. "And the doctor says they are monitoring them, and it looks like they may be fine despite the fall. I think that's the good news. But it all depends on whether you think that news is good or bad. And then you might have to flip the bad and the good."

"Well, that's good, right? What's the bad news?" Kassie gripped Chris's arm.

"Her leg. We still don't know how bad her leg is or how they'll treat it. Surgery may be an option. Depending on what the orthopedist has to say. And then an obstetrician will need to weigh in on whatever the orthopedist recommends. And then Lexi will—I mean—we'll have a decision to make."

Chris knew he was rambling, digging himself an even bigger hole than he was in when Lexi showed up the night before. He couldn't help it. More than anything, he wanted to pull Kassie into his chest, wrap himself around her, ask for her forgiveness, and cry.

Kassie beat him to it.

An Honest Offer

"Two babies, Chris!" Kassie swiped the back of her hands across her cheeks, wiping away a stream of tears.

She pulled away from Chris and went to Lexi's bedside.

"Oh dear, Lexi, how are you doing?" Kassie said, placing her hand on Lexi's forearm, stopping short of leaning in and giving her even a friendly cheek kiss. "Twins. Aren't you excited?"

"Still getting used to the idea, aren't *we*?" Lexi half smiled at Chris.

"She didn't know," Chris said, sounding more than a bit defensive. Or was it a guilty conscience coming to light? "We just found out together a few minutes ago when Dr. Alexander told us the twins are okay so far."

"Dr. Alexander? *The* Dr. Alexander?" Kassie rolled her eyes toward the ceiling, recalling her own memory of Dr. Alexander's eccentric bedside manner during Mike's hospitalization. "So far? What does he mean by that? Chris? Lexi? What does he mean by that?"

Chis and Lexi exchanged looks and head shakes.

"You didn't ask?"

"No, we didn't. We were in shock, I think, about the twins. He did say Lexi needs to stay in the hospital for a few days."

"Three to five days," Lexi chimed in.

"To monitor the babies or because of the leg?" Kassie wanted to know, and she wanted to know now.

"Probably both, wouldn't you think?" Chris said, appearing out of his element.

"Didn't he say that I might have to stay home for the rest of the pregnancy? That has to be about the leg. Right, Chris?"

"Of course, that makes sense." Chris shrugged, looking at Kassie for confirmation.

"Maybe I should have a little chat with Dr. Alexander and get the skinny on what's going on here. We have history. I'm sure he'll remember me."

Lexi said, "You would do that, Kassie?"

"Certainly, she would. You're lucky to have her here. She'll be your best advocate."

The curtain screeched as Kassie pulled it back and marched down the hall, pushing past a half dozen scrubs with stethoscopes around their necks, most likely making rounds. Neither she nor Chris noticed Lexi put her hand over her mouth and whisper, "More like adversary."

Waiting at the ER's front desk behind a taxi driver asking about a pickup, Kassie inhaled, pushing Bad Kassie as deep into her body as humanly possible. From her experiences with her mother's illness and ultimate death a couple of years ago, in addition to Mike's hospitalization recently, Kassie knew she'd get more with honey than vinegar.

When it was her turn, Kassie peered over the desk on her tiptoes. She recognized the emergency room nurse who glared over her glasses as the same nurse who had been on duty the Good Friday Kassie rushed Mike to the ER the year before. That should be a good thing, right?

"Excuse me. I'm here with Lexi Moore, the pregnant woman with her leg in a sling."

"And?"

"Oh, I need to see Dr. Alexander." Kassie tapped her left foot.

"And why is that?"

"We have some questions."

"And who is *we*? Are you related to the pregnant woman with her leg in a sling?"

"Umm. I'm not. She arrived from San Francisco yesterday.

"And?"

"She's staying with *me*. She fell down *my* stairs." Kassie's foot tapping accelerated.

"Oh, is that so?"

"She's carrying my fiancé's babies."

Oops. As soon as she blurted it out, Kassie wished she could swallow those words. Who could blame her, though? She'd had less than twenty-four hours to construct a reasonable, less scandalous way to describe the Chris/Lexi relationship. Was it really possible that she was about to trade the mantra *"I'm having an affair with my husband's son"* with *"My fiancé is having twins with another woman"*?

"Sounds like you've got a problem."

"Ha! Ya think? Can you help me with Dr. Alexander, please?"

"Mrs. Ricci—"

"Oh, you remember me? You can call me Kassie." Kassie tilted her head. Recognizing that the nurse had more than likely switched her bullshit detector to high alert, Kassie smiled as sweetly as possible and went for the emotional angle.

"So, you must remember Mr. Ricci? He died right here in this hospital a week ago."

"I'm very sorry to hear that. You, of all people, know about privacy laws."

Damn it. She's not biting.

"I just thought under the circumstances … " Kassie said, ratcheting it up a notch. "I mean, how many wives bury their husband in the morning and discover in the evening their fiancé impregnated someone while on a break in Greece?"

"I'll say that's quite a soap opera you're living through, Mrs. Ricci. So, I'll save you some more heartburn. I know the doctor won't discuss Ms. Moore's health care with you or with your fiancé. All I can do, *under the circumstances,* is tell Dr. Alexander that Ms. Moore needs to see him at his earliest convenience."

"That's the best?"

"That is the best. Next?"

"Thanks," Kassie said, drumming her fingers twice on the counter and then swirling around on her heels. *Fuck.* She regretted failing in her quest to become a hero to both Lexi and Chris.

"Well, seems I hold little sway around here these days," Kassie said as she pulled the curtain open, walking in on Chris and Lexi. She ignored what she sensed was an intimate moment between the two of them, hoping her instincts were wrong for once.

"I tried," she said. "But the nurse insisted privacy laws won't let me talk to Dr. Alexander. So, I requested he come to see you, Lexi."

Chris offered Kassie the chair he'd been sitting in nearest Lexi. "At least you tried. Right, Lexi, at least Kassie tried?"

Lexi nodded, raising her eyebrows slightly.

"Both of you should know that it's not just me Dr. Alexander won't talk to alone. Technically, Chris, you're not part of Lexi's family circle either. Your sperm to the contrary."

Kassie thought they'd laugh. They didn't. If she could make light of the situation, why couldn't they?

She switched to a more mature tone, at least for Kassie. "So, Lexi, you need to add Chris to your list of next of kin if you want him to be informed of your condition or make any decisions on your behalf."

"You're okay with that, Kassie?" Chris squared his shoulders.

"It's not my call. It's up to you, Lexi. But from where I stand, as long as you're in Boston with no family here, it probably makes sense. You don't have family here, right?"

"No one close," Lexi whispered.

"Once you return to San Francisco," Kassie said, "you'll want to be sure your family there is looped into your health care directives."

Both Kassie and Chris waited for Lexi, who sat upright and tight-lipped, hands folded on her lap, to respond.

"What are you thinking, Lexi?" Chris leaned across the bed and lifted her chin. "Tell us."

"Where am I going to live when I get out of here?" Lexi said. Her eyes watered. "That's what I'm thinking about right now."

"Don't you spend any of your energy thinking about that. You need to nurture those babies of yours and tend to getting that leg in good working order," Chris said.

"Of course, while you're in town, you'll stay at my house," Kassie blurted.

"With those stairs?" Chris said.

"With that cat?"

8

No, No, Nana

Kassie almost tripped over the metal chair she'd been leaning on as Chris gripped her arm and ushered her out to the hallway for a second time since she arrived.

"Excuse us a minute, Lexi. We'll be right back," Chris said.

"Excuse *me*, Chris. What are you doing?"

"How in God's name do you think this will work? Lexi's probably going to be in a cast for a couple of months. She can't navigate those stairs of yours. And the memory alone of falling down them could make her queasy enough to fall again, breaking her other leg and harming the babies."

God only knew she'd never do anything to harm Lexi's babies. In her attempt to be a Good Samaritan, Kassie hadn't considered the stairs. Now that Chris had raised the issue, an image of one of those popular contraptions flashed through her mind. She envisioned the television ads of elderly people sitting in a chair smiling and then, with a push of a button, motoring up the stairs. Easy peasy. She tried to picture Lexi, big bellied and all, propped up in one of those gizmos with her left leg outstretched in a cast.

"That's it!" Kassie said. Problem solved.

"What is?"

"What if we hooked up one of the motorized chairs that chug up and down the stairs?" Her eyebrows raised, trying to gauge his reaction.

"For what, two or three months? Does that even make sense? Not even sure that would work if her leg's in a cast. And the cost of installing such a thing. Come on, get real."

Kassie walked six paces up the hallway and turned around, scratching her neck just below her right ear. There just had to be a logical solution.

"Perhaps you're right. What about family? Does she have any family on the East Coast? Doesn't have to be right here in Boston."

"No family here. You heard her."

"What about friends she could stay with for a couple of months?"

"No other friends than us out here. I don't think so, anyway."

Kassie shook her head, wondering if Lexi considered her a friend. Obviously, Chris was Lexi's friend with benefits. What kind of friend was he now?

"Wow. You're a big help. How well do you know this woman? And I don't mean in the biblical sense."

Chris coyly admitted their colleague-with-benefits relationship was more work-related and physical. He and Lexi spent most of their time together either dishing on people at the office or taking care of business in the sack. He satisfied her needs, and vice versa, especially in the year he and Kassie were apart.

"What about her parents? Her mother? Father? Shouldn't someone call them?"

"That's up to Lexi. And her father's dead. Her mother's back in California. I met her only once, briefly. Barely a conversation."

"You can bet that's going to change."

"Guess I didn't know her well enough. I assumed she was on the pill. Aren't most sexually active women these days?"

Kassie cringed and then reminded him it took two and by not protecting himself, Chris was as responsible for the situation as Lexi was. Obviously, in the Chris/Lexi relationship, neither behaved as the adult in the room, though they probably believed they acted as such. Now, it seemed, Kassie was destined to play that role.

"Maybe we could talk with a hospital social worker. Even if Lexi wanted to and could stay at my place, you and I would both be at work. She'd be alone and have to fend for herself for eight, ten hours a day. And what if you have to travel?"

Chris stared at the floor as if the scuffed-up linoleum held the answers. "I just won't travel while she's here. Bill can cover the out-of-town clients."

With her majority-owner's hat on, Kassie figured that might work, since most of the current clients knew Bill better than Chris at that point.

"What about a rehab hotel?" she said, offering a new alternative. "Social workers know about those kinds of places. With all the hospitals right here in the Boston area, there must be several reputable facilities where she could stay and be very well cared for night and day, 24/7. Don't you think?"

Chris got up, arms crossed, shifting his gaze to the ceiling tiles, seeming either not to have heard Kassie or to have ignored her. She could hardly blame him; she didn't like the taste or sound of the words flowing out of her mouth either.

"Okay, here's an idea. There's a full bathroom on your main floor," Chris said. "Why don't we turn either the family room or one office, maybe Mike's, into a bedroom? We could buy a futon or rent a bed for her, and she could camp out in there for the time being until she can travel back home."

The more she thought about it, Kassie wasn't sure she was ready to turn the house she was considering her own again into a long-term bed-and-breakfast for Lexi. Look what happened after just one night.

"You obviously didn't listen to anything I said. Who'd take care of her while you're at work? And I'm in Paris?"

"Paris? Did I hear Paris? What about Paris? Didn't you two just get back from there?"

Kassie winced and closed her eyes, wishing she could close her ears. She'd recognize that menacing voice anywhere.

"Karen, hi. What are you doing here?" Chris said.

"I didn't get a chance to tell you, hon," Kassie said. "Karen called this morning to talk to you. She wanted to stop by the house. Who knows why?" Kassie rolled her eyes. "I had to tell her we wouldn't be home. And then I slipped and said you were here with Lexi."

Chris rubbed Kassie's arm. "Not a slip. What else could you have said? It's the truth."

"So, Chris, both your girlfriend *and* your fiancée are here? Sounds like your problems surpass anything Mike, Charlie, and I ever had. At least we kept, or at least tried to keep, the interested and competing parties separated." Karen chuckled, shifting the strap of her purse from one shoulder to the other.

About to open her mouth and give Karen what for, Kassie was grateful that Chris stepped up instead.

"From where I stand, Karen, you three are not the ideal role models I should adopt now, or ever, as my own," Chris said.

"You could do worse," Karen said, glaring at Kassie.

"Let's not do this here," Kassie whispered. Literally chewing her lip, Kassie feared Chris would end up eating his words once Karen learned that Lexi's injury to her leg wasn't the only reason she was in the hospital.

"Catch you later, Karen," Kassie said as she reached for Chris's hand, nudging him toward Lexi's room and away from any further conversation with his mother.

"Wait just a minute," Karen piped in. "As soon as I heard your girlfriend was in town and in the hospital, no less, I rushed here to give you some support, Chris. See what I could do to help."

"We don't need your help," Chris said.

"But I also came here to meet Lexi. Any girlfriend of yours is a friend of mine." Chirping in her usual style, Karen followed them down the hall. "Chris, aren't you going to introduce me to Lexi?"

"Now's not the time." Chris squeezed Kassie's hand. "And Lexi's not my girlfriend. Not that it should matter to you."

Kassie stopped the mini-caravan near two empty chairs and faced Karen. "Why don't you take a seat here, okay? I need to talk to Chris. Privately."

She dragged Chris to a corner of the hallway, out of Karen's prying ears and the ER traffic that seemed to be getting more congested as the day progressed.

"What?" Chris asked. "I don't think Lexi wants visitors, do you?"

"Probably not, but we have a choice. Either we bring her in and manage the introduction, or Karen leaves now and returns when we're not around. You know she'd do that."

Just as Chris agreed she had a point, Kassie slumped against the wall, its coldness doing nothing to soothe the heat that started from her head and traveled quickly down her body. As Kassie slipped toward the floor, Chris grabbed her by the waist.

"Are you okay? What's the matter with you?" Chris said as he eased her to the floor and sat beside her. "Are you going to faint?"

Kassie shook her head. "Oh my God, Chris. Don't you see? We're never going to get Karen out of our lives. It's not bad enough that Mike gave her a job at the company for life and that she's your mother, but she's the *grandmother*. To your babies." She rested her forehead on her knees.

"Crap. I hadn't thought about that. But so what? Lexi lives in San Francisco. I'm sure she'll head back there as soon as she can. And then, after the babies are born, she and the kids will rarely see Karen."

Kassie gave him a teary, unconvinced glance. "How can you be sure of that?"

"Easy. Don't forget, she didn't want me for forty years. Sure as shootin', she's not going to cozy up to *two* rug rats. Especially at her age."

Kassie wasn't quick to buy into Chris's theory. She considered his rationale, which had some truth to it. Truth about the past. After all, Karen freely gave Chris up for adoption, acknowledging him only when Mike needed a kidney transplant. On the flip side, Chris was no soothsayer; he couldn't predict the future. Who could've ever predicted Karen would volunteer to be Mike's kidney donor, let alone be a match?

"Two rug rats," Kassie murmured, shifting her mind from the future unknown to the present reality. "It's not fair," she thought she said to herself. But evidently Chris heard her, or maybe he read her mind or body language, because he hoisted her to her feet and pulled her into a full bear hug.

"I know, I know. I'm sorry. This is happening so fast. Somehow I'll make it up to you. I promise."

A little late, Kassie thought, keeping those three words to herself this time. They needed to handle the current situation with Karen, whom she spotted still sitting alone with her eyes glued on Chris.

"Should we do this?" Kassie tilted her head toward Karen.

9

Baby, It's Cold Inside

One-hundred forty-four square feet. By counting the ceiling tiles and estimating they were twelve inches square, Lexi calculated the size of what she designated "the ER staging area." She could've been wrong, but she rarely was when it came to practical matters. It was affairs of the heart that were her nemesis. Obviously.

Shivering, she rubbed the goosebumps on her arms. With her left leg exposed like a pork loin at the butcher, she pulled the starched white sheet up past her waist nearer her neck the best she could. *Brrr.* She felt chilled, as compared to the disdain she sensed from the audience at Kassie's house the night before when she made the big announcement. Oh, they tried to be warm, friendly, welcoming even. But Lexi knew a fake front when she saw one—like the one-hundred and forty-four tiles looking down on her.

Maybe it was whatever medication they were pumping through her veins, or perhaps the whirlwind of the morning—the fall, his blue eyes, the ambulance ride. She'd never seen so much diagnostic equipment in one small space. Whatever, by now Lexi's thoughts bounced like a ping-pong ball on steroids, never quite finding a comfortable resting place. Between the dull, throbbing pain in her leg and visions of not one but two babies floating around in her tummy, she struggled to focus.

Her mind drifted to a few days before. Lexi recalled humming Ed Sheeran's "Shape of You," one of Chris's favorites-to-have-sex-by, while packing her bags for her trip to Boston with purpose and conviction. Chris had asked her to wait a couple of weeks before making the trip, explaining he and Kassie were in no mood for entertaining guests beyond who showed up for the funeral. Let them get past Mike's death, he'd said.

On the one hand, she was relieved he hadn't pressed her on why she was heading to Boston, and on the other she understood his request that she postpone her trip. But that would never do. Lexi couldn't wait until he got a load of her new shape. And she had her own objectives. For once, what she needed and wanted had to come first.

Lexi had meticulously charted her journey, booking an early morning flight out of San Francisco that would land her in Boston and at Kassie's doorstep as Mike's mourners were heading home. She could text Chris before her flight took off so he wouldn't be caught off guard. That much she would do.

She rationalized that informing him she was with child—his child—would lift whatever spirits of his were down after the death of a man he'd known for only a year. And if that didn't do it, she had other ways to get a rise out of Chris.

She retrieved a short blue lace nighty from her "fun-with-Chris-drawer," folding and tucking it between two cotton shirts to prevent it from slipping around and getting wrinkled in her suitcase. When she refreshed the contents of her cosmetic bag, which had sat idle in her closet since she returned from Greece, she tossed the nearly empty shampoo and conditioner bottles, along with the pink foil package of partially consumed birth control pills.

"Don't need *those* any longer," she'd said, as the three containers clanged, hitting the bottom of her small metal trash can. For the life of her, Lexi couldn't remember when she took the last pill. It was so unlike her to skip any, or forget when she last took one, but she conceded it must have been before the trip to Greece. She hadn't consciously planned to tempt fate, so it must have been happenstance. Vacations have a way of relaxing norms. Different time zones. Disrupted routines. Oodles of sex. Whatever the cause, the deed was done.

Granted, the trip to Boston wasn't absolutely necessary. There were other ways to tell Chris she was pregnant. She could conspire with one of their mutual friends to lure him to California under some false pretext—some special anniversary or birthday party he just couldn't pass up. "Everyone would love to see you!"

Or she could tell him over the phone, maybe even on FaceTime. Perhaps she would concoct a game, like show-and-tell; give him some clues and make him guess. See how long it took him to figure it out on his own. He was a smart guy. That could be fun; she played it out in her mind. A onesie, a diaper, a baby bottle.

There were other moments, though, when the image of Chris scrolling through his phone on the balcony in Santorini and his admission that Kassie was the one, not her, that rattled her self-confidence. Would he be thrilled at the prospect of being a father? Would he engage, accept responsibility? Or would he be an asshole and challenge her as to whether or not he was, in fact, the sperm donor? Had she been with anyone else before or after their vacation? If so, had they used protection?

She considered not telling him at all. After all, why would she want to be with someone who didn't want to be with her, let alone raise a family with him?

That idea horrified her mother. Though Sherrie Moore had met Chris only once a couple of years ago when she rudely barged in during one of their regular Thursday-night fuck-fests, her mother was old-school and adamant in her belief that exciting, life-changing news like having a baby was best delivered in person.

"Chris seems like an upstanding young man," her mother said. "And you have to admit, Chris and Kassie's relationship is on shaky ground. If their love was that intense and stable, they wouldn't have been on a break in the first place. He certainly wouldn't have made his way back to you. Whisked you away on a romantic vacation to the Greek isles."

Lexi never told her mother the jaunt to Santorini was her idea.

Her mother's biased opinion was based on a brief hello and mostly on Lexi's recitation of Chris's bio, during which she emphasized how his adoptive mother, Sarah, was a philanthropist—well heeled, well connected, and thus *wealthy*. Not that Lexi's mother was a gold-digger; she just wanted what was best for her daughter—and grandchild.

Grandchildren, as was now the case.

Precious bundles of joy. That's the ticket.

Now, lying in a bed in the ER, Lexi stared at the monitors, sending her methodical signals she was ill-equipped to interpret. Except, the reality of the moment began to settle in. Where she thought she could handle being a single mom with one child, two children were an entirely different ballgame. She was dealt a hand she never expected, and she had doubts about just how much of a commitment Chris would be willing to make.

Tumbling down Kassie's stairs that morning changed every-thing. Now Lexi was convinced her not-so-concealed weapon to capture Chris's heart had doubled. He would have to come to terms with the fact that she was more worthy of his love than a woman ten years older than he was. After all, what could Kassie offer him? Not even one child, certainly not two at once.

What choice did Chris have now with two babies—his babies—in her belly? She continued massaging her tummy. He'd not only have to provide child support, but he'd surely want to live nearby and be in their lives on a daily basis. Right? Help with 2 a.m. feedings, change diapers, build jungle gyms, choose schools.

Maybe once he slept on it a few nights, he'd send Kassie to parts unknown, pack his bags, and take up where he and Lexi had left off—not in Santorini but in San Francisco—where Kassie would be out of sight, out of mind, and hold little to no influence over him.

If Kassie was as smart as Chris claimed, perhaps she'd take the lead, see the writing on the wall herself. She might decide on her own the best course of action for everyone, especially the kids, would be to just let Chris go free. Break their silly engagement. Let Chris be a father, a gift she'd never be able to give him. After all, Kassie had given him up once. She'd do it again. Especially once the babies were born and she saw a light on his face she could never ignite.

Perhaps that morning's fall was preordained after all. If she hadn't fallen and been rushed off to the hospital, she wouldn't have known she was carrying twins until her next visit with the obstetrician back in San Francisco. And if Chris had refused to return there with her, the impact of that reality would have been lost.

But it wasn't lost. The existence of the twins was a found opportunity. It was out of her control, not her fault. Certainly not a scheme she'd cooked up to steal Chris.

Rather, Lexi conjured, the twins inside her womb behaved like a magnet that would pull Chris toward her from now until forever. If she couldn't convince him to be with her, his two offspring would be more than enough to win his attention and affection.

As a bonus, falling down Kassie's staircase, over her cat, would surely instill considerable guilt within do-gooder Kassie.

Lightly stroking her belly with a deep sigh, Lexi welcomed being alone for the first time since the tumble that changed her life that morning. She craved some me-time to think. Where would she stay after they released her from the hospital? Could she care for herself? Would she need help?

Her me-time came to an abrupt and sudden halt. Soon after Chris and Kassie scurried away to talk about a problem called Lexi, a nurse arrived to check her vital signs. So far, so good, she guessed. The nurse summarily turned down her request for something to silence her growling stomach, despite her plea that she hadn't had any breakfast. Intravenous feeding was all she could have, especially if surgery was the ultimate, agreed-upon outcome. The only upside to the fluids-only regimen was that her morning sickness appeared to have subsided, at least for the moment.

Held hostage by tubes and wires, and her leg immobilized, Lexi turned on her charm. "I know you're busy, but could you please get my purse out of the cabinet for me? I can use my phone in here, right?" She congratulated herself for having the forethought to ask the nurse, who complied with a friendly smile before she rushed off to some else's bedside.

With absolutely no privacy since Dr. Alexander broke the news he thought she already knew, having Chris and Kassie out of the room should give her at least some time to reassess her original grand plan of snatching Chris from Kassie's clutches.

But first things first. She scrolled through her contacts, stopping at V—for Aunt Venus.

10

Daydream Believer

Visiting Aunt Venus in Rhode Island was one of her mother's brilliant ideas. That would've been a pleasant side trip for Chris and her to take if she hadn't broken her leg. Now, she had to keep Aunt Venus a secret as long as possible.

Texting her aunt was an option Lexi considered only briefly. She had no clue how soon Chris and Kassie would grace her bedside once again. And even Lexi, though jacked up on drugs, could predict texting Aunt Venus was fraught with peril.

Lexi sensed her mother's sister was a chatterbox like Chris, so texting back and forth would take too long. And if, God forbid, Chris caught a glimpse of her messages, he'd figure out quickly enough that she wasn't as alone on the East Coast as she wanted him to believe. Relying on him and taking advantage of Kassie's sympathy and hospitality suddenly became as important as Chris's knowing she was pregnant.

Instead of texting, she called her aunt.

As she waited for her aunt to answer, she murmured, "Make it snappy. Keep it short and sweet. No side trip to Rhode Island. At least not in the near term." She tapped her recently manicured fingernails on the rolling table that straddled the bed.

Lexi's plan kind of worked. In less than a minute, she recounted the story to her aunt— she'd tumbled over the stupid cat and would probably require surgery. If nothing else, she expected to receive at least an effusive response of sympathy from her aunt. And frankly, at the moment, Lexi welcomed all the sympathy she could get, whatever the source.

Right on cue, Aunt Venus took the bait, almost too much so. "Oh, you poor dear. I'll head right up to Boston this afternoon. I'm less than an hour due south of you. Be there in no time. I should arrive in good ol' Beantown by suppertime," her aunt said, as if she'd make dinner reservations for the two of them as soon as they hung up.

"Why do that? If I need surgery, I'll be in the OR this afternoon most likely. And my fiancé, Chris, is here with me. He's why I'm here. I'm in good hands."

"Fiancé? You didn't tell me you were engaged!"

"True. I wanted to surprise you. In person. Have you meet him."

"Oh, that's nice, dear. Well, under the circumstances, I'll forgive you for that, you naughty girl."

Lexi grunted, acknowledging the name-calling more than the pardon her aunt bestowed.

"What did your mother say about your fall? You called her, didn't you?" Aunt Venus switched gears, peppering her with questions Lexi didn't want to take the time to answer.

"No, not yet. Been a bit busy this morning. Not to worry. I'll call her. There's nothing she can do from California. I wanted you to know first, so you won't be expecting me this coming weekend. Maybe not for a while. I'll call you when I know more. Gotta go. Bye."

Lexi neglected to tell Aunt Venus about her pregnancy when she invited herself to visit. Just as with Chris, she planned to give her aunt the good news in person. She patted herself on the back for planting the seed on this call that she was engaged. That bit of good news should soften the reaction she imagined her aunt would have when she learned her niece was an unwed mother.

Moreover, Lexi surmised the news that she was having twins would thrill not only her aunt but also Lexi's mother—Aunt Venus's identical twin sister.

There was always the possibility that Sherrie, Lexi's mother, had a premonition that getting on the good side of Aunt Venus could be beneficial to her daughter. Perhaps Sherrie had an ulterior motive when she encouraged—well, mostly insisted—Lexi break the news, not her leg of course, to Chris in person. Lexi figured that, in her mother's mind, if she couldn't be there to support Lexi herself, Aunt Venus was as good a surrogate as any. Especially with Rhode Island being a hop, skip, and a jump away from Boston.

"Don't buses and trains run between Providence and Boston?" Sherrie asked Lexi, attempting to show how simple and quick it would be to pay her artsy-fartsy aunt a visit.

Sherrie was convinced it wasn't too late for Lexi to sever the relationship between Chris and Kassie once and for all. And crafty Aunt Venus would surely have some clever advice to get Chris back once and for all.

"She'll roll out the red carpet for you and Chris," her mother insisted, leaving it to Lexi to call and invite herself.

"She hardly knows me," Lexi argued. "It's been years. Why would she want to see me now?"

"Because blood is blood," her mother had said. "If she ever found out you were in Boston and hadn't stopped by, I'd hear about it until the day you all scatter my ashes off the shores of Carmel."

So Lexi yielded to her mother's witchy wishes and made the call because she knew between the sisters, however estranged they sometimes had been over the years, there was always a mutual, unspoken invitation to visit. Until now.

11

Cleansing Breath

"You're not *all* going in there?" a voice from behind stopped the Kassie-Chris-Karen parade in its tracks. Turning, Kassie recognized the shrill tone of her "favorite" nurse who somehow escaped her front desk perch. "This is an emergency room, not a Starbucks! I'll allow only two at a time, and even that's one too many. Mrs. Ricci, shame on you. Of all people, you know better."

Bad Kassie stifled the obvious rejoinder, knowing being called Mrs. Ricci was the least of her problems and not really the nurse's problem either. She was only doing her job. In all the time Mike spent in the hospital, Kassie had rarely corrected the staff or asked them to address her as Ms. O'Callaghan. Now was not the time to start.

There'd be time in the future for that. After she and Chris married, would she become Kassandra Gaines? *Not! No way!* She had her own identity. Kassie O'Callaghan had built a professional reputation in Boston and in Paris. Certainly, Chris would understand, wouldn't he?

Yet, they never discussed it. Something else to add to her to-do list.

"What do we do now?" Chris asked.

At that moment, determining who was going in to see Lexi was the number one priority. If it could only be two, would it be Chris and Karen or Kassie and Karen? Neither combination was ideal.

Chris, she knew, was too invested to handle the introduction of his mother to Lexi. And with his tendency to fumble his words, what would he say?

Lexi, this is my mother Karen. I told you about her. She gave me up for adoption more than forty years ago, and I just met her last year.

And then. How would he continue?

Karen, this is Lexi, the girl I slept with while I was having an affair with Kassie. Oh, by the way, I knocked her up last March when we were in Greece, while I thought Kassie and I were on a break.

If Kassie accompanied Karen, she'd have to explain why Chris wasn't with them—the nurse set the ground rules at only two at a time. She feared even that brief explanation would provide Karen an opportunity to ambush the conversation.

It had to be all three of them, and it was up to Kassie to make that happen. Without question, Kassie knew she had to step in and quarterback the scene with as little intrigue and emotion as she could muster. She had to convince the nurse that three really wasn't a crowd.

She inhaled deeply, hoping to strengthen her resolve with fresh oxygen to her brain and her lungs. Instead, she inhaled an overabundant stench of hospital-grade bleach. Coughing turned into gagging. Gagging triggered tears.

Still in the hallway with scrubs and gurneys, the trio reversed course and found the two chairs Karen had occupied minutes before. The nurse rushed away, returning with tissues and water in a tiny paper cup that looked like a white dunce cap turned upside down.

Karen moved to the side, tapping her right foot and checking her watch.

"If you've got some place you need to be, Karen, we can do this later," Chris said.

"No. That's okay. I'll wait until Kassie recovers. I'll be right back. Don't go in without me."

"Sorry about this. I thought I could convince the nurse that we all needed to see Lexi. Together. I was trying to be helpful. Look at me. Next thing you know, they'll be sticking me with an EpiPen." Kassie wiped the moisture under her eyes, thankful she hadn't gone full make-up that morning. No raccoon's eyes for her.

"What the hell happened?" Chris asked.

"I think I sucked in a can of Lysol fumes. I'm fine. Really. I could use some more water, if you wouldn't mind."

It seemed to Kassie that Chris was gone a long time just to fetch her water. Maybe he was searching for a large cup, or perhaps he ran into Karen along the way and convinced her to go home. Too much drama for one day.

"Here you go," Chris said, returning and standing in front of Kassie with a red Solo cup. "Where's Karen? She not back yet?"

"Your guess is as good as mine. I thought maybe she was with you." Kassie pulled out her phone. "Let's give her two more minutes. If she's not here, we'll go in to see Lexi. Perhaps she's seen the doctor again. Karen can meet her another time."

"Sounds good. Promise me something, though," Chris said, bending to kiss her forehead.

"Anything, bubbie."

"Don't breathe."

They laughed. Two minutes passed. No Karen.

12

FAQs

Chris latched onto Kassie's hand as she navigated the rush of humanity and the jungle of supply carts and rolling beds and led them toward Lexi's side.

"Is it always this crazy?" Chris shook his head.

"It's an emergency room, Chris. What do you expect? Get with the program."

"She's gonna be pissed," he said, following Kassie's footsteps.

"Who? Lexi? Why?"

"No. Karen."

"Do you really care?"

"Not sure. I'll have to think about it."

"Come on, Chris. We waited. Her loss." Kassie kept moving.

Knowing his mother as he had come to know her this late in his life, Chris had a hard time trusting her. Sadly. More than likely, he expected Karen would freak out when she returned to their designated meeting place and discovered they'd left her there. He made a mental note to call her as soon as they left the hospital.

And do what? Apologize? Reschedule a meetup with Lexi? Ask her where the hell she disappeared to and why she'd left them waiting for her?

Just over Kassie's shoulder, Chris spotted Dr. Alexander and a nurse heading in their direction. Their heads leaned toward each other jibber-jabbering about something, not noticing Kassie or Chris. He would've liked to stop the doctor but accepted the reality that he had no standing in Lexi's treatment.

Kassie's head turned ninety degrees. Not much got past her. Chris followed her eyes, which followed the doctor.

"Ouch!" Chris said, reacting to Kassie's fingernails digging into his hand.

"Look, it's Dr. Alexander," she said.

"Don't. Go. There." His right hand gripped hers. His left hand rested on her shoulder, directing her forward.

"I only want to know—" She swerved sideways, but he kept her moving. "Shouldn't we ask what's going on with Lexi? Will they operate today? When can she leave? We'll need to know that in order to make plans."

They halted just outside Lexi's curtain.

Chris shrugged. "Who knows? Maybe Lexi's got all the answers. Shall we?"

13

Family Feud

Kassie pulled back the curtain just enough to enter, protecting Lexi's privacy. Standing to his right, Kassie seized Chris's hand with her left hand and grasped his arm with the other.

Hold on tight. Don't say a word. And for heaven's sake, don't breathe.

She gave Chris's arm a slight jolt, a jumpstart.

Say something, Chris. Anything. Uh-oh. Too late.

"Well, hello there." Lexi laughed. "We've been waiting for you, haven't we, Karen?"

Sitting upright in the bed, Lexi was turned slightly toward the wall to her left so her back was to Karen, who stood beside her with a cat-who-destroyed-the-catnip-toy grin and a hairbrush in her hand.

"Actually, Lexi," Chris said, "we were just around the corner waiting for Karen. We intended to come in here together. To properly introduce the two of you. That was the plan, right, Karen?"

"The plan? That may have been your plan. I couldn't wait all day! I have places to go, people to see." Karen continued to pull the brush through Lexi's locks. "With your coughing fit, Kassie, I reckoned there was a mighty good chance they might just check you in here," Karen said with a laugh and a wink toward Lexi.

"That won't be necessary," Chris said. "Kassie just needed some water."

"And with that fine nurse restricting visitors," Karen said, "I decided not to wait until you two got a move on."

"If you're so busy, Karen, what are you doing here?" Kassie asked, releasing Chris from her clutches.

"She's brushing my hair. What does it look like she's doing? Do you have a problem with that?"

Kassie shook her head, remembering her mother doing the same for her each morning before she headed off to fourth grade. But, Lexi wasn't ten years old.

"Are you that helpless?" Chris interceded, perhaps reading Kassie's mind. "I know you're perfectly capable of brushing your own hair."

"Oh, come now, Christopher, I offered. After all, it's the least I could do for the mother of my grandchildren."

Mother of my grandchildren hung like a cloud, a thundercloud ready to burst, over the gathering holding vigil around Lexi's bed. Karen smiled at Lexi. Lexi raised her eyebrows at Chris. Chris let out an audible sigh. Kassie closed her fists, keeping Bad Kassie in check.

The monotonous beeping of the monitors reminded Kassie why they were there. Lexi was the priority, not Karen. Unwilling to elevate Karen to Queen for the Day, Kassie changed the subject, if only slightly. "We just passed Dr. Alexander. Was he in here with you? Did he give you any news?"

"Yes, he stopped by to see Lexi," Karen said. "In fact, he's got an excellent memory. He remembered me from when I visited Mike while you two were off gallivanting in Europe. Must be the red hair." Karen ran her fingers through her own locks.

"That wasn't so long ago, Karen, that he wouldn't recognize you," Chris said, apparently sharing Kassie's reluctance to further pump up Karen's outsized ego. "I mean, what? It was just last week, for cryin' out loud. Give me a break."

On the one hand Kassie was pleased Chris stood up to Karen; on the other she knew that wouldn't help.

"Okay, guys. Let's not do this here. Not now. This is about Lexi. Not Karen. Or what Chris and I were doing in Paris," Kassie said, consciously or subconsciously putting her left hand with her engagement ring on her chest for all to see, as if to say, "Well, there is this."

"Kassie's right. Lexi, tell us what Dr. Alexander had to say," Chris said.

Karen opened her mouth. "It's really good news."

"I asked Lexi, not you, Karen. Please."

"Well," Lexi started, "I do need surgery. That's for darn sure. The leg is broken. Thanks to your cat." On that remark, Kassie sensed Lexi's animosity toward her was still alive and cooking. Rather than continue to give her any reason to ratchet it up a notch, Kassie switched her focus, eyeing Karen.

"Good news, Karen? You have an odd way of sizing up situations. She's pregnant and needs surgery! How is that good news?" Kassie placed her purse on a side chair and her hands on her hips.

"Oh, but it is good news, Kassie," Lexi said, defending Karen. "For your information, it's perfectly safe for me to have surgery."

"Then, again, dearest Kassie, you wouldn't know about this never having been pregnant yourself. Am I right?" Karen said.

Kassie's eyes grew as big as turkey platters, struggling to maintain some decorum in the ER, when what she wanted to do was pounce on Karen and wrestle her down to the cold tile floor and beat the shit out of her.

"Don't bite," Chris whispered in her ear. "I've got this."

Standing straight up with shoulders square, Chris said, "Okay, ladies. Let's stay focused here. This is about Lexi, right? Not ancient history. And certainly not about Kassie."

"He's right," said Kassie, lifting her palms to the ceiling. "Lexi, why don't you tell us the rest of what the doctors told you? Like, when will this perfectly safe surgery take place?"

Lexi rehashed the conversation with Dr. Alexander and the orthopedic surgeon. They'd check the schedule, but they thought they could get her into the OR late that afternoon—four or five o'clock.

"Did they say how long the surgery will take?" Chris asked.

"Depends," Karen blurted.

Chris's shoulders slumped and his head dipped as if to say "Come on, just stifle it!" He lowered his voice, staying focused. "Lexi, how long?"

"Anywhere between three and four hours. So Karen was right, Chris. It depends on how bad the break is. And maybe you could all do me a favor and lighten up on each other a little here, okay?"

Three heads nodded, eyes rolled.

"Easy to see why more than two visitors is a crowd, eh?" Kassie said. "I think we'd all agree it's not a great idea to upset Lexi ahead of surgery."

To her surprise, Lexi mouthed *thank you* toward Kassie and placed her hand to her chest.

"What about recovery, Lexi? What did they say about recovery time, physical therapy, stuff like that?" Chris asked.

Lexi repositioned herself squarely in the bed as best she could, taking the brush from Karen. She gazed at Chris; her eyes twinkled as she continued brushing where Karen had left off. Lexi said the surgeon had explained that recovery may not be a linear path.

"What did he mean by that?" Kassie asked.

"Under normal circumstances, I could go home in a couple of days. But you have to agree, my circumstances aren't normal," Lexi said, massaging her abdomen.

Oh, dear. Another drama queen.

"We get that, Lexi. Go on," Chris said.

She reached toward her leg but stopped, Kassie thought for effect, and said, "All depends on what they find during surgery. But the doctors sounded hopeful."

"See, I told you there's good news," Karen said, pumping out her chest like a peacock.

Neither Kassie nor Chris bit.

"Only one problem," Lexi said, lingering there for more than a pregnant pause.

Here it comes.

"Problem is, where's home? Obviously, I'm not getting on a plane back to San Francisco anytime soon." She went on. "Depending on the fracture, I could be in a cast for six weeks or more. Not exactly how I imagined spending my pregnancy."

No one spoke. Kassie assumed Chris and Karen were assessing and devising their responses, just as she was. She tried to put herself in Lexi's shoes, or the hospital gown, because Lexi wasn't wearing any shoes.

Here Lexi was. Broken leg. Pregnant. In a strange city. Apparently, with no relatives nearby to come to her aid, to take her in. No place to go to recover and recuperate. And here the three of them were there, feuding over her. Was no one going to step up and be the adult in the room?

"How awful for you, Lexi." Kassie finally opened her mouth, trying desperately not to insert her foot for once. "Let's just get you through today and the surgery, and then tomorrow we'll work together to figure everything else out. How's that for a plan?"

"Sounds good, except for one thing. I'm scared. What if I lose these babies because I fell over your cat?"

14

Words Matter

"You've got to be kidding, Lexi. You fell down Kassie's stairs because you tripped over her cat? That's how this happened?" Karen asked, glaring at Kassie.

Kassie opened her mouth, trying to decide whether to defend herself or Topher. Instead, Chris decided for her, somewhat.

"We're not really sure what happened," he said, stepping toward Karen, brushing her to the side. "It happened so fast. No one saw it." He clung to Lexi's hand. "You're not going to lose these babies. Why are you even going there? Did Dr. Alexander mention that as a possibility?"

"No, but—" Whatever rendition of her tumble Lexi was about to describe was interrupted by a nurse with a stethoscope, a clipboard, and an attitude. She frowned at the three visitors individually and gave a nod for them to leave.

"Pre-op preparation, right?" Kassie asked as she passed the nurse, who nodded once again.

"Let's go get coffee or something. We'll be back soon," Chris said. Kassie noticed he kissed the back of Lexi's hand before placing it on her lap and patting it three times.

"I wouldn't hang around the hospital, if I were you" the nurse said finally. "It'll be awhile before Mrs. Moore can have visitors." In a few curt phrases, the nurse explained that Lexi was now in her able care as she readied her for surgery. Then, once the surgery was over, she'd be in post-op for a while. Eventually, probably in the middle of the night, she'd make it to a proper hospital room that already had her name assigned to it.

"When can Chris come back?" Lexi asked, reaching for his hand.

"Tomorrow morning. Plan on your husband coming back tomorrow morning."

Kassie stopped, almost tripping. "Oh, he's not her husband. He's going to be mine." She waved her ring toward the nurse.

"Okay. Your brother can come back tomorrow morning."

Karen grinned. "Oh, he's not her brother. He's my son."

"Well, whoever you are," the nurse said, tilting her head and gawking at Chris, "tomorrow morning earliest, ya hear?"

As they moved toward the open curtain, Kassie overheard Chris ask the nurse how he could find out how the surgery went. The nurse recommended he call Mr. Moore, Lexi's husband, to find out.

"There is no Mr. Moore," Lexi said, shrugging her shoulders. "I'm visiting from San Francisco. No family nearby. I'm here all alone."

"You're not alone." Kassie turned to face Lexi, eager to stifle her pity party. "See, we're all here for you." Kassie swept her hand toward Chris and Karen. "And if I recall correctly, I think you have to designate someone for the doctor to call after the surgery, right?" The nurse grunted affirmatively. "So, give them Chris's contact information, and you'll be all set. He'll know. I'll know. And we'll let Karen know."

The nurse handed the clipboard and a pen to Lexi and flipped through two documents she'd have to complete in order to proceed. One to admit her, the other to give permission for surgery.

"Would it be okay if I stayed and helped Lexi with all this paperwork?" Chris asked the nurse. "It's the least I can do since I'm the babies' daddy. That makes me family, doesn't it?"

Wide-eyed, the nurse said, "Well, now we're getting somewhere. The other two of you—out."

"We should just leave. Chris isn't going anywhere for a while." Karen snickered at Kassie as they left Chris behind to help Lexi fill in all the blanks.

Kassie didn't need Karen to tell her what she already suspected. And she resented Karen inserting a motherly sentiment toward the son she'd known for just over a year. As long as Lexi and those babies were under the knife, Chris wouldn't be far away. She knew him well enough—certainly better than Karen ever could or would—to know a phone call away would be much too far away to be acceptable.

Kassie agreed with Karen for once, saying she'd text Chris and let him know they were leaving and she was heading home. Then she remembered. He had her car keys, and the car was parked somewhere in the hospital garage. She assessed her options as they approached the elevator.

If she went back and got the keys from Chris, he'd be without wheels, and she'd either have to come back into town to get him or he could take an Uber home. Or she could just leave things as they were.

"If you don't mind," Karen said, interrupting Kassie's internal monologue, "can I meet you at your house?" Kassie tried to hide her startle along with the realization the situation either got more complicated or could easily be solved. Would Karen give her a ride home? Not an ideal solution. Sitting cooped up in a car with Karen, even for twenty minutes, was the last thing on her list of things that would propel her into a happy dance.

They walked in silence toward the elevator. Neither of them pressed the button, and when the doors opened and the car emptied, neither stepped forward.

Kassie wasn't ready to make any definitive move yet. Before asking Karen for a ride, she needed to figure out why Karen wanted to come the house. "Why? Why do you want to meet me at my house?"

"Oh ye of short memory. When we talked this morning, I said I needed to come by the house. Don't you remember?"

"Vaguely. A lot has happened since then. But what's at the house? I thought you removed everything that was yours the other day?"

"Mostly. But I may have left something there after the funeral."

"And pray tell, what would that be?"

"A gift from Mike."

"Really? What is it?"

"Oh, it's a surprise. I didn't even open it. Do you remember me holding a small bag while we talked in your office?"

"I do remember, now that you mention it."

"Oh, good. I thought I was losing my mind. I've looked high and low around my place and in the car, and I can't find it anywhere. I'll just die if I lost it. Mike had those two guys in the Cape make me something special."

"You mean Guy and Dolly?"

"Yes. Those two chaps. Fine fellows—"

"And Karen. It's *on* the Cape." Uh-oh. If Karen remembered Bad Kassie correcting her like that the afternoon Mike died, and then calling her a "stupid slut," any chance Kassie would get a lift home could go downhill in a flash.

The elevator doors opened, inviting them to take the next step.

"After you," they each said.

15

Frenemies?

Oddly, there wasn't another soul in the hospital elevator. As etiquette dictates, Kassie and Karen stood side by side, facing forward, a few feet apart. Each having her own personal space and respecting, or avoiding, the other. As the elevator lowered itself through the shaft, the only sound was the ping as it passed each floor. Whatever they were thinking, they kept to themselves.

When the door opened to the lobby, they paused, turning toward each other. Kassie swept her hand gently in a *you first* move. Karen obliged, holding the fast-closing elevator door open, so it didn't crush Kassie.

Once safely among a throng of people buzzing about and scattering to various wings of the hospital, Karen said, "Well, what do you think? Can I swing by the house now? You are heading home, aren't you?"

"About that." Kassie stopped by an unoccupied blue-and-green plaid couch, the pattern she recalled from prior hospital visits. She rested her purse on its back and subconsciously willed Bad Kassie to remain incommunicado. She conjured up Chris's habit of droning on and on. Although Kassie found it endearing when he did it, she suspected Karen would think differently.

"Here's the deal, Karen. I don't have a car here. Well, I do. But I think it would be best if I leave it for Chris. You see, he drove my car to the hospital this morning. Lexi's rental blocked his car, and she rode off in the ambulance with her key in her purse. They wouldn't allow him in the ambulance. We should've thought about that. But we didn't. So I told him to take my car. Which he did. And now he has the key. And he knows where he parked it. At least I hope he knows. I certainly don't. So, it wouldn't do me any good even if I had the key."

Kassie felt flushed, starting with her neck. Was it really so difficult for her to ask a favor of Karen? If Karen drove her home, would that mean Kassie owed her one? And what favor would Karen demand in return? *It's just a ride home, for cryin' out loud*, Bad Kassie nudged her, but apparently not enough for her to make the request.

"Well, Kassie, seems like you need a ride to the place *I* want to go. And I have a car, keys, and I wrote the garage location on the parking ticket." Karen riffled through her purse, waved the ticket, and then jingled her key chain. "Shall we?"

On the way to the car, Kassie found it hard to keep up with Karen's pace after using up a lot of her oxygen on her no-car explanation. She tried slowing her down by thanking her over and over for the ride. But with no reaction from Karen, she hadn't a clue if she even heard her. Maybe she was ignoring her. Yet, they were both getting what they wanted. Kassie, a way home. Karen, a way to find her missing gift from Mike. Kassie prayed the bag was in plain sight somewhere on the main floor, so Karen could retrieve it and get the hell out of there. One could only hope.

Kassie heard two chirps before reaching Karen's silver Lexus hybrid sedan. She remembered Chris telling her the story of driving Karen to pick it up at the car dealer, somewhat astonished Karen could afford a luxury car on a receptionist's salary. Kassie reminded him that donating a kidney to the boss probably came with some perks beyond what the regular rank and file received. Now that Kassie was the big boss, would Karen expect some grandiose gesture under the category of RWB—Receptionist with Benefits? Or would Karen make Kassie some offer she couldn't refuse in return for something of significant value? *Fat chance.*

"Get in. The door's open," Karen yelled from the driver's side.

Slightly winded and out of out-of-control thoughts, Kassie welcomed the opportunity to sit. She slid into the black leather passenger seat, got her phone out, and buckled up for more than just safety. Noticing Karen had slung her purse in the back seat, Kassie retrieved her wallet and said, "Here, let me pay for parking," as she handed Karen her platinum Amex card. When she said, "It's the least I can do," she failed to notice Karen's raised eyebrows.

"No argument here. Thanks." Little did she know Karen was mostly thankful she didn't have to pay with Mike's Visa card.

Once out of the garage, Kassie focused on her phone. "I should let Chris know where I am."

"Where we are, you mean. Don't want him wandering around the hospital looking for me."

"Right." *As if he would.*

Kassie considered how best to tell Chris what was going on in the fewest words.

Hey. You have my keys. Karen's driving me home.

Sorry about that. Nice of her though.

How long you staying?

Til they kick me out or until 3ish when they begin prepping her, methinks.

Will you head home then?

Kassie inhaled deeply, fearing Chris would ultimately decide to stay at the hospital overnight, and fearing something had broken, not just Lexi's leg.

"What's he saying?"

"He thinks they'll start getting Lexi ready for surgery in about an hour." Kassie neglected to share his *nice of her* sentiment, as she chewed the inside of her lip, waiting for his reply.

Then it came.

Of course. Dinner tonight with Mom and Dad. Remember?

Indeed. With all the Lexi drama, Kassie forgot about their dinner plans with Sarah and Charlie. It heartened her to realize Chris had his priorities straight.

"Why the smile?" Karen said.

Kassie concealed how happy she was that Chris would head home shortly instead of hanging around the hospital until the middle of the night, when Lexi was due to be out of post-op and in her room. Instead, she cited their dinner plans, which would be of no interest to Karen, as the reason for the positive shift in her mood.

"He reminded me we're having dinner with his father and mother ..." As soon as she said *mother*, she knew her blunder, and her smile turned to a grimace faster than a rocket lifting off a launch pad. Kassie stared out the side window, expecting Karen to burst into one of her famous tirades about being Chris's actual mother.

"Oh, dinner? Tonight? Before Charlie and Sarah leave, I guess?"

Perhaps Karen didn't catch Kassie's faux pas?

"Yes. It'll be nice for the four of us to be together. As you know, we didn't have much time to chat after the funeral. I suggested Chris have dinner with them alone, but he insisted I be with him. To be honest, I think he just wants me there to navigate the way to the hotel. He's still learning his way around Boston. You know how men are with directions."

"Hotel? You're picking them up?"

"No, we're meeting them and having dinner there."

"Where's there?"

"The Lock and Key Hotel. Relatively new. It once was an old house of detention."

"I've read about that place. A historic jail. Hmm. Sounds like a good time. Today, that is. Not back then." Karen laughed. "Do they have parking?"

Kassie's head snapped back ever so slightly. Parking? Why would Karen ask about parking?

"Yes, of course. Why do you ask?"

"Umm. Well, uh. Just curious. Mike often complained … uh, about parking in downtown Boston … uh, when he went in to meet with a client."

That was news to Kassie. Mike complained about a lot of things. Parking for a client meeting was seldom one of them. Kassie scratched her head, deciding it was best not to challenge Karen. Assuming she hadn't really missed the mother reference, heading it off at the pass might be Kassie's best opportunity to avoid Karen's likely wrath.

"Sorry about referring to Sarah as Chris's mother. Didn't mean to offend you." Kassie hesitated and counted on her fingers, wondering how high she'd get before the verbal fireworks began?

"No offense taken. Aren't we becoming quite the twenty-first century family?"

"How so?" Kassie goggled in shock and awe; she'd only counted to her middle finger. Who was this person impersonating Karen?

"Think about it. Chris has two mothers—me and Sarah. There was a time he had three, but now that we know Mike's not his real father, you're no longer his stepmom."

"Thank goodness for that." Kassie tried to chuckle, not knowing exactly what direction Karen was going with this line of reasoning.

"I agree. How weird that must have been for you! And for Chris. How would he have introduced you to his friends? This is my fiancée, who is also my father's ex-wife?"

The words *I'm having an affair with my husband's son* whizzed through Kassie's mind. Obviously, she hadn't successfully erased that tape yet. *You'll need to work on that.*

"It's easy to imagine, isn't it, how he must've explained things to Lexi last year? I'm sure she thought our relationship was in the rearview mirror when we split after we all thought I was having an affair with my husband's son." *Damn those words again.*

"You must regret that now."

"Regret what? My affair with Chris? Or breaking up with him when I thought he was Mike's son?"

"Maybe both?"

Kassie decided not to go there. She'd never regret meeting Chris in Venice and falling in love with him—though on more than one occasion, she wished she'd divorced Mike sooner, before he discovered, or rather revealed, his chronic kidney disease. Had she been free of Mike sooner, she and Chris would have already been married for a few years. He wouldn't have had a fling with Lexi in Greece. The truth of Chris's lineage would still be buried. And she wouldn't be sitting in traffic with a woman attempting to psychoanalyze her.

"You're probably right about Lexi," Kassie said. "We can't blame her for being in love with Chris. I can't, anyway. He's great. It's just a shame everyone's timing was off. I'm afraid this is all going to get very complicated."

"It doesn't have to be complicated. I think our own version of *Modern Family* can succeed. Don't you?"

"How so?"

"Just think about how blessed those two babies will be, especially because they're being born into a family that seems to be larger than Lexi's. Chris and Lexi's children …"

Kassie grunted hearing those four words. She hadn't said them out loud yet.

"You listening, Kassie?"

"Yes, Karen, of course. Go on."

"Chris and Lexi's children will have two grandmothers—Sarah and me. As well as a mother *and* a stepmom, if you want to be referred to as such, if and when you and Chris finally get married."

Lucky kids. Lucky for Kassie, they'd pulled into her driveway, saving her from having to respond to Karen's outrageous assumption.

16

Hide-and-Seek

Karen wheeled the car into Kassie's driveway. As she drove over the bump at the bottom, she released her foot on the gas ever so slightly, almost like holding your breath when you hiccup. Muscle memory must be a real thing.

She parked behind Lexi's rental car, which blocked Chris's car, just as Kassie had said it did. Not that she ever doubted Kassie's story about not having a car at the hospital, but if she was going to finagle her way into the legacy of whatever Michael Ricci left behind, it was becoming crystal clear to her she'd need to start cozying up to Kassie. No matter how much it frosted her ass to do so.

Fortunately, the driveway was long enough to hold three or more cars, so she didn't have to park on the street. As Karen got out of the Lexus, she followed closely on Kassie's heels. When she stopped to the right of the garage door, Kassie keyed in the code. Her fingers moved so fast, Karen failed to pick up the sequence of numbers. If she had only asked Mike for the code when he was alive, she wouldn't feel as if he short-changed her in his will.

Despite the scraping and creaking garage door, she heard Kassie say into her phone, "House list. Garage door. Greased."

"Who you talking to?"

Kassie laughed as she explained in way too much detail for Karen's liking about how she was able to create lists on the Alexa app. Apparently, besides the Post-it notes she was most famous for, Kassie kept digital lists to manage not just the house, but also the cat, groceries, birthdays, and all things related to her going to Paris for her company. One of her companies, anyway. Thankfully, not Ricci and Son, where Karen had decided she'd continue being gainfully employed, not just for monetary reasons. She needed to keep her son close and her enemies closer. The more she knew what was up, the more she could protect her own interests.

Upon entering the house through the garage door, which led into a small hallway and mudroom, Karen couldn't help but notice the cat back away from the door and skedaddle into the family room, meowing the entire way.

"You hungry, Topher?" Kassie stopped in the mudroom, retrieved a small pouch of what looked to Karen like a bag of Goldfish crackers from a cabinet above the washer and dryer, and followed him. "Here, this should hold you for a while."

At sixes and sevens on how to behave in a house she should be living in but wasn't, Karen moseyed into the kitchen, sat down at the oak table at the far end, and waited for Kassie to find her there. Rather than scurry around on her own searching for the small shopping bag, she decided she might as well take her cues from Kassie. It was her domain now—again.

"What are you doing in here?" Kassie joined her in the kitchen, but at the other end, next to the refrigerator.

"Oh. I thought I'd wait for you before looking around the house."

Did Kassie just smile?

"Perhaps we should reconstruct your movements. That's what my mother always suggested I do when I couldn't remember where I put something."

Bang. Bang. They both swung their eyes toward the lower cabinet next to the stove.

"What was that?"

"Probably just some lids shifting. Or mice flitting around." Kassie laughed, most likely thinking she'd made a joke.

Karen let the reference to mice pass, knowing full well there'd be no mice in that house with the cat lurking. That much she knew about cats.

Seeming to want to change the subject, Kassie said, "You ready to see what we can find?"

"Okay, let's start in your office."

"Good idea. That's the last place I remember seeing you with the bag. As I recall, you tore an edge of it when I told you what Mike had left for you."

All Karen remembered was Kassie's saying, "A thousand dollars a month for five years." Words that meant she'd have to continue working for the rest of her life. Not the future she envisioned had she become Mrs. Ricci. Somehow, she needed to convince Kassie and Chris that Mike really did appreciate her donating her kidney to him. What she once did for love must be worth more than sixty thousand dollars, paid out over time. After all, because of her unselfish act, Mike probably lived a year longer than he would've otherwise. And during that year, Chris learned the ins and outs of Ricci and Son, and Kassie was free to focus on the career she claimed to love. All that must have some monetary value they could bestow on her.

Following in Kassie's footsteps again, Karen arrived in Kassie's office, feeling more nostalgic than she had a right to feel. This was supposed to be her room to do with whatever she wanted. And now it just looked and smelled like wishful thinking gone sour.

Kassie walked behind her desk, pulled out the rolling chair, and bent down, looking underneath. "Not here."

One by one, Karen tilted back the other chairs in the room, willing the bag to be underneath one of them. Nothing doing.

"Check the wastebasket," Karen said as she scoped out the area behind the office door and ran her fingers across the shelves on the tall bookcase. *Does she really read all of these?*

"If you're ever looking for something good to read, let me know. I'd be glad to loan you—"

"Thanks. I'll keep that in mind," Karen said heading her off at the pass. Getting into a discussion with Kassie about the latest *New York Times* bestseller was the furthest thing from her mind. Finding that necklace and hot footing it home to change for dinner were job one.

Karen threw her hands in the air, conceding the bag wasn't in Kassie's office. "I think I was holding it when I walked out of the room."

Continuing the hunt, Karen tried to visualize what had happened next, leading Kassie into the family room. "Charlie, Sarah, and I chatted here for a few minutes. Then I went to the bathroom."

Nothing seemed out of place in the family room, as Karen recalled from the days she'd spent there. The end tables had the requisite lamps, books, and tissue boxes. The only thing different was that a picture of Kassie and Chris had replaced one of her and Mike. She walked to it and picked it up, wondering if Kassie had eighty-sixed theirs?

"Venice?"

"Yes."

"Second trip?"

"No, first. We weren't there long enough to take pictures last time. For that matter, we weren't in Paris long enough to take many pictures there either."

As Karen placed the frame back on the table, Kassie came up next to her and slid open the drawer in the table. "Here, take this. It's yours." Karen felt a warm hand on her arm.

Did she read my mind? Mike often said she was good at that. Freaky!

"I better not put it down anywhere, huh? I might lose it too."

Kassie tried to assure her she hadn't lost the necklace. They just hadn't found it yet. It had to be somewhere in the house if it wasn't in her car or at the apartment.

"Unless someone snatched it," Karen said.

"Highly unlikely. The few folks who were left at that point yesterday are all people I trust. And you should trust too."

After looking behind the chairs and coming up empty-handed, Karen checked the bathroom just in case. Of course, it wasn't there.

"No luck?"

Karen surrendered, slumping onto Mike's BarcaLounger, a.k.a. his Pleasure Chair, which wasn't pleasing her much at the moment. She leaned forward and buried her head in her hands. Tears, not her usual reaction, appeared from nowhere.

She sensed Kassie's hand on her shoulder and looked up. "This really sucks," Karen said.

Kassie sat across from her on the couch and ran her hand through her hair. If she'd meant that as a brush, it fell short, in Karen's opinion. But by now, she figured hers wasn't in great shape either. *Are we becoming two peas in a pod?*

"How about something to drink? It's five o'clock somewhere, so how does a glass of wine sound?"

Kassie didn't wait for her to answer, disappearing into the kitchen with Topher scampering alongside her.

While Karen didn't want to hang around the house longer than necessary, she also didn't want to leave empty-handed. She just had to find that necklace.

"I'm thinking," Kassie said, handing her a glass of chilled pinot grigio and settling back on the couch. Topher must have taken it as his cue to insert himself into the fray, as he jumped on her lap.

Kassie stroked his back, and he purred so loudly she had to raise her voice to continue her thought. "I should just contact the people who were still here when you walked out of my office. Maybe someone saw you put the bag down, or put it somewhere for safekeeping, thinking it was mine, and forgot to mention it to me. That's always a possibility, right?"

Karen wasn't sure of Kassie's thought process, but she didn't have any ideas to offer, so what the heck?

Kassie offered to text Teresa, Vicki, and Amelia, who all had stayed behind to get the house in order following the funeral. And she was planning to call Annie anyway before heading out for dinner. Oh, and then she could certainly ask Sarah and Charlie at dinner if they'd seen a small bag with Guy's and Dolly's Galleria of Jewels printed on it.

Whatever Kassie wished the wine would do for Karen didn't work. She welled up in tears again at the mention of dinner, realizing her plan had gone down just as fast as the drink had.

Karen grabbed the picture frame and started toward the garage to leave. It was getting late, and if she was going to show up at the dinner as she promised Charlie, she'd have to readjust her game plan without the necklace as proof of Mike's undying love and forever commitment to her.

Just as she stepped into the hallway, Karen felt a breeze sweep by her right leg. Glancing down, she caught a glimpse of Topher rushing past her.

"Wait for me," Kassie said, catching up with them. "Don't want Topher getting out through the garage."

Abruptly, Topher skidded. A door in the mudroom stopped his forward trajectory. At that, he raised his rear haunches and banged his body against the door, mewling loudly.

Unexpectedly, Topher brushed his body around Karen's right leg, and then her left.

"Maybe he doesn't want you to leave?" Kassie laughed.

He stretched out on the floor, blocking Karen, and slid his paw underneath the closet door.

Karen wondered if Topher had pulled a similar stunt on Lexi, which was why she was probably on her way to surgery that very moment.

17

FWPB

After the nurse granted him permission to assist Lexi fill out the paperwork with a curt "Make it snappy" and Kassie and Karen had left, Chris settled into a chair at the foot of Lexi's hospital bed. With only the two of them left in the room, the *beep ping beep* of the monitors reminded him why he was there. Constantly. He didn't need Lexi to do it.

So, when Lexi said, "Why don't you sit up here next to me?" Chris claimed he didn't want to disturb any of the wires they'd hooked her up to. She gave him a you-gotta-be-kidding-me look, shrugged, and accepted his feeble excuse, for which he was grateful. He didn't want to give her any false impression of why he stayed behind instead of leaving with Kassie when he could have. Yes, he cared about Lexi, but they weren't a couple.

Chris was simply an FWPB. Friend with Parental Benefits.

He could just as easily help her fill in whatever blanks stumped her sitting eight feet away as he could up close and personal.

From his vantage point, Lexi didn't seem as stressed as he imagined he would be if he were sitting where she was. In all his forty-some-odd years, he'd never had surgery or spent an overnight in the hospital—all thanks to the good ol' mothering skills of Sarah Gaines. Despite her philanthropic commitments to Chicagoland and her role as an active associate at the Chicago Museum of Art, Sarah always put Chris's needs ahead of her own.

He tried hard to picture the woman in the bed in front of him as the mother of his children. He'd never given that possibility any thought. But there Lexi was, pregnant. Humming. Her pen seemed to be making headway through the sheets of paper on the clipboard.

"How can I help?"

"You're here. With me. That's more than enough." Lexi smiled, then chewed the pen.

He inhaled deeply as his right foot took to tapping. Though never a hospital patient, he was becoming a regular visitor. How many times had he been there in the last week? Too many for his liking. And what about from now on? How long would they confine Lexi after surgery? Two, three days? A week? How much time would he need to be there each day assuring her he was committed to the kids, though not necessarily to a romantic relationship with her?

And then there was the office. How would he handle all the work he'd put on the back burner—starting with his trip to Europe, then Mike's demise—and now this? He took out his smartphone to text Bill, who thought Chris was taking time off to put some of Mike's affairs in order and to spend some quality time with Kassie—meaning in bed—making up for cutting their trip to Paris short. Bill needed to know that none of that was happening.

Contacting Bill would have to wait.

As if she sensed he was thinking of her, Chris received a text from Kassie letting him know she hitched a ride home with Karen, of all people. He'd wait to get the lowdown on their ride on their way to dinner with Sarah and Charlie that night. Once he got home to Kassie, he'd have one thing on his mind. And it didn't involve talking … or Karen.

Chris steadied his right foot. His left foot took over as he moistened his lips.

Lexi said, "You okay over there? Whatcha thinking about?"

"Just work." That was the best and safest answer he could give, not wanting to tell Lexi all the shit clamoring through his mind and that making love to Kassie was his latest thought. That way, he didn't lie or get into a conversation he wasn't at all prepared to have.

Lexi resumed her pen chewing.

Chris addressed the easiest problem on his plate—the office. Though he'd been at Ricci and Son just over a year, he knew the team would have his back and pick up whatever void his absence caused.

As he was about to text Bill, he realized Bill wasn't up on all the latest news. He didn't know Mike wasn't his father and wouldn't know who Lexi was since he left the house before she arrived on Kassie's doorstep. So rather than start something he couldn't finish, he simply wrote:

At the hospital with a friend. May need you to cover me for a few days. I'll call later to set up time to talk. Give my regards to all.

No emoji added. He saved those for Kassie.

"You texting Kassie?"

"No, Bill," Chris said, keeping his head down. Her remark sounded more like an accusation than an inquiring mind, so he added, "At the office."

As he waited for Bill's response, he lifted his head to see how Lexi was doing. Her pen continued its progress through the documents. She probably didn't need his help after all.

His phone pinged.

Sorry to hear that. Hope Lexi's going to be okay, Pops.

Chris stared at his phone, reading Bill's message three times and swallowing hard. How did he know about Lexi? And what was with the fatherly reference?

Okay. Who spilled the beans?

Cecilia stopped by the office.

Chris let out an audible "Huh." He guessed Cecilia was exploring the possibility of starting her internship sooner rather than later.

So much for secrets.

Sorry, bro. Sounds like you have your hands full. Call whenever. How's Kassie handling things?

Thanks. Later.

That was all Chris could say at the moment, unable to answer Bill's question because, frankly, he didn't know.

Only a couple of weeks ago, he had no women problems. He was happily engaged to Kassie, and Lexi was three thousand miles away and comfortably in his past. Now there were two women expecting something, though each different, from him.

Given their discussions in Greece and her untimely arrival after Mike's funeral, no less, Chris believed Lexi's plan was as clear as a shot of tequila he wished he had in his hand. Lexi intended to use her pregnancy to pry him away from Kassie. And for her, the ace, or aces, in the hole were the babies. But Lexi's scheme had one fatal flaw: leaving Kassie was not in any of the cards Chris held. He wouldn't play or be played.

Decidedly, the best alternative for managing Lexi would be for him to set boundaries, like sitting out of her reach, as he did then. And be consistent with the messages he gave her. He could do that, couldn't he?

Everything was happening so fast; he wasn't sure where Kassie stood on the entire situation. She welcomed Lexi into her home the night before, accepting Chris's mistake almost as if it were just another of life's problems she could control and solve, starting with inviting Lexi to spend the night in the guest room. For sure, he'd have to share his boundary-setting idea with Kassie before she turned her house into a bed-and-breakfast.

It hadn't surprised him, though, when she jumped to Lexi's aid when she fell that morning, or when she showed up at the hospital to support both Lexi and him. But crying and fawning over Lexi when she learned twins were involved was not the reaction he expected from the woman who'd never have children of her own, yet would someday soon be a stepmother to his children.

Nevertheless, there she was. Kassie, the forever optimist.

That was, until Karen entered the picture. Their plan to stage an introduction between Lexi and her quickly evaporated. So much for Kassie's planning prowess. Even her clairvoyance failed her. Maybe Mike's and her mother's aura lingered in the hospital duct work, clouding Kassie's power to control the situation, no matter how distressful.

Once they got through that day and the surgery, he'd have a heart-to-heart with Kassie. If she needed any reassurance from him, he'd give it. If she needed to vent concerns she harbored about their relationship, he'd let her vent. If she challenged him about how he was going to balance long-distance parenting, he'd admit he still had to work all that out, assuming Lexi would return to San Francisco as soon as the doctors allowed. Which, of course, he expected would happen. No reason for her to stay in Boston, especially since he was committed to Kassie.

He glanced at Lexi, still humming something he didn't recognize. *What's taking her so long?*

Rubbing his forehead was all he could do as he reflected on how complicated his life had become in the last twenty-four hours.

Besides the Lexi dilemma, he wondered if Mike would have changed his role in the company, or at least changed its name, had he known the truth before he died? Chris hoped not. But what would happen once Bill got wind that Mike was not his real father?

Would that affect their relationship at the office? Or their friendship that was growing? Would it affect the way they co-managed Ricci and Son until Kassie returned from Paris and reclaimed the mantle at a renamed O'Callaghan, Mahoney, and Gaines?

"Hey, babe, I think I need your help." It startled him when he heard Lexi's voice. Before he responded, he typed *Call Annie* in his Notes app—though this was one reminder he didn't really need.

"Look at this. I'm almost finished. But here's something I can't answer."

"What's that?"

"My local address and who to contact in case of emergency."

Lexi pouted and put her free hand on her tummy. Chris got the message. He gave her the address of his Charlestown apartment and told her to put down both his cellphone and office telephone numbers.

So much for boundaries.

As if on cue, the nurse returned to pick up the paperwork. She flipped through it and said, "Looks like you're good to go." Two orderlies came in, shifted Lexi onto a gurney, and repositioned her wires. She was on her way.

She gazed at Chris as if he was all she had in the world. All he could muster was his hand on his heart and a small kiss blown through the air.

As he was about to follow her out of the room, Chris heard the familiar ping of an incoming text message. He grabbed his phone from his pocket. Nothing there. He heard the ping again, this time locating the sound coming from under a blanket on the hospital bed. He picked up Lexi's phone and read:

Getting on 95 now.

See you tomorrow.

He stared in the direction the orderlies had wheeled Lexi. *Who's Aunt Venus?*

18

Music to Her Ears

Once Karen hustled off to wherever she was heading in such a hurry, Kassie plopped onto the couch in the family room and poured herself another glass of wine. What a day. Usually she wouldn't have more than one glass of wine before going out for dinner, but today was far from usual.

With Topher stretched out alongside her, his head on her lap, purring, Kassie wished she knew for sure if he was the culprit. Had he caused Lexi's tumble?

"Was it you?" Kassie stroked the spot between his eyes. He closed them as if sleep was near and his motor grew louder. "What are you thinking, my sweet?"

With no certitude about what had transpired that morning and with Topher unable to shed any light on the topic, Kassie resigned herself to accept Lexi's explanation of what had happened. At least for now.

What other choice did she have? She only just met Lexi. There was no way to determine whether or not she was telling the truth.

One lesson she recalled her father teaching her in the ten short years they had together was to never call someone a liar.

Unless, of course, you could prove otherwise.

Like the time when she was seven years old and had woken up in the middle of the night for no apparent reason. Even at that young age, Kassie knew going into her parents' room to wake them up wouldn't be a good idea. As a Boston police officer, her dad needed all the rest he could muster so he could be *awake, alive, and enthusiastic* on the job. That's what he said, anyway; she believed him.

That particular early morning or middle of the night—she never knew which was which—Kassie was bored. Quietly, she turned on the light next to her bed and rummaged through the blond toy chest in her walk-in closet for a box of crayons. Searching for her favorite cowgirl coloring book or at least some plain white paper was futile. She came up empty-handed. All of those essentials must have been on her art table in the living room. She contemplated creeping down the stairs but decided that, too, was unwise.

So she did the next best thing. She looked around her bedroom with its baby-powder-white walls; the color she'd picked out with her father. No girly pink for her. Sitting on the floor next to her bed, she found a brown crayon and drew her interpretation of a horse on the wall. She leaned back, admiring her artwork. She named him Hercules, after the next-door neighbor's German Shepherd—printing *Herkulees* on an angle near its head. The horse looked handsome, but lonely. He needed company. With a blue crayon, she sketched a long-legged, stick-figured cowboy with pointy boots. Soon her eyes grew heavy. She'd finish drawing *Hero* later.

Kassie opened her eyes to her mother and father hovering over her.

"Did you do this?" her father asked, as he bent down and picked up the Crayola box, handing it to her mother.

Kassie leaned over to look at whatever he was referring to. "No."

"You sure?" her mother said, giving her a second chance to fess up.

"Nope. Not me."

Her father told her to get dressed and meet him and her mother in the kitchen. "You've got five minutes."

Pulled away from the kitchen table was a chair with her name on it. Literally. Her father made it out of oak once she'd graduated from a high chair and painted her name in purple and green across the back. Three yellow flowers surrounded *Kassie*, one for her and one for each of her parents.

"Listen, missy," her father started once she slid into the chair. "We asked you twice if that was your handiwork on the wall. You denied it. How do you think it got there? Did Casper the ghost slip in through your window during the night, find your crayons, and make that exquisite drawing?"

"No." She started to giggle but stifled the urge.

"Then it had to be you, Kassie," her mother said. "Don't lie."

"Don't call her a liar, Patricia, unless you can prove it."

"I'm not a liar."

"We'll see," her father said, pulling out the brown and blue crayons from his pants pocket. "I guess I'll just take this evidence down to the station and check for fingerprints."

Wide-eyed, Kassie knew her goose was cooked. She admitted she made the drawing. What else was she supposed to do when she woke up at three in the morning?

"Read a book," her mother and father said in unison, followed by her mother saying "Jinx," and her father telling her she owed him a Coke.

Grown-ups.

Now as an adult herself, Kassie couldn't grasp why she lied back then, but she always remembered her punishment—no chocolate chip cookies for a week. And that her dad had slipped a vanilla wafer to her as she sat at the kitchen table printing one hundred times on lined three-hole punched paper—*Thou shalt not tell a lie.*

"Lies," Kassie said out loud to no one but Topher, who apparently grew tired of the little attention she was giving him and had curled his body in a circle on Mike's BarcaLounger. His front paws crossed over his eyes. So many lies in the last couple of years—little ones, big ones, white lies. Too many to count. She was sure she could write a book about them. Perhaps when she retired.

Kassie looked around the family room. She and Mike had spent years in there; some good times, some not so good times. How many Red Sox/Yankee battles did they watch? How many Sundays had they cheered on Tom Brady and the Patriots?

Picking up her wineglass, she went over to a media cabinet that was almost as tall as her. She flipped open the Bose Wave music system she gave Mike one Christmas, expecting to pick out a CD from the stack sitting beside it. Since there was one already in place, she pressed Play.

A chill formed around her shoulders and goosebumps spread down to her fingertips; her thighs tingled through to her calves and to her toes. She could name the song and the artist in one drumbeat. Standing with one hand on the cabinet and her eyes glassing over, she let "Mack the Knife" play through.

Rumor had it Mike was sitting in his BarcaLounger when the ambulance arrived to take him to the hospital the week before. Had he been looking through their wedding pictures and listening to Bobby Darin's *That's All* album when he had that initial heart attack? The album was the first present he'd given her way back when she was a student at the University of Missouri, and he was her Italian professor.

"I want you in my fan club too," he'd said. Those were the good times.

Needing to steady her legs, Kassie found the couch and soaked in the family room again. She remembered placing the picture of her and Chris on the table but couldn't recall removing pictures of her and Mike. More than likely, Karen confiscated them a while ago. Mike would've left them on display, because he was too lazy to pack them away, or he assumed Kassie would collect whichever pictures she wanted after the divorce. Didn't matter now. She'd look for the pictures later.

As Bobby Darin crooned on, so did Kassie's thoughts about Mike. She hadn't grieved or expected to feel the intense sorrow for Mike the music raised up in her. Granted he was a prick, especially doing everything possible to ensure she wouldn't get pregnant. Those were the not so good times.

She gathered her thoughts. Her heart and mind needed more than a sip of wine as she confronted the unexpected emotions welling up inside.

Wait a minute? Was her discovery of the CD a sign Mike left for her, even if unwittingly? They'd forgiven each other their transgressions when they last spoke in the hospital the day before he died. Recalling it now, Kassie was sure if Chris wasn't in the picture and Mike had recovered, he would've tried one more time to win her back.

In some ways, she reckoned Mike died fulfilled.

He was still officially married to Kassie, and maybe that was enough for him. After all, he lived out their vow of 'til death do us part. So had she, come to think of it.

And Mike died believing Chris was his son. Though it would've never been her truth to tell, she was certain had he known the truth before his heart attack killed him, nothing would've changed between him and Chris. Surprisingly, despite his relationship with Kassie, Mike genuinely liked Chris and was proud and pleased he instilled an upbeat, contemporary vibe into the firm since he'd joined. The obvious competition between Chris and Bill raised Bill's game to a higher and more profitable level.

Just in time.

Now, as CEO of Ricci and Son, in name only, Kassie would need to rely on Chris and Bill to carry the load, so there was a viable company for her to return to when she completed her commitment to Calibri in Paris.

With both fists, Kassie wiped any wet or dried tears that lingered on her cheeks. She needed to snap out of her doldrums. No time to wallow in the past, a past she could not change. It was time for her to shower and get ready for dinner with Sarah and Charlie. Tomorrow she'd sort through the CDs and put them in the same box as the pictures. And then she'd figure out how to solve the Lexi dilemma. All in due time.

Right now, she needed her BFF.

19

Is That All?

Wait for me! Topher meowed and jumped off the BarcaLounger as soon as Kassie picked herself up and headed for the stairs. Instead of turning right toward the master bedroom, she veered left and froze in the doorway of the larger of two spare bedrooms, the one in which Lexi slept the previous night.

Topher sat on his haunches in the hallway, waiting for Kassie's next move.

She intended to relax in the chaise lounge in that room as she talked to Annie. Spotting Lexi's clothes strewn across the bed, Kassie stepped back, shrugging off her original plan. That was, until she noticed her mother's multicolored afghan on the floor in a heap next to the chair.

Privacy be damned.

In a huff, Kassie marched into the room and snatched the afghan. *How dare she?*

She craned her neck slightly into the guest bathroom, half expecting to hear water running or sensing the toilet needed a good flush. Neither happened. Of course, she found a white towel balled up on the floor. *Does she think this is a hotel?*

Kassie picked up the towel to hang it on the rack. Instead, she tucked it under her arm beneath the afghan. Since the towel was damp and had sat all day on the floor, she reached into the vanity cabinet and hung up a fresh, dry towel on a hook behind the door. "There you go," she said, fluffing it up a tad. She grabbed the used hand towels and washcloths and wrapped the bath towel around them. *Might as well.*

She noticed a small, amber-colored prescription bottle next to a paper cup on the sink. Naturally, she read the label. The words *morning sickness* jolted Kassie back into reality. Gently replacing the bottle where she found it, she left the bedroom, closing the door behind her.

With the wet towels in a ball, Kassie braced herself at the top of the stairs and heaved them down to the tiled entryway below, missing Topher's fluffy bed in the corner near the front door. She'd pick them up and put them in the wash later.

Before she called Annie, Kassie stripped, intending to shed any residual germs or stench she'd picked up at the hospital. She checked her phone for the time. 3:08. *Darn. She's probably still at work.*

Kassie pulled a lightweight terry-cloth robe out of her closet, slid into it, and sat on the floor with her back to the waterbed frame. Not the most comfortable position, but it would do for the moment. Anyway, her call with Annie wouldn't be as long as their calls usually were with Chris expected home shortly. She made a note on her phone to move the chaise lounge back into the master bedroom as soon as Lexi was out of there.

Annie answered on the first ring. "You home?"

"Yes, finally. You still at the museum? I can call later."

"I am. But I can talk. It's quiet here today. Just me, the fossils, flowers, and the forests."

Just like Annie to joke about her work as an archivist at the Cambridge Natural History Museum. With new collections arriving daily, Annie was never bored and always full of stories, some true and some conspiratorial, about the nature of man and how we're heading for a climate disaster. To know Annie meant to always be in the know.

On more than one occasion, Mike urged Kassie to ask Annie to introduce him to the museum's marketing director. He'd have loved to get that account. She'd remind him the museum would be a plum account for her firm as well. So if she was going to do anyone's bidding, it would be for Calibri. *So there.*

But Kassie would never take advantage of her friendship with Annie. She was confident if the museum was in the market for a new advertising relationship, Annie would know and, in turn, would give Kassie a heads-up. In some ways, she was glad that had never occurred. In that way, they could keep their professional and personal relationships separate and sacrosanct.

Nevertheless, Kassie enjoyed Annie's stories about packages she received from people who believed the bones they dug up in their backyards were dinosaur fossils, when they actually were from cats and dogs buried in years past.

Now, she had a doozy of a story for Annie.

Kassie prefaced her tale by saying she expected Chris home shortly, so she'd call her at home later that night after dinner, if she had to jump off suddenly. Not that Chris would care she was talking to Annie, but Kassie wanted to give him her undivided attention when he arrived. As she talked, she wiggled out of her undies and tossed them toward the hamper.

Annie prefaced her remarks with "It's about time you called. You left me in the lurch this morning."

Kassie apologized.

"Did Lexi lose the baby?"

"Not quite. She fractured her leg. They're operating this afternoon. And, Annie, you sitting down?"

"Yes. Why?"

"There are two babies. Lexi's pregnant with twins."

Silence. Kassie held her phone at arm's length. Had the connection failed?

"Annie, you there?"

"Yes, Kassie, I'm here. Of course, I'm here. Sooo, I guess an abortion is out of the question?"

"Annie! Are you kidding me? An abortion was never *in* the question."

"You sure about that? Chris looked pretty stunned last night. I'd be surprised if the thought didn't cross his mind. But then there you were all googly-eyed about being a stepmom."

"Was I that bad?"

"Yup, you kind of were. Twins, huh? One kid would be complicated enough. Two is a whole new ballgame."

Kassie sat with her phone in one hand and her forehead in the other, as Annie listed all the obvious issues and dilemmas Chris and Kassie were about to face with Lexi and the babies. "Your marriage will be under incredible stress and strain even before you take your wedding cake out of the freezer to celebrate the end of year number one."

"Aren't you being a bit melodramatic?"

"Me? Melodramatic? Never. That's your shtick. But remember what I asked you this morning when I thought there was just one bun in the oven? Do you really think this is a good time for you to fly off to ol' Paree?"

Silence.

"Kassie, you there?"

"Yes, I'm here. You know I love you, and you're making all good points. I just don't know what I'm going to do. Would you believe before I called you, I flipped on the stereo and there was Bobby Darin reminding me of Mike and me back in Missouri? I actually cried. Annie, I think he was listening to it when they wheeled him out on a stretcher. It's a sign."

"Have you lost your mind? A sign of what? That he was an asshole?"

"Okay. Maybe I am losing my mind. What if he's telling me it's time to put it all behind me and move on? The name of the album is *That's All*."

"So he's saying what? That's all there is?"

"Right. Not to dwell on how we screwed up our marriage. Somehow giving me permission to marry Chris and to take the business forward to new heights."

Annie reminded her she already accepted Chris's marriage proposal, and she certainly didn't need Mike's permission.

"Except, by giving you the business, Mike must've thought you'd leave Calibri. So maybe the message he's giving you is *that's all over* at Calibri."

"No, I don't think that's it. Mike knew how much I wanted to put my mark on Calibri at the highest level possible. And I've made a commitment."

"Commitments are made to be broken. Just look at your marriage vows."

"Don't be such a cynic. I think Chris and I can figure all of this out. Including Paris. We've been apart before and found each other again."

"He found you, remember that. You walked away when the going got really tough."

"That's not fair. I thought he was Mike's son."

"Did you ever hear Chris say, 'I'm having an affair with my father's wife?'"

Silence.

"No."

"That's because it didn't matter to him. He loves you, Kassie. He always has and he always will. It's about time you figure out how you can be there for him when he needs you most."

"I'll think about it. I really don't want to lose Paris."

"Okay, you do that. In the meantime, I pray you don't lose Chris. Gotta go. Another call's coming in."

20

Center Stage

Chris searched his pants pockets front and back, trying to find the damn parking ticket. He easily found where he left the car in the hospital garage that morning. The ticket was another matter. He hoped he hadn't lost it. As he reached the car, he pulled out his wallet, and there it was. Right where he'd put it.

He took his Amex card and the ticket and tucked them into the cupholder next to a Starbucks cup. They'd be ready when he was. In a hurry earlier to get to Lexi, Chris hadn't noticed a sour smell in the car, which now wafted into his nostrils. He lifted the cup, got out of the car, held it at arm's length, and tossed it into a trash can near the stairwell. After heading out of the parking garage, he opened all four windows to give both the car and himself some much-needed fresh air.

Chris also needed to talk to a friend. Confused as to which problem to tackle first, at the first red light he inserted his earphones and called Annie. He prayed she wasn't tied up in some management meeting at the museum or on another call with a donor trying to convince her to acquire their butterfly or beetle collection. Thinking back, he'd attribute his preference to Monet over Triceratops when he was growing up to his mother, Sarah. With her life's work and philanthropy focused on art history, rather than natural history, it's no wonder he sought a career in art design and advertising. *Thank you, Mom.*

Annie answered on the fourth ring. "Where are you?"

"On my way home—why?"

Before Chris could fill her in, Annie told him she knew about Lexi's leg and the twins, thus relieving him from recounting all the gory details.

"So, you talked to Kassie? How do you think she's handling things?"

"Which things? That you knocked up an old girlfriend?"

"Kassie and I were on a break."

Annie didn't give him one. She continued: "Or that you're going to be the father of twins when you're supposed to be the man she plans to marry. Preferably unencumbered."

"We will be married."

Not reacting, she went on. "The easiest of the breaking news in the last twenty-four hours for her to digest was that you're not Mike's son."

Chris picked that topic and ran with it. "Shocking, huh? I'm still trying to sort through all the ramifications of that."

"Like what?"

He put up the windows, turned on the A/C and poured out his concerns about running the business and working with Bill under the new circumstances. Technically, Ricci and Son was suddenly a misnomer.

"Kassie's given you and Bill your marching orders. They're pretty clear. And from where I sit among the dinosaurs, you sit squarely in the nexus of all problems you're worried about. So, my dear friend, how are you planning to handle things?"

Was he at the center of everything? Certainly, Kassie held some sway in their future. Didn't she?

"You know how Kassie wants to change the name of the firm to O'Callaghan, Mahoney, and Gaines?" Chris said, testing the water.

"Yes, but OMG won't happen until she leaves Calibri next year."

"What if … she doesn't go to Paris? What if … she stays here, quits Calibri, and takes over the firm *now*, not a year from now?" Before she had a chance to respond, Chris shared with Annie how he never wanted Kassie to take the job in Paris in the first place. Annie would have to agree that a lot had changed since Kassie received the Paris offer. Certainly, she could tell the board she had second thoughts. Couldn't she?

He waited for Annie to concur with him. He needed her on his side.

"Kassie might agree a lot has happened, but I'm not sure she'd accept that it means she has to give up a dream opportunity, and in Paris—"

"But Mike didn't know about Paris before he left her the business. He assumed if something happened to him, she'd jump right in and take the reins. That was his succession plan. He didn't intend for either me or Bill to take over."

"I'm not sure she'll see it quite that way. Kassie has her own career. She's worked long and hard at Calibri to make a permanent mark there. This is her chance to do that before taking on a new challenge like running Mike's company."

"Okay, but what about the twins? They're due to arrive while she's in Paris. She wouldn't want to be thousands of miles away when that happens, would she?"

"Won't you be thousands of miles away from Lexi then?"

"Oh Christ. Annie, hold on." He hated talking while driving, and despite the air-conditioning, he began to sweat. Focus, he told himself. He turned into the Stop & Shop parking lot, pulled into a space along the perimeter, and let the engine idle to keep the car and himself cool in the afternoon midsummer heat.

He grabbed the steering wheel at ten and two o'clock and rested his head at twelve. An image of a globe filled his mind. If Kassie went to Paris and Lexi returned to San Francisco, he envisioned a red dotted line running from one place to the other. There'd be nearly six thousand miles separating them. And he'd be smack dab in the middle.

Chris tried to pull himself together and breathed deeply. He exhaled so loudly he was certain Annie heard him.

"You okay?"

"Honestly, Annie, I haven't figured out how to handle the Lexi situation. I've barely had time to grasp that I'm going to be a father, let alone the father of twins. Except for one thing I do know. I want to be involved with their life as much as possible. I want them to know who their father is."

"Unlike you, you mean?"

"How weird is that? I grew up thinking Charlie had adopted me when all along he was my real father."

"Will you look at him any differently now? Do you think that'll change anything between the two of you?"

Chris shrugged his shoulders. "Probably not. You know how guys are. We roll with the punches." As soon as he said that, he realized how ludicrous he must sound. He was far from rolling with any punches being thrown his way lately.

He tried to clarify his remark. "Guess we'll see about that. The first test will be tonight. We're having dinner with Charlie and Sarah."

"Would love to be a fly on the wall."

"I'm not worried about them. I'm worried about Kassie."

"Really? Or are you worried about yourself?"

Chris tugged the earphones off his right ear and then the left and tossed them onto the passenger seat. *Damn it.* His call with Annie didn't quite go the way he expected. He thought she'd agree with him that Kassie should stay put in Boston, take care of responsibilities there, support him when his world was upside down. Become an involved, perhaps loving—not wicked—stepmother, even if it was long distance.

On the rest of the drive home, Annie's question gnawed at him like an itch he couldn't reach. Was he just worried about himself? Growing up an only child, life was all about him. Did that make him selfish and unlovable? Is that why he hadn't found the right gal to settle down with until he met Kassie?

"She's an only child too," he said to the announcer on WBOS 92.9 radio who introduced Bon Jovi singing "Livin' On A Prayer." Maybe that was the tie that bound them together. They each knew what they had missed as kids. Were they the ultimate epitome of yin and yang? If that were true, she'd have to see things his way; understand how much he needed her. Wouldn't she?

Chris belted out the song, releasing the tension that had built inside him as he got closer to the house. Not knowing what he was walking into, he felt down on his luck, like the song said. Perhaps he should've called Kassie instead of Annie. If he had, he'd know before walking through the door whether she was as committed as he was to holding onto what they've got.

The house was quiet when he went in through the garage door. Topher wasn't there to greet him, as he sometimes did. Standing in the kitchen, he listened for any sign of Kassie. He could hear water running through the pipes and then a sudden clunk of the shower upstairs being shut off. That made sense. She was getting ready for dinner.

A nearly empty bottle of pinot grigio sat on the kitchen counter. Two wine glasses lay on their side in the sink. Had she and Karen shared a bottle of wine? Would wonders never cease?

Not letting the rest of the bottle go to waste, he grabbed it and chugged down the room-temperature remnants. He rinsed out the glasses, put them in the dishwasher and dropped the empty wine bottle in the recycling bag in the mudroom.

He delayed encountering Kassie long enough. Heading for the stairs, he almost tripped on a pile of white towels. He picked them up and placed them on top of the washing machine.

Walking back through the house to the stairs, he could hear Stevie Wonder singing the last few stanzas of "All in Love Is Fair." He stopped in the entryway to catch what song was up next. Stevie started the same song again. He knew she played it in a loop when she felt melancholy and in the mood. They'd made love to it too many times to count.

Chris unzipped his trousers and dropped them where the wet towels had been. He pulled the polo shirt up over his head and then climbed the stairs two at a time.

Kassie posed by the waterbed, wrapped in a yellow waffle towel with a hairbrush in her hand and wearing a slinky smile. When she tossed the brush toward the hamper next to her bureau, Topher took his cue and scampered out the bedroom door for safety.

Chris tugged at the towel, which fell to her feet.

"I see you heard my message," she said as he led her back into the shower.

21

Need You Now

The shower was just the appetizer. A steaming one, to be sure. Clearly, Chris and Kassie had some pent-up passion from the events of the last few days they needed to release. More than once.

Luckily, she set the alarm on her phone for six o'clock, not because she expected they'd fall asleep but simply because she didn't want to be late for dinner. Setting alarms or timers was how she got through her days on time, so she could always be awake, alive, and enthusiastic, like her father.

Her habit worked like a charm. As they awoke, they kissed in a hurry and jumped out of their respective side of the sloshing waterbed.

"Don't you think it's time you replace this bed?"

Kassie sighed and then agreed some memories were meant to be put to bed for good. Even if they replaced the entire bedroom suite of furniture, memories of Mike would still haunt her as long as she lived in that house.

"I'll put it on my list of things to do before I leave for Paris. We'll need to find time when you're available to go shopping with me, since you'll be the one breaking it in while I'm gone. And when I say breaking it in, I mean sleeping in it, not breaking it in in the colloquial sense. You'll need me here for that."

"Speaking of Paris …"

Kassie supposed Chris's mention of Paris was his way of suggesting she wear one of the dresses she'd bought at La Maison de Paris. She grabbed them out of her closet and hung them on the hook behind the powder room door. Holding up the black dress, she shook her head. *No can do.* She wore that the day before to Mike's funeral. It would have to be the midnight-blue, tulip-shaped dress she had worn to dinner in Paris—the night Chris proposed, or tried to propose, until her pomegranate rash rudely interrupted.

Standing in front of the full-length mirror, she held up the hanger with the dress in front of her. *Too fancy?*

"If it's good enough for 58 Tour Eiffel," Chris said, reading her mind. "It's good enough for dinner at the Lock and Key with my parents." He patted her rear.

Yet, she wasn't born yesterday. She knew better than to believe Chris had any interest in her clothing. Annie's warning that Chris would want her to turn down the Paris offer and stay in Boston echoed in her mind. Her goal was to convince him how much she needed Paris. Her crowning achievement. Perhaps if she approached the subject as a *fait accompli.*

"Oh Paris," she said as she turned her back to him so he could zip her up. "You're right. Mike's dying and the Lexi news interrupted my planning. Only temporarily. I need to get myself into the office … perhaps tomorrow … to start reassigning my local clients and to set up a meeting with the board …"

"So you're still intending to go?"

"To the office tomorrow? Why wouldn't I?" She handed him the white-gold chain that held both the gondola and Eiffel Tower pendants.

"No, to Paris?" Chris clasped the necklace and kissed the back of her neck as she slipped on her engagement ring.

She spun around in a tease. *"Mais, oui."* Kassie sashayed around the bedroom, pulling up the duvet cover so it would be somewhat orderly when they climbed back in later that night. Topher took that as his cue to jump on the bed and settle his body against Kassie's pillow.

"Why wouldn't I go to Paris?" She said the word, so there was no mistake about the topic at hand. She checked herself again in the mirror and applied her favorite plum-colored lip gloss.

"Why? Because I need you here," Chris said as he led their way down the stairs. *Thump, thump.* Topher stayed close behind Kassie.

"What? To pick up the pants you leave in a heap?" Kassie bent down, grabbed the trousers he left there earlier, and headed toward the kitchen.

"I was in a hurry. I heard your siren call."

"I'm glad it worked." She leaned up and gave him a full kiss on the lips. "Here, put these on the washer while I feed Topher."

"You taste good. Better watch it, or I'll take you back upstairs."

Kassie reminded him they were already cutting it close and had the rest of their lives together.

Before leaving the house, Kassie asked Chris to turn a light on in the family room for Topher as she flipped on the light over the kitchen sink. "It'll get dark before we're back."

"Cats can see in the dark. You know that, don't you?"

"What I know is if we don't get going, we'll be keeping your parents—my soon to be in-laws—waiting. Whose car are we taking?"

Walking out to the driveway through the garage, Kassie answered her own question. Actually, make that *questions*. The answers to both involved Lexi. They'd have to take Kassie's car because Lexi's rental car still blocked Chris's car. And as to why she wouldn't go to Paris? The answer Chris wanted from her was that she'd stay because of Lexi and the twins. She wasn't prepared to do that then, maybe ever.

"I guess I'll drive," she said, clicking the fob to unlock the doors.

"You sure? I can drive."

Though she loathed driving with a man sitting next to her, at that moment she needed to be in the driver's seat. Especially if Chris decided having her captive in the car was an appropriate venue to continue pressing about Paris. What could he possibly say—"I'm not going into the hotel until you promise not to leave me"?

KO, change the subject, her inner voice, or rather her mother's voice, commanded. She paused longer than normal at a stop sign, looking both ways more than once.

"So, how was Lexi when you left her? They'll call you when she's out of surgery?"

"Oh crap! See what you've done," Chris teased. "I turned off my phone when we got out of the shower and forgot to turn it back on." He reached into his blazer, retrieved it, and powered it up.

As he did, his phone chimed, indicating a message waited. Driving, Kassie could only glance sideways at Chris as he listened. Curiously, he didn't play the message so they both could hear.

"Is it from the hospital?"

Chris held up his right-hand index finger, indicating she should hold on, and then placed it on his lips, telling her to stay quiet so he could hear.

Now who's in the driver's seat? Kassie wondered.

"She's in recovery. The surgery went faster than expected. Lexi and the babies are doing fine. I can go see them in the morning."

"You mean *her*. You mean you can see Lexi? The twins aren't here yet."

Kassie pulled up in front of the Lock and Key Hotel, deciding to take advantage of valet parking. Before getting out of the car, she grabbed his hand and squeezed it tight. When he looked at her, she could see slight tears and his chest swell as he let out an enormous sigh.

The valet asked if they had luggage. She said no, they were there for dinner and handed him a twenty-dollar tip. She went over to the passenger side, opened the door, and gave Chris her hand.

"See. I need you, Kassie, here with me."

Well, not quite "I'm not going into the hotel until you promise not to leave me," but a variation on the theme, for sure.

She looped her arm through his. "Ya know, we've had enough excitement for a few days. Let's table that discussion for now and go in and have an uneventful dinner with Sarah and Charlie."

22

The Intern

Earlier that day, Ricci and Son was on the verge of getting a makeover. Though they'd lost Mike, their fearless leader, the firm was about to gain Cecilia Howe, a beautiful and bold intern.

Cecilia cut her shift at Boston Clinic short. She jumped on the T and made tracks home to change into what she figured had to be more appropriate business attire than her hospital garb. She slipped on a floral pencil skirt that sat a couple of inches above her knees, but long enough to keep her private parts private if seated. A white cotton sleeveless blouse, as sheer as she thought she could get away with, covered a pale violet, spaghetti-strap tank top.

Checking herself out in the mirror, especially above the waist, she gave her ample breasts a bouncy lift and hoped her decision to go braless on this scorching last Wednesday of July was wise. Expecting to meet people who'd form an initial and lasting opinion of her, she fastened a couple of buttons in the middle and rechecked that everything that needed to be tucked in and secured was indeed.

She pulled her long, gloriously dark auburn hair into a high ponytail, positioning it just slightly to the right, and securing it with a brand-new electric-purple scrunchie she recently bought at Claire's in the CambridgeSide mall. *Oh fiddlededee, no.* Wrong shade, especially against her hair color. *What was I thinking? Too late to return it.* Shrugging her shoulders, Cecilia tossed it in the drawer in the nightstand, riffled through ribbons, mascara, and empty birth control packs until she found Old Reliable, a white scrunchie she told the face in the mirror served two purposes: utilitarian and ornamental.

Almost, but not quite ready to hit the road, she held the bottle of Chloé L'Eau at arm's length, spritzed it three times, and walked through the spray with her eyes closed. With that, she grabbed her day bag and her keys and pointed her chest and her ten-year-old VW Beetle, which her father had bought used, toward nirvana. Actually, with the scent of grapefruit and roses lingering, she told Siri on her iPhone to play Nirvana's "Smells Like Teen Spirit." No matter how inappropriate the lyrics, she liked the beat. In sync with the music, Cecilia pounded the steering wheel as she navigated the insane midday Boston traffic, crossed the Longfellow Bridge, and pulled into the Ricci and Son parking lot.

For once, she agreed with her mother. When you're given a gift from heaven above, as Mr. Ricci had bestowed upon her, you don't wait to begin your new journey. You begin it as soon as possible.

This was an opportunity she'd been waiting for. Volunteering for the last two years at Boston Clinic, Cecilia often prayed in the chapel there that she'd meet someone influential, someone who could open a door that would otherwise be closed. Someone who appreciated that someday she could be somebody.

While it was less than twenty-four hours since Mrs. Ricci ushered her into her office after Mr. Ricci's funeral to tell her the mind-blowing news, Cecilia still felt the buzz. "I feel like I've won the lottery," she texted a friend. "Not a scratch-off ticket, the real thing. The Powerball."

A commercial plumber all his life, her father beamed and said, "You go, girl," when Cecilia told her parents of the gifts Mr. Ricci had left her. "Make sure you write a proper thank-you note. First impressions are critical to success. If your mother doesn't have some fine stationery, buy a nice card," he said, pulling a five-dollar bill out of his money clip. And then he added, "Never forget the people who give you first chances. You owe them."

For a starter, Cecilia owed her father a lot. For as long as she could remember, he'd worked overtime and taken on side jobs for neighbors and friends—untangling miles of funky hair from drains and unclogging unmentionables from toilets—so that she could continue her education past high school and fulfill her dream of being a famous writer one day. The twenty-five thousand dollars Mr. Ricci had stipulated should apply to her last year in college meant her father could use the home equity loan he was about to discuss with his banker to replace the roof instead of paying her college tuition.

Cecilia's news of her financial windfall seemed to barely register with her mother, who had her eyes glued to her Chromebook, reordering the weight-loss products she didn't need then or ever. She got hooked on them after Cecilia's brother was born, deciding it was time for her to contribute to the family's income now there were two mouths to feed.

Two months after her mother started spraying perfume on little cards and handing them to women more focused on cutting through Filene's Department Store in Downtown Crossing to get to the T than to buying perfume, the store announced it was closing. Right then, she pledged to get behind the counter at the new store.

"I'm destined to serve serious customers who come in to replace their favorite fragrance or buy a new scent they sampled from a small packet tacked inside their latest copy of *Vogue*," she'd told the family at the dinner table every night for a week. They all just nodded. Cecilia wondered if her mother had ever seen a copy of the upscale magazine. *People* was the only magazine her mother subscribed to annually.

Nevertheless, her mother assessed her competition and came to the conclusion, however misguided, that she needed to get her figure back and keep her weight down in order to jump to the other side of the counter when the new store opened. Apparently, she was right. She'd been selling Chanel No. 5 there for more than a decade.

"Look here, young lady," her mother said. "It says right here: 'For your future self.'" Cecilia humored her mother and glanced over her mother's shoulder at the Shaklee website.

She'd heard it all before. She touched the top of her mother's head and said, "I know, Mom, 'The best way to predict the future is to create it,'" she said, in a singsong sort of way.

"You got that right. And don't you go disparaging Dr. Shaklee. You know he created the very first vitamin in these United States. That's not for nothin'." Her mother adopted his sacred words and spouted them to Cecilia on a regular basis, almost it seemed, concurrent with Cecilia's period. Over time, she couldn't tell which was more distressing.

So, while Cecilia would've preferred not to add anything to her day-to-day schedule over the next five weeks before classes started, she pulled into an area in the Ricci and Son parking lot marked Visitors, imagining one day she'd have a space out front marked especially for her.

No one was at the first desk she encountered upon entering the Victorian-style home that Mr. Ricci's mother-in-law had redecorated. She knew that nugget of information because one day at the clinic when she'd delivered lunch to him, Mr. Ricci told Cecilia the story of how he gave Patricia O'Callaghan the opportunity to redo the office. "My mother-in-law was so traumatized that her daughter went to Italy without me. Crazy woman. As if her adult daughter couldn't take care of herself. Putting her to work helped occupy her worrying mind."

"That was profoundly solicitous of you," she recalled telling him. Now, she was about to examine the fruits of Mrs. O'Callaghan's handiwork and judge it for herself. Too bad Mr. Ricci wouldn't be around to hear Cecilia's opinion firsthand.

It was in a separate conversation during Mr. Ricci's hospital stay last year that Cecilia learned Mrs. Ricci was more than capable of self-care and hadn't put herself in harm's way, as her mother feared. And he told her it took five years for Mrs. Ricci to reveal her secret that she'd met a man who had given her more in Venice than a ride in a gondola. And then, when Mr. Ricci needed an organ donor to save his life, he learned Chris wasn't just his wife's lover, but also the son he'd given up for adoption when he was in college. *Phew.*

Thinking about Chris, she glanced around the open work environment, trying to get a feel for how she'd fit in. While Cecilia knew Mrs. Ricci, now known to her as Kassie, was following Mr. Ricci's directive in giving her this awesome opportunity, she was confident Chris played a role as well. And with Kassie hotfooting herself to Paris in short order, Chris would be her day-to-day boss. At least she thought he would. *Don't fuck this up. Daddy was right. I owe it to both Kassie and Chris.*

She cleared her throat, a trick her mother said her customers used to get her attention at the store. Funny. It didn't work for Cecilia. No one looked up from their computer monitors or removed their earbuds or put down the plastic spoons as they ate their Greek yogurt. Was she that invisible? Her eyes scanned the top of the desk, searching for one of those small, silver bells often seen at libraries or in delicatessens. She was about to press the red-and-silver Staples Easy Button when she noticed a name plate sitting next to it. *Karen Copperman, Receptionist.*

She scratched her cheek. In a blink, Cecilia contemplated turning her twenty-year-old body around and heading for the exit. Maybe this internship wasn't such a good idea after all.

When Kassie, the new CEO, and hot-man-about-town Christopher Gaines gave her this prodigious opportunity, she forgot that the surly, ill-bred strumpet worked there as well. But apparently not that day. Was Karen still mourning the death of the man she cheated on right under his nose? Not a snowball's chance in hell. More than likely, she was getting a mani-pedi at the trendiest spa in town.

Her mother's incessant pep talk reverberated in Cecilia's brain. She vowed, if only to herself, to accept how her stars were aligning. She would create her own future and make a conscious choice as to whether or not to make nice with Karen. After all, she was Chris's mother. Cecilia owed him at least that much.

From a distance, some might call Cecilia *thirsty*, a social climber. Not so. Her mother, perhaps, but not her. Though her father had worked his way up the plumber's ranks, his take-home pay and the extra money he brought in, combined with her mother's hourly pay, were never enough to fulfill her mother's expectations.

"You can do better," her mother whispered to her every other week since she was old enough to stay home alone after school. When her mother would drag her to the bank branch on the corner so she could deposit their checks, she always reminded Cecilia, "You can just as easily fall in love with a rich man as you can a poor man."

Since she hadn't yet fallen in love with any man, rich or poor, Cecilia decided to be responsible for her own future, like Dr.

Shaklee said, and become successful in her own right. To do better than her parents, no matter how hard she had to work at it. For right now, working at it meant interning at Ricci and Son. No one could take that away from her or stand in her way. Not even Karen Copperman.

"Excuse me," Cecilia said to the air-conditioned open office. Still, no one looked at her. She cleared her throat again. Still, nothing.

She walked toward a corner office. The grandfather clock chimed once. *What the hell?* Almost coming out of her Roxy Rory Slip-Ons, she dropped her day bag. Her phone hit the floor with a thud. "Fuck." She grimaced. *Oops. I better watch my language here.*

Looking up, she saw signs of life. Finally. A tall man appeared in the corner office doorway. She recognized him. She first met Mr. Mahoney a year ago on Easter when he visited Mr. Ricci at the hospital. Cannolis were involved. And then at the house yesterday, he droned on about his son, the lacrosse superstar.

"Well, hey there, Cecilia," he said, waving. "Come on in. Wasn't expecting to see you today."

They walked toward each other. She stuck out her right hand to give him a firm shake, just as her father taught her. "No one likes to shake a dead fish," he'd said.

She must've done okay as Mr. Mahoney smiled and tilted his head toward his office as if to say "Follow me."

Keeping her mouth closed, she grinned—no big teeth show-ing—and took his lead. "I hope I'm not interrupting anything. I'd really like to start my internship right way."

"You're not interrupting. Your timing is good. My son, Leo, is here. Remember I mentioned him yesterday? Let me introduce you."

As she entered Mr. Mahoney's office, a guy she assumed was his son pushed his chair back with a clunk and stood, reminiscent of when Mr. Darcy greeted Miss Elizabeth Bennet at Pemberley in the *Pride and Prejudice* movie. To her recollection, no person of the male persuasion had ever risen when she walked into a room before. Their eyes met. Briefly. Cecilia bowed her head to the floor and smiled from ear to ear. *This guy is hot. Don't lose your shit now, girl.*

Trying to control her blinking, she recovered. In a sign she knew as much etiquette as Leo, she stuck out her hand to shake his.

"Cecilia, this is Leo. Leo, Cecilia Howe." Mr. Mahoney swept by them and sat behind his desk.

"Leo, as in Leonardo?"

"No, as in Leopold. I'm neither an artist, actor, or activist." He held her hand, and they stood, eyes locked for longer than either Miss Manners or her father would approve.

"Nor activist," she muttered.

"Excuse me?"

"Neither an artist, actor, *nor* activist. To be grammatically correct."

"Nor activist then," Leo said, giving her a wink and a sly grin.

She'd swear on a stack of St. James Bibles that the air between them sizzled. Afraid her hair might stand on end, she touched the white scrunchie and then ran her hand through her ponytail, chewing her lower lip the whole time.

"Why don't you two take a seat? I was just talking to Leo about his internship here. So your timing, Cecilia, is spot-on. Except …"

Here comes the oh-but clause. Is he going to drop a bomb? Maybe it's not a paid internship.

"I'm sure Chris would like to be the one to introduce you to everyone and personally explain what he has in mind for your internship. But he isn't here today."

"Oh, I know that. I saw him at the hospital this morning with Lexi."

23

Paul Revere

Near the top of the escalator, Kassie spotted Sarah and Charlie sitting in the Lock and Key lobby bar before they saw her and Chris. Still holding Chris's hand, she tugged on his arm, led him back down the escalator and pushed him through the revolving door to the sidewalk outside the hotel.

"What the fuck?" Chris said in a voice she was sure he meant only for her.

"They don't know."

Chris looked at her as if she'd gone mad.

"Sarah and Charlie left the house before Lexi arrived last night. They don't know about her, the twins, or that she's in the hospital." Kassie stepped to one side to let others pass.

Chris stayed with her, letting go of her hand, and crossing his arms in an X in front of his midsection as if he were protecting something. "Actually, two out of three. They don't know two out of three," he said.

"Which one of the three do they know, Chris?" Kassie's mind computed, sorting through the options. Logically, they couldn't have heard about the twins or the hospital unless they knew about Lexi.

"Lexi. My parents know about Lexi." Chris confirmed the result of her thought process. "Basically, that I dated an old colleague and friend named Lexi in San Francisco and that we went to Greece together in March."

"Oh," Kassie said as she bowed her head. "Friends with benefits."

"We were on a break, Kassie."

"I didn't screw around while we were *on a break*," she said through her clenched teeth, anticipating Bad Kassie was about to make an inconvenient appearance. Should she tamp her down or let her erupt like Pompeii would if it came alive again?

"Come on, KO, how many times are you going to make me apologize? I can't take it back. There's no redo, do-over, or whatever you want to call it."

"Perhaps if Lexi weren't pregnant ..." *Down, girl.*

Uttering the word *pregnant* flipped a switch, helping Kassie regain control. She hadn't rehearsed the words *my fiancé's ex-girlfriend is pregnant* enough so they'd roll off her tongue, let alone adding *with twins.* Nor had they discussed how they were going to break the news to his parents at dinner.

Chris stared up at the evening sky, perhaps wishing for divine intervention to make this all go away. He could ignore her all he wanted. Kassie wasn't ready either to let him off the hook or to make nice with his parents at the moment.

"You're right. You can't erase what's been done." She'd give him that, except she filed her never-ending need for more than words of apology in her mental list under *Paris.*

"Can we go in now? We're late."

"Not yet." Kassie grabbed the pole of an empty luggage cart someone had left in the middle of the sidewalk. It followed her footsteps as she paced in a circle. "It feels to me everyone was aware of the other woman in your life but me. How do you think that makes me feel?"

Chris seized the cart to make it and Kassie stop.

Kassie didn't give him a chance to answer. "You could've told me when we were in Paris. When she called you that night at 58 Tour Eiffel. But no. You waited until we got home. And then, in the midst of Mike's turmoil, you tell me about Lexi only because she called and said she wanted to come to Boston. To visit you."

Chris reached out to her and pulled her in for a tight embrace. "I'm so sorry. If I could redo *that* I would. Believe me, I would. I promise not to keep things, anything, from you in the future."

She leaned her head into his chest, fighting back tears. "Not sure what's gotten into me, Chris. It seems like overnight I've become a widow, a manager of a foreign subsidiary, a CEO, and a future stepmother. A stepmother of a different kind."

"And I'm going to be a father." He lifted her chin and kissed her sweetly.

"That's a lot to digest, don't you think?"

"I get it. And we'll get through this together. Speaking of digesting, I'm famished." He clasped her hand and escorted her into the hotel's lobby. For a real redo.

The server couldn't bring the cosmopolitan Chris ordered for her fast enough. Mimicking an itch on her arm, she'd whispered to him, "Make sure they don't make it with pomegranate juice." Part of her considered switching her cocktail of choice to white wine, preventing the possibility of getting another rash as she had the night Chris proposed to her in Paris. *That's a stupid idea.* She quickly eighty-sixed that notion.

Ready to go another round of wine, Charlie asked the server to bring a bottle of whatever Sarah and he had started drinking an hour before.

"We thought we'd get the party started," Charlie said, raising an almost empty glass in the air. "Hope you don't mind."

"Looks like you're making headway with the appetizers too," Chris said as he put two shrimp on a napkin and handed it to Kassie and then helped himself to a scallop wrapped in bacon.

"*Cicchetti*," Kassie said, smiling … sort of. First the cosmo, now the little appetizers. Was everything that evening going to remind her of their time in Venice and Paris?

"At least here in the States, you know what you're eating," Chris said, laughing and sharing her memory.

"Speaking of traveling," Sarah chimed in, crooking her index finger so they'd lean in closer to her. "Looks like we'll be going overseas ourselves this winter."

"Why are you whispering?" Chris said.

"Because it's confidential. A secret." With that, Sarah filled them in on the outcome of her recent visits to Boston. Three local museums had formed a consortium, and through Sarah's philanthropist network, they raised millions of dollars to acquire new art and artifacts from around the globe.

"Two other art experts—from Rhode Island and New York State—will be joining me on this exciting adventure. 'The Great Art Hunt,'" she said with air quotes.

"Sounds like an Easter egg hunt to me," Charlie said.

Sarah laughed. "You never know. Perhaps one of us will find a long-lost Fabergé egg."

"Wouldn't you have to go to Russia to find one of those?" Kassie said with great hesitation and a slight hiccup she tried to stifle. Art history was never her strong suit.

"Not necessarily. There were sixty-nine original Fabergé eggs. Fifty-seven supposedly still exist. We can either accept that a dozen are lost or destroyed, or we can keep our eyes open and antennas up for the possibility of discovering more. But Charlie made us digress. As he often does."

Charlie lifted his palms to the ceiling. "At least I'm good for something."

No one picked up on his remark, so Sarah continued.

"When I get back to Chicago, I'll start working with our travel agent. I'm very excited. Europe here we come!"

Kassie was about to ask if Paris would be on their itinerary. If so, she'd have to invite her future in-laws to visit while she was there. Not wanting to upset Chris with the mention of Paris, she swallowed her thoughts along with a mouthful of deep-pink liquid.

"Wow, that's an incredible opportunity. Shows how much they respect and value your expertise," Chris said.

"And trust her not to abscond with the consortium's funds," Charlie added.

Sarah gave him a mini-punch in the arm. "I'd never do that."

Kassie believed that to be true. Sarah was beyond reproach. Someone Kassie could look up to. She couldn't ask for a better mother-in-law. Even though they didn't live nearby, Kassie looked forward to a fond relationship with her. Of course, Sarah would never replace her own mother in Kassie's heart, but they could be friends, couldn't they?

Above the dulcet sounds of Muzak and chatter of patrons who unwisely extended their happy hours beyond one or two drinks, Kassie heard a sudden crash of a glass breaking. The fellow behind the bar bent down as if to clean something up.

"Did you hear that?" She nudged Chris.

"Hear what?"

Maybe Chris's ears weren't as sharp as hers, but Kassie recognized her mother's calling card. Gone, yet not forgotten.

Without consulting with Kassie, Chris raised his drink. "Let's make a toast."

"To your mother?" Charlie said.

"No actually. To me."

"To yourself? Whatever for?" Sarah said.

Kassie gasped. *What's he up to?*

"I'm going to be a father," Chris said straightaway.

More than a few pregnant pauses passed. No one said a word. Maybe they didn't hear him. *Oh God, please don't make him say it again.*

His parents' eyes shifted from Chris to Kassie, then to Chris, and then back to Kassie. Their mouths flapped like guppies.

"Kassie, really? How wonderful!" Sarah exploded and jumped to her feet. She reached across the table as if to give her a hug. Charlie bounded off his chair as well, heading around Sarah's chair to make his way to his son.

Instinctively, Kassie retreated, holding up both hands in front of her to fend off Sarah's embrace.

"No! Not me! Look. I'm drinking." She held up her cosmo. "See. I'm sorry, actually very sorry to say, it's not me. I'm not pregnant." She shifted her body toward Chris. "Take it away, Paul Revere. Start spreading the news."

And so Chris did. A little too prideful if you asked Kassie. He reminded them about his friend back in San Francisco. The one he went to Santorini with in March. Their heads bounced like two bobbleheads, going along with Chris on his journey.

"Well, after you left the house last night, Lexi showed up."

"I figured out right away she was pregnant." Kassie seized the moment. If she left it up to Chris, they'd never get to dinner. "You see, she wore an outfit eerily similar to one Mimi wore."

Sarah and Charlie strained their eyes as if to say, "Who the hell is Mimi?"

Catching their drift, Kassie explained: "Mimi Couture. The managing director of Calibri in France. The woman I'll be filling in for when I go to Paris." Kassie made sure to emphasize the Paris angle. "And when Lexi wouldn't accept a glass of wine, well, I knew."

Kassie felt Chris's hand on her back. *Is he comforting me or wanting me to shut up?* She was on a roll. He opened the floodgates with his big reveal. Obviously, his parents thought he meant Kassie was pregnant. If she could scream, she would. Instead, the floor was hers, and she was going to keep going.

"Obviously all of us, well maybe not all of us," she glanced at Chris, "were shocked when she told us Chris was the baby daddy. I mean, my goodness, they're not teenagers. Didn't they ever hear about birth control?" Kassie signaled the server to bring her a refill.

"That's enough," Chris said. "I'll take it from here." He reached for Kassie's hand, held it, and squeezed gently. He began with Lexi spending the night at Kassie's house and continued with her falling down the stairs that morning.

"Did she faint?" Sarah said. "Pregnant women faint, I hear."

"Maybe she was on her phone. You know how these young people think they can multitask," Charlie said.

"Lexi blamed Topher," Kassie said, putting a kibosh on their guessing game. And adding, "My cat."

Chris picked it up from there, not dwelling on the cat. Instead, he leapfrogged all the way to Lexi being rushed to the hospital in an ambulance, apparently by the same EMTs who helped Mike when he'd had his heart attack.

"The long and short of it is Lexi fractured her leg and had surgery this afternoon," Chris said. "She's resting comfortably at Boston Clinic."

"She and the twins, that is, are resting comfortably," Kassie said, putting an exclamation point at the end of the story.

"Your table's ready," a voice said as it floated over the four of them. "I can take your drinks, and the wine, into the restaurant for you, if you like."

"Oh, we like." Charlie said.

Kassie got to her feet. Her legs felt like pickup sticks. Sarah must've noticed.

"We'll meet you in there," Sarah said to the men, slipping her arm through Kassie's. "We've got a stop to make first."

24

One Option

Annoyed at everyone touching her—Chris squeezing her hand, rubbing her back, and now Sarah locking her arm through hers—Kassie swayed down a long hallway seemingly distracted by historic photographs of the old jail and its "guests."

"Wonder what they'd think about this place now?" Sarah said, stopping to read the inscription under a photo.

"They'd probably steal the silverware." Kassie giggled at her own inside joke as an image flashed through her memory: a fork with tines shaped like the Eiffel Tower that found its way into her purse during dinner just a couple of weeks ago.

"What's so funny?"

"Oh, nothing. You had to be there."

"Well, we're here." Kassie felt Sarah's hand grip her bicep, leading her into the ladies' room. "Let's freshen up before dinner, shall we?"

Kassie was all for that. She did her thing in the loo and joined Sarah at the sink. One look in the mirror, and she pulled a brush through her hair, swished warm water through her mouth, which tasted like a desert, and splashed a scant amount of cold water on her face—enough to sober her up without noticeably smearing her makeup.

"You okay?" asked Sarah.

Kassie suspected Sarah's reason for the pit stop was about to become as clear as her diamond ring, which reflected merrily off the bathroom's luxury chrome fixtures.

Kassie wanted to believe Sarah's concern centered on whether she'd had too much to drink. Which, of course, she had when you counted the wine at home and the cosmos she downed in a matter of minutes. Clearly, she wouldn't be the designated driver on the way home.

But Kassie wasn't born yesterday. There'd been no time for either Charlie or Sarah to react to the twins bombshell she dropped. Clever of Chris to not include that in his Lexi story.

Perhaps you didn't give him enough time. Was that Bad Kassie scolding her or was Kassie anticipating how Annie would admonish her when she related the incident whenever they next spoke?

She couldn't argue that the liquor messed with her tongue. With her wits about her, she decided to play along.

"Oh, I'm okay. Just give me a minute." She applied fresh lip gloss and blotted her lips together. "There. Better." Kassie rotated away from the sink and the truth in the mirror and faced Sarah. "Agreed?"

"That's not what I mean. You okay with all of this—Lexi, twins? Were you kidding when you said twins?"

This time Kassie reached out and touched Sarah's forearm. "I wouldn't kid about a thing like that. Once you know me better …" She clicked her heels like Dorothy and started for the exit door.

"Don't go, Kassie, not yet. Let's sit a minute."

Kassie checked out the comfortable-looking two-seater and opted to stand, fearing if she sat, she might not get up.

"I'll stand, if you don't mind. But you go ahead and sit," she said, leaning against the wall next to the couch.

For whatever reason, Sarah stood too, which Kassie interpreted to mean their conversation would be short and sweet. Other than the brief chat she had with Annie earlier, she hadn't needed to explain how or why her fiancé was in the predicament he found himself in. Or how she was feeling about it. All that was about to change as she felt imprisoned in the ladies' room of the Lock and Key Hotel.

Problem was Kassie wasn't sure how she really, really felt about the situation. The thought of Chris making love to Lexi in Greece pained her heart beyond anything she'd ever experienced. Flashbacks scrolled through her psyche like the photo gallery on her iPhone. Their first time in Venice, their last time in Venice, the morning after he'd proposed in Paris. Then a distorted vision of Chris and Lexi on a private veranda in Santorini interrupted the passion she was reliving. She could've cried if she weren't standing face to face with Sarah.

"I know you love Chris. God only knows the trials and tribulations the two of you have endured. But soon he'll be the father of twins. Doesn't the fucked-up mess of a family we already have give you pause? If you really love him—"

Kassie raised her right hand as if she were a traffic cop. "Wait." What stopped her in her tracks was Sarah's use of the f-word. In the few times she'd been around her, Kassie had never heard such blunt language from this well-bred aristocrat. With that and with what she perceived as the beginning of an ultimatum, Kassie's eyes bulged, her bloodstream diluting the booze at warp speed.

"I can understand this seems complicated to you. It certainly is to me. If anyone's fucked this up, it's your son. Literally. With all due respect, Sarah, maybe you should be talking to Chris."

"Of course, I'll talk to him. I thought first I'd appeal to your better angels. If you and Chris marry, under the best scenario, he'd be a part-time father and a part-time husband. What kind of stress do you think that'd bring to your marriage?"

"Are you asking me, or telling me, not to marry Chris? Despite all the *trials and tribulations* we've gone through? You can't be serious."

"Well, it is one option." Sarah lowered her head.

Does she realize she's gone a step too far, that she's out of bounds?

"You're right. It is one option. And not one Chris or I would consider viable."

Kassie walked back to the sink, inspecting her lip gloss once more and giving her time to figure out how the hell she was going to go into the restaurant and eat dinner with this woman who just suggested she split with Chris for a second time in their lives so he could be the type of father Sarah wanted him to be. Any thoughts she had of inviting Sarah and Charlie to visit her in Paris went bye-bye as quickly as the doors would've slammed shut on the prisoners who once lived in the jail cells there.

Confronting Sarah eye to eye, she said, "I know you're trying to be helpful, and the last thing you want is for Chris to be subjected to family drama like you all have recently. I get that. But from where I'm standing, this situation is between me and Chris."

"And Lexi."

Fuck. She's right again.

There was no touching on their way back down the hallway and through the lobby. There were no words. No stopping to inspect the historical photos they passed on their way to their impromptu tête-à-tête. But lips were licked, side glances given, and their steps fell remarkably in unison.

The maître d' greeted them. Sarah said they were there with the Gaines party. "Right this way, ladies. I moved you to a larger table. One that would comfortably accommodate five."

"Five?" Kassie's question was asked and answered in a flash.

Chris must've spotted Kassie as he and Charlie got to their feet when she and Sarah approached. Indeed, they were a party of five.

"Look what the cat dragged in," Charlie said, grinning quite Cheshire-like.

25

Green Is the New ...

Scorching temps shouldn't have made Karen sweat buckets. She spent many a July in Elephant Butte, New Mexico, where the mid-90s were as common as tourists making fun of the town's name. But there was always the lake where she could take a dip to cool down her body.

This was her second July in Boston—where makeup melted faster than a stick of butter for your evening popcorn and a dip in the Harbor was never an option—so she should be used to the heat and humidity.

After arriving at the Charlestown apartment from Kassie's, she swung by the mailroom and picked up her mail. Or let's say, she picked up one piece of mail. The electric bill. *Ugh.* She tossed it aside unopened onto her dining table, where she'd stack all the incoming bills and wait until next month to find out the price of keeping cool. During her first year in Beantown, she never worried about running the air conditioner or the heat. She had her sugar daddy. But now he was six feet under. From now on, paying her rent, utilities, food, etcetera, etcetera was all up to her. Which was why she needed to increase her monthly income if she was going to continue to live in the manner she intended to become accustomed to by marrying Michael Ricci.

She sang the few familiar lines of Queen's "I Want It All" as she considered what she'd wear to dinner at the Lock and Key Hotel that night. First, she carefully placed her favorite white linen pants across the queen-size bed; ironing was out of the question. Next, she slid two orange tops off their hangers and tossed them in a pile in the corner of the closet. They'd been her favorites once upon a time, but her recently acquired red hair would have neither of them. She considered a black-and-white wide-striped shirt and then thought better of it as well. If she wore any of the first three options, somebody might think she took the whole jailhouse theme of the hotel and restaurant a step too far. Though she probably wouldn't have been the first to do so.

"You know, Karen, you're going at this ass backwards," she said. "Match the necklace to the shirt."

Stripping down to her undies as she headed into the kitchen, she retrieved the Guy's and Dolly's Galleria of Jewels' shopping bag, which ended up even smaller than it was originally after Topher, Kassie's cat, had chewed two corners. She tipped the bag over and dumped the contents on the bed. Then she rolled the bag into a ball and tossed it toward a white Lucite wastebasket in the corner of the bedroom. She missed.

Karen was eager to see the result of Guy's and Dolly's creative genius. Several weeks had passed since Mike had found the pale-pink rock during their adventure on the dunes in Provincetown. Looking back on that day and all that had gone down since, she was grateful Mike suggested they stop at the local jewelry store there to have it made into a necklace. It had been a good day, even though it was their last good day together. She'd always have the necklace to remember what could have been.

Luckily, the rectangular package inside the bag survived the cat's curiosity, with no teeth or claw marks anywhere. She tore open the rainbow-colored wrapping, scrunched it into a ball, and lobbed it at the same wastebasket. Missed again. Michael Jordan she was not.

Sitting on the floor, Karen opened the padded white box and discovered a green pouch. She slid the necklace into her hand and laid the pouch on the ghastly light-beige carpet, standard issue in apartments these days. Dangling the eighteen-inch Argentinean silver snake chain above her head, Karen appreciated for the first time why Mike insisted only Guy and Dolly had the talent to transform the rock into a pendant.

"Fucking amazing," she said, reaching for the side of the bed for leverage getting up. She rested the pendant against her chest, gazed into the mirror, smiled, and then spun around. As she did, her foot kicked what she thought was the padded white box. Bending down to pick up the pouch and the box, she found a shimmering silver envelope with her name on the front and an imprint of the galleria embossed on the back flap. Not sure how she missed it to begin with. Didn't matter.

Gently, she stretched out the necklace on the bureau and opened the envelope. Her eyes caught the closing signatures at the end of the note: *We're here for you, Guy and Dolly.*

"But how?" Karen retraced the events of the last few days. Thinking, she touched her index finger to the outer corner of her right eye. "Of course." They had expected Mike and her to return to the store to pick up the pendant and choose an engagement ring. Except Mike mucked up that plan and had a friggin' heart attack. Rather than send the necklace in the mail, Guy and Dolly used the funeral as the perfect opportunity to deliver it to her in person. Which they did, until she left it—probably in the family room—for Topher to swipe and hide in a closet with the rest of his fuzzy and saliva-matted toys.

She read the message on the card.

Dearest Karen,

We crafted this gem of a necklace especially for you on behalf of Mike, who was the pirate of your heart. We hope you'll wear it with lasting memories of him and, of course, with PRIDE. Do good when you wear it.

We're here for you,

Guy and Dolly

The reference to pride was so on the nose, she gulped as she laughed out loud, appreciating their own personal and professional pride. Though when she read the note again, the words—*Do good when you wear it*—struck her as odd. Was it a warning? A threat? A prophesy?

Pish-tosh. Where was this coming from? They hardly knew her. She met them twice. At their store in Provincetown and at the funeral.

"There's a postscript. Of course, there's a postscript!" She read it out loud.

P.S. Hope you love this Crayola Green pouch. It accentuates the bold flamingo pink of the stone and complements your fabulous titian hair.

Karen slid the pouch under the stone. They were right. She grabbed the pouch and marched into the closet. Holding it against three green shirts, she chose the one that most closely matched.

Her wardrobe for the evening was ready for prime time.

Pulling into the circular drive in front of the Lock and Key, Karen had another decision to make: self or valet parking. Either way, parking would cost something. She stared at the placard that listed the prices, calculating a fifteen-dollar difference between her options. Fast forwarding in her mind to the end of the evening when the merry band would retrieve their cars from the valet,

Karen didn't want to say goodbye on the sidewalk and then shuffle off all by her lonesome to the garage.

And she still had Mike's credit cards. Valet parking it would be. She handed the fellow who opened her door a card and five singles.

Nearing the top of the escalator, Karen spotted Charlie and Chris alone, walking toward her. This was the first time she'd seen them together officially as father and son since the paternity test results the day before ruled out Mike as Chris's real father. Her eyes widened as her heart expanded. It was as if she were seeing them for the first time, seeing what she lost because she gave them both up to Sarah.

Karen always knew there was a fifty-fifty chance Charlie had gotten her pregnant. She could've rocked the boat and insisted on a paternity test back then. But neither Charlie nor Mike was Jewish, so her parents would've never let her marry Charlie even if she'd split up him and Sarah. Despite their mutual animosity now, she couldn't have hurt Sarah then. Especially because she'd offered to save her from her parents' fury and adopt Karen's child. Her only child.

Curiously, in all her years, no one—not her parents, not her husband Barry, not even Mike—asked Karen how she felt about giving her baby up for adoption.

She blinked as Charlie and Chris approached. How had she missed the physical resemblance between the two?

People see what they want to see.

People at the office, and even she and Kassie, for that matter, said Chris and Mike shared similar traits. They didn't, really. Mike couldn't see what others did. He even remarked about it occasionally. He accepted Chris as his son out of the pure joy of having a child, and he took that joy to his grave.

Observing Charlie and Chris now, Karen felt pride, and it had nothing to do with the necklace she wore. Both men were ruggedly handsome and tall, though Chris had an inch or two on

Charlie, who either slouched a bit or was shrinking as he aged. She remembered Charlie's graying hair was once similar to Chris's chestnut-brown color, though Charlie would've never worn it as long as Chris did.

As they got nearer to her, they were even in lockstep.

Charlie's crystal-blue eyes caught sight of hers first. He beamed as he elbowed Chris to notice her. He did, but with raised eyebrows. Obviously, Chris wasn't as happy to see her as Charlie was.

Oh God, I hope Charlie doesn't say he's glad I made it. Or. There you are! That would let the cat out of the bag in more ways than one.

Almost in a panic, Karen stumbled getting off the escalator. Chris grasped her right arm, saving her from doing an unladylike face-plant in the middle of the lobby bar.

"What are you doing here?" Chris gave her a moment to gain composure and to come up with a believable answer. She opted for the truth, at least a partial truth.

"Oh, thank you, Chris, for catching me. I should've been looking where I was going. But I saw you both ..."

They stepped to the side of the lobby bar entrance. Karen readjusted her shirt and pants and checked that the strap on her sandals hadn't snapped apart. She touched the pendant. Still intact.

"Why are you here?" Chris continued to press.

"Well, I heard you were all having dinner here tonight. So, I wanted to come by and wish Charlie and Sarah safe travels. Now that we are all one big family, it's time for me to do my part to make it a happy one."

Karen paused and looked beyond the men. "Speaking of a happy family, where are Sarah and Kassie?"

26

Love Bites

Rather than give Chris directions home, Kassie fixed her blood-shot eyes out the passenger side window and let him find his own way.

If she were driving, she'd have taken Memorial Drive along the Charles River, past MIT and Harvard. Even though the schedule Mike kept pinned on the refrigerator door with a Patriots magnet showed the Red Sox were playing in Baltimore that night, there was always a chance there'd be a concert or some event at Fenway that would jam Storrow Drive like a gummed-up garbage disposal. It'd take them hours to get home.

Such was not the case, perhaps because it was a Wednesday night, and hump day wasn't typically a great night for concerts, since the following day was a workday for most people.

"The Foo Fighters were at Fenway over the weekend," Chris said as they cruised past Kenmore Square and the lighted Citgo sign.

Is he really reading my mind? Scary.

"I saw in the *Boston Proper* Jimmy Buffett and Billy Joel will be there in a couple of weeks," Kassie said.

"Together?"

"No, I don't think they tour together. That would be a hoot." Kassie let out a little laugh. "But Journey and Def Leppard are performing together after Billy. Maybe going to a concert would be a great thing for us to do before …"

She didn't complete her thought because if Chris was truly on her wavelength, he'd connect the dots and land on Paris all by himself.

He kept his eyes on the road and his voice mute. She hummed the first song that entered her mind, hoping to break the ice.

"What's that?"

"Don't you recognize 'Love Bites'?"

"I didn't know you were into Def Leppard."

She was about to ask if he remembered the song involved a love triangle. Instead, she laughed and said, "Good to know there's still a lot for us to learn about one another, don't you think?"

Apparently, Chris had no opinion on the subject. Kassie resolved to change the conversation. She couldn't imagine the idea of going to a concert stifled Chris.

"Well, that was fun." She glanced at Chris, suspecting her sarcasm would be more discernible than her humming. Just in case, she added, "I mean tonight. Don't you think?"

"Which part do *you* think was fun?" Was Chris throwing shade or was he serious? "Karen crashing our dinner party? Or you not being able to hold your liquor? In front of *my* parents."

Kassie straightened her back against the seat, catching his drift loud and clear. "Or maybe, just maybe, it's the part where your parents immediately assumed *I was pregnant*. Liquor or no liquor, I had to set the record straight."

"You didn't give me a chance to explain."

"What's done is done. And you know what, Chris?"

She cast a brief look at him to be sure he was paying as much attention to her as he was to the road. "You're not always going to be around to *explain*. It's up to me to dream up some pithy response to all our friends and our colleagues, including the staff at both firms, to justify why I think it's okay by me that you're about to be the father of some other woman's children at the same time you're marrying me."

Chris said absolutely nothing as he reached across the console to touch her left hand. She kept it on her lap, entwined with her right hand.

"I think I was in shock last night when Lexi arrived pregnant," Kassie said. "Facing death and life on the same day could do that to a person. At first, I was excited for you, and for me, that there would be a child in our new life together even if it wasn't mine, biologically or legally. Sure, it would be complicated. Optimistic me thought we could figure it out."

She could see him shaking his head, looking everywhere— ahead, side to side, at the road, the traffic—everywhere but at her.

"Then this morning, when I learned she was having twins, I was both overwhelmed and concerned about Lexi's surgery at the same time. A double whammy. On top of that, add Karen bursting in and putting her grandmother stake in the ground. What a fucking shitshow."

"Speaking of—" Chris started to switch the conversation to Karen, but Kassie was figuratively in the driver's seat of this little talk, and she was full steam ahead.

"Hold that thought. We'll get to Karen."

She adjusted the seat belt that had crept up her chest toward her neck and placed her fist underneath it. Being strangled by polyester or Chris's attempt to muzzle her was not on the agenda. She was determined to get whatever emotion she'd squashed all day out in the open before they reached the house.

"How could I not be thrilled about two babies?" Kassie said.

"You acted thrilled."

"Honestly, I think I was. At first. Now I think I'm jealous."

Finally, that got Chris's attention. "You have no reason to be jealous."

"Listen to what you're saying. You know exactly how much I wanted to be a mother. For crying out loud, that was the biggest barrier between Mike and me. And here you are getting a built-in family plopped right in your lap. Except it's not with me. At a time we're supposed to be starting a family, you'll have two. One on each coast. Presumably. Lucky you."

Kassie shook her head and looked out the window. They'd gotten off the exit and were now passing through neighborhoods where the U.S. Census Bureau claimed an average of 3.15 persons lived in each American home. Maybe not happily ever after, but as a family, in any case. How would the census count the family that Lexi and Chris created? As three or four, if they counted Chris as a part-time father? And then would they count her household as one person? Hardly a household; hardly a family.

Snap out of it, KO, her mother's voice rang inside her mind. *Stop feeling sorry for yourself. This dude's in a hoot of big trouble, and you're not helping things.* Kassie outstretched her arm and patted his.

"I'm sorry, Chris, for my pity party. I'll figure this out and be fine. You just watch."

"I know you will. We will."

Kassie reached above Chris as they pulled into the driveway and pressed the door opener so they could enter through the garage. She stepped out of the car, not waiting for him to come around to open her door, as was his custom.

The more things change, the more things must *change.*

Except, as usual, Topher was waiting on the other side of the door in the hallway between the mudroom and the kitchen.

Well, it's about time you two got home, his loud mewl seemed to say.

He stuck his furry tail in the air as he brushed first around Kassie's right leg and then the other, totally snubbing Chris.

Kassie busied herself rinsing and refreshing Topher's water bowl, giving him his vitamins and a small helping of canned food.

"What's with Topher?" Chris powered up the Keurig and sorted through the K-Cups until he found decaf coffee for him and green tea with mango for Kassie.

"What do you mean?"

"He ignored me when I walked in. He gave me the cold cat shoulder."

Kassie guffawed at his attempt at a joke. *At least he didn't try to trip you.*

"Big or small?" Chris held up Mike's favorite large white Nantucket mug and the small white Seattle mug that had sketches painted in black of Mount Rainier, Pike Place Market, and the Space Needle she bought, not pilfered, during a trip to Washington State.

She chose Nantucket, not because it reminded her of Mike but because she anticipated needing more tea than the smaller cup would provide to discuss the two elephants in the room: Karen and Sarah.

Chris was still unaware of what had gone down between her and Sarah in the ladies' room. He had no reason to think anything newsworthy happened. Kassie realized she needed to tell Chris about it before Sarah had a chance to. God forbid Sarah filled Chris's head with her cockamamie idea that Kassie should give him up, walk away from their engagement, and instead give his hand willingly and freely to Lexi. What was Sarah smoking?

Would it come down to Chris's loyalties? To Sarah? Lexi? Her? Kassie feared she walked a dangerous tightrope. If she slipped, she could lose him for good.

27

Modern Family

Chris carried their steaming recuperative drinks into the family room. Kassie waved her index finger at him, signaling she'd be just a minute. She rummaged through the vanity drawers in the first-floor bathroom, searching for a toothbrush. In the decades she lived in that house with Mike, she kept a spare there so she wouldn't have to run upstairs just to brush her teeth. Someone, probably Karen, disposed of it and the other paraphernalia she left behind when she moved out the year before. Made sense for Karen to let bygones be gone.

Passing the family room, she glimpsed Chris standing near the far end of the coffee table, holding his coffee cup in one hand, the television remote control in the other. "I'll be right down," she said.

"Take your time," he sang out.

Topher followed her upstairs, into the bedroom, and jumped onto the waterbed.

"Don't get too comfortable. Just brushing my teeth." Which she did. And then she gargled, slipped out of her clothes, donned fresh undies, wrapped a three-quarter-length powder-blue silk robe around her, tied it tight, and drew a brush through her hair. A quick pinch to her cheeks and she headed downstairs to Chris.

As did Topher.

Chris had staked out the far end of the couch, stretching his legs onto the coffee table. Kassie settled in at the other end, curling her legs beneath her.

Topher chose the BarcaLounger. Mike's Pleasure Chair.

In a habit she abhorred when Mike did it, Chris clicked aimlessly through the television channels. She opened her mouth to say *Like father, like son,* but promptly ate her words. Perhaps she realized it would be an inappropriate, outdated thing to say. Perhaps, too, some other memories of Mike should be tossed aside, just like her former toothbrush.

They stared at the television, Kassie contemplating her next move.

"What should we watch? What are you in the mood for? The Red Sox game must be over. Can't find it."

"Rain out. Already checked." She held up her phone to prove her point. "Would you mind turning that off?" She jutted her chin toward the big screen.

Chris shrugged and leaned toward her, misinterpreting her request.

She poked him away.

"What? No kiss?"

"I think we should finish what we started in the car."

Chris asked her to refresh his memory.

"We digressed a bit, don't you think, after I asked if you thought tonight was fun?"

"Fun? That depends on how you define fun," Chris said.

Oh God, is he going full Bill Clinton on me?

Not wanting the conversation to veer sideways off the rails, Kassie said, "Okay. Let's begin with Karen and go from there."

"All right. I'll start. You and Karen seemed pretty chummy tonight. What was that all about? Just this morning at the hospital, you were at each other's throats."

"Let's see. Technically, I'm now her boss, and she's going to be one of my mothers-in-law. I think it's about time we bury the hatchets, don't you?"

"So, you're saying you had a kumbaya moment when she drove you home?"

Kassie sipped her tea. "I wouldn't go that far."

Obviously, Chris wanted to take it even further. "You didn't look surprised to see Karen sitting at our table. How come?"

Opting for the *Reader's Digest* version of her afternoon with his mother, his actual mother, Kassie fessed up that she'd mentioned their dinner party to Karen. "Actually, now that I think about it, it's your fault she showed up."

"Mine? Impossible. I only talk with her when I absolutely have to. Sure as shootin', I would've never invited her to dinner."

"If you hadn't texted to remind me we were having dinner with your father and your 'mother'—" She put mother in air quotes.

"Oh, that must have gone over real well."

She admitted she expected fireworks, or actual fire flaming out of Karen's mouth, like a dragon. That got a chuckle out of Chris, at least. So she continued. Much to her surprise, Karen empathized with both Kassie and Lexi about the dilemmas each found herself in.

"She thinks we're a modern family," Kassie said. "Is she right?"

Chris excused himself, headed into the kitchen, and returned with his coffee mug refilled. In his absence, Topher jumped to his place on the couch, curled up to Kassie and, when Chris returned, purred as if to say, *Where's hers.*

Kassie ignored the slight, figuring it was unintentional, a guy thing. She stroked Topher starting at the top of his head between his ears and down the length of his back. He lifted his hind quarters for more.

"Not sure we're a modern family," Chris said.

"If not modern, what are we then, Chris? Picture this. A round table, like King Arthur's. But at this table, there's you, your biological mother, your adoptive mother, your father, and your fiancée, all expected to break bread in a congenial and polite manner. On top of that, less than two miles from the hotel, there's a woman recovering from surgery carrying your two babies. What, or rather who, is the common thread that binds everyone together?"

"Me?"

"Right on! Sounds pretty modern to me. And I'll let you in on a little secret. Since I'm marrying you, if I decide it's in my best interest to bond with Karen, I don't expect shade from you. Got that? She doesn't have cooties, ya know?"

Chris scratched his left ear. "Maybe you're right."

"Maybe? Of course I'm right. It might behoove you to show her a little of the respect you're showing Lexi. Imagine what a sacrifice it was for Karen to give you up when you were born and to have to beg for even a little attention from you now that you're finally in her life."

Sarah's proposition whizzed through her mind. The digital clock on the cable box read 10:38. It was getting late, especially if she was going to head into Calibri the next day to start her transition to Paris. Except she wasn't done with Chris. She had more to say before the night was over and another day full of unknowns dawned.

"I hear you. But you have to admit, I'm not all bad. I did compliment her on that huge pendant she was wearing and caught her as she nearly fell getting off the escalator. Don't I get points for all that?" He shooed Topher off of Kassie, lifted her legs, and placed her bare feet on his lap.

A déjà vu moment flashed inside her mind.

How to seduce Kassie. — Rule No. 1. Must give foot massage.

"Yes, kudos to you for pointing out the necklace. Clearly, she relished telling the story of how Mike proposed to her on the dunes in Provincetown and how important it was to Mike that Guy and Dolly created that beautiful pendant especially for her."

"She didn't dwell on it, though. Amazingly."

"True. I think she got more of a kick out of telling everyone how Topher saved the day."

"Did you notice? She kept touching it all evening. Like she's afraid of losing it."

Kassie massaged Chris's arm as he continued caressing her feet.

"I wouldn't doubt Karen's afraid to lose it. She lost you. Her first husband. Then Mike. Maybe from now on, the necklace will be her lodestar. Karen needs to cling to something. We all do."

How to seduce Kassie. — Rule No. 2. Must disrobe her.

But Kassie had a better idea, or so she thought.

28

New Rules

"Wait a minute, Kassie. Chris followed the *Rules of Seduction*, and you shut him down midstride? Is that what you're telling me?"

Kassie glanced at her college diploma hanging next to her desk in her home office. *Those were the days.*

She fiddled with the pink four-by-nine-inch lined pad on which she organized each day. Except that Thursday, she digressed from the order of her to-do list. She called Annie first; not Calibri, or Bill at Ricci and Son, who she initially considered her first two priorities.

It wasn't unusual for Kassie to reach out to Annie at the museum first thing in the morning, especially if there was juicy gossip to share. Or she had a problem to solve. More often than not, Kassie could count on Annie to be her conscience, providing her with an unbiased, healthy dose of reality. A comeuppance she couldn't get from anyone else. Even Chris.

"Rules are made to be broken, Annie."

Anticipating Annie's impending rant, she placed her phone on the desk and pressed Speaker. It was Annie's honest reaction to all of last night's events she sought, not her voice blaring in her ear. Why she ever started the conversation by telling Annie how she curtailed Chris's advances was beyond her? Perhaps it gave her a way to glide into the real issue haunting her: a fear that forces beyond her control were fracturing her relationship with Chris. She could've started with party crasher Karen or buttinsky Sarah, but she chose instead to admit she'd broken the *Rules*.

"Whoever the fuck said that was a moron. Especially when it comes to our *Rules of Seduction*."

Let the games begin.

Kassie, and Bad Kassie, kept quiet, intending to give Annie more airtime to rant. Instead, Annie whispered. "Oh, please tell me it wasn't your mother with all her quotes to live by."

Relieved, Kassie sighed. "Ha! Not my mother. Good guess, though. Try General Douglas MacArthur."

"You're making that up. Trying to impress me with your knowledge of military history, are you?"

"What knowledge of military history? Not me. If you don't believe me, go look it up in your Funk & Wagnalls."

Kassie knew she'd gotten Annie's goat on that one. She wouldn't have to remind her of the source of that remark.

"Tell me again. From *Laugh-In*, right? Was it Rowan or Martin who said that?"

"If memory serves me … Dan Rowan. Today, he'd have to say, Go Google It!"

They both hooted. Kassie loved moments like this when she could share special memories with her BFF.

During her life with Mike, Kassie rarely thought about the *Rules of Seduction*. It wasn't necessary. Thirty years of marriage will do that.

She did recall sharing them in jest with Chris the first time they hooked up after Venice. He said she was charming and couldn't wait to meet Annie, her partner in crime. Now, assessing the current calamity with Lexi, it was crystal clear he never abided by Rule No. 3 with Lexi as he had with Kassie in their early years together. *If he'd only taken the rule seriously.*

Over a bottle or two of cheap red wine on a beach on Cape Cod, Annie and Kassie had concocted the *Rules of Seduction* the weekend before they went their separate ways to their freshman year in college. Kassie flew off to Mizzou, a.k.a. the University of Missouri, where she focused more on her Italian professor, a.k.a. Michael Ricci, than the pursuit of a diploma. Annie, bound and determined to get a degree in museum studies, stayed in-state, attending Tufts University in Medford.

The *Rules* enabled the girls to share their sexual adventures, or misadventures, in private through a code, a short checklist. Right in Kassie's wheelhouse. Throughout the semesters when they were apart, each Sunday afternoon at precisely four o'clock Eastern time, one would call the other. Sitting cross-legged on the floor in their respective dorm hallways, they swapped turns describing their weekend escapades. Whoever scored the least number of rules would go first, saving the most scandalous story for last. Most often that honor went to Annie.

They judged their dates by how they made their way through four sequential behaviors:

Rule No. 1 — Must give a foot massage. If they won't touch your feet, don't let them touch anything else.

Rule No. 2 — Must disrobe you. If they want you bad enough, make them work for it.

Rule No. 3 — Must provide protection. No protection, no nooky. Better to take preventative measures than be sorry.

Rule No. 4 — Must spoon. Post-coitus is as essential as foreplay and a key predictor of potential future hook-ups.

If a guy passed muster through all four rules, his odds increased that he'd get the chance for a repeat performance. However, because the guys were clueless about the rules, if there was a next time, most of them skipped Rule No. 1, thereby disqualifying them in the future. Only after, of course, the girls had their fun. But rules were rules. At least for a time.

"So let me get this straight 'cause I don't believe what I'm hearing. After Chris rubbed your crusty middle-aged feet and took off your clothes, you didn't jump his bones right there on the floor? You took him to your bed instead, right? Please tell me I'm right."

"Nope. You're not right," Kassie said. "He went to bed. I curled up on the chaise lounge and fell asleep reading the damned book you assigned to your Banned Book Club. Really, Annie, *Ulysses*? Couldn't you choose something else, like *Lady Chatterley's Lover*?"

Annie groaned. "Don't change the subject. Did you say you curled up on your chaise? I thought it was in the spare bedroom. Isn't that where Lexi slept the other night? You invaded her privacy?"

"Well, I guess kind of. Not intentionally, though. Turnabout is fair play, I think. She certainly has invaded mine. I went in the room to shoo Topher out of there, and I fell asleep on the chair instead."

"Okay, I can forgive you for skipping Rule No. 3, which doesn't apply to you any longer, anyway. But failing to end the evening wrapped around Chris is deplorable. Sounds to me like you have your priorities more than a little bit mixed up, girl."

"Oh, I don't know about that. You were originally third on my list today, and yet I called you first."

Kassie let that hang between them until Annie poked the bear.

"So be honest with me, Kassie. You didn't call me to give me a blow by blow of your sex life. What's going on? Really."

Kassie rubbed her eyes, holding back tears. "I'm afraid it may be Chris who's struggling with his priorities right now. And honestly, I'm not sure how to handle it. I've never been in love with a man who got another woman pregnant."

"Well, except for—"

She stopped Annie before she said *Mike*. "First, the truth is, as we all know it now, Mike did not get Karen pregnant. Charlie did. And second, Mike's first go-round with Karen was long before I met him."

"None of this explains why you didn't jump Chris's bones last night. Shouldn't you take advantage of the time you don't have a houseguest?"

"You mean Lexi?"

Kassie could envision Annie's "Who else?" eye roll.

"We haven't solved that. With the stairs and Topher, she can't stay here. I need to figure things out."

"Knock it off, lady. Until *you* can figure things out? Remove those blinders you're obviously wearing. This is more about Chris, not you. Can't you see what he's going through?"

"Going through? Of his own making."

"That's a fine attitude. No wonder he hustled off and climbed into that warm waterbed without you."

Kassie wasn't about to take the blame. She swallowed hard and just said it: "I don't think Chris and I will be getting married."

"You're kidding. I don't believe you just said that. What gives you that idea?"

"You met Sarah the other day, right? Well, she's a piece of work. Pull the veil back on her sweet elitist exterior, and there's quite a tigress there. Protecting her cub."

"How so?"

Kassie described the incident in the ladies' room at the hotel the night before. "In a nutshell, Sarah wants me to break up with Chris so he can be with Lexi and the kids. One happy family."

"She said that?"

"Yup. And she didn't mince words."

"I thought she'd be on your side."

"Me too."

"You had Chris first."

"Maybe I did. Maybe I didn't. He and Lexi worked together in San Francisco. They had a friends-with-benefits relationship for some time, I gather. Maybe he was with her before we met in Venice. I can't be sure. I never asked."

"Did you tell Chris what Sarah is asking of you? He can't possibly agree with her."

Kassie explained she hesitated saying anything to him because of his loyalty to Sarah. And then, when things started getting hot and heavy on the couch, she'd accidentally kicked her phone off the coffee table onto the floor. It came to life with her calendar app in view.

"I was afraid of planting ideas in his head. Sarah's ideas. So when I saw the calendar, I had one of my own."

"Tell me. You decided not to go to Paris in September."

"Don't start, Annie. I'm going. Come hell or high water. Actually, I had a better idea."

"Let's hear it. I'm all ears."

"Glad *you* are. Chris didn't seem to be. I suggested we get married before I leave for France."

Annie listened.

"He knocked that down for two reasons. Too soon after I buried Mike. And he had no clue when Lexi would head back to San Francisco, if she could even fly back there in the near future."

"Okay. That all makes sense."

"So, I quickly came up with plan B. There always has to be a plan B, right?"

"If your name is Kassie O'Callaghan, there is."

Kassie chuckled and moved on. "I suggested the holidays. Around Christmas or New Years. I'd be back home then for vacation."

"As good a time as any. We could reserve the clubhouse here at my condo now for a reception."

Kassie warned Annie not to get ahead of her skis, just because she was.

"He didn't bite on that idea either. Apparently, I forgot Lexi was due around that time."

"Fuck." Annie apologized for her reaction.

"No problem. That's what got him into this trouble to begin with."

Annie asked if she had a plan C?

"There's no such thing as a plan C. When there are two options, one should work. But neither is good for Chris. Which makes me want to puke."

"Where is Chris now?"

"On his way to the hospital to see Lexi."

"I think there needs to be some new rules."

29

The Uninvited

For the second day in a row, Chris pulled out of the driveway, heading for the hospital in Kassie's car. He promised not to stay long, only long enough to be sure Lexi and the babies were okay and to find out when Lexi would be released. He also promised to get the keys to Lexi's rental car so tomorrow wouldn't become like the movie *Groundhog Day*.

Kassie promised to text him so he wouldn't forget.

Good thing too. He had so much bullshit on his mind. Lexi's keys were not on top of his list, despite being high on Kassie's.

The last twenty-fours were as tumultuous as any he'd ever experienced in his life: twins, one of his mothers—the crazy one—showing up uninvited to a dinner party, Kassie pressing him to set a sooner-rather-than-later date to get married.

Under the circumstances, he was in no position to set a firm date for a wedding when he didn't know the date his children would be born. Given his luck lately, Lexi would want to set a date to baptize the kids to coincide with his wedding date. He had to get his ducks in a row. Figure out what *first things first* meant when it came to his life.

To confuse things even more, last night Kassie set Chris back more than just on his heels when she put a kibosh on his attempts to let off some steam with hot sex in the family room. What was up with that?

He swept his hair out of his eyes. *I don't know.* Maybe he shouldn't have brushed aside her suggestion to get married sooner than originally planned.

Earlier that morning when Chris got up and headed for the shower, Kassie appeared to be sleeping peacefully, rolled on her side with Topher tucked in next to her. By the time he wrapped a towel around his waist to dry off, she'd made the bed.

He found her in the long white terry-cloth robe he gave her two years before, shuffling around the kitchen in her favorite blue Snoozies slippers with the face of a black cat on one, an erect tail on the other. His coffee sat cooling on the kitchen table.

"How'd I get to bed? Did I sleep walk?" She held her cup of tea and stared out the window over the sink.

"Don't you remember? You were asleep on the chaise. I found you there around three and brought you to bed." He left his coffee mug on the placemat and moved behind her for a morning kiss.

"Oh, right. The chaise. No wonder my back's killing me." She placed her hand in the middle of her back, stepped to one side, and opened the medicine cabinet.

She mumbled something like "Hope Karen didn't throw the aspirin out too." He had no clue how to answer and decided it was best not to go down that path.

He could've brought up what happened when they got home last night, but chose not to do that either. Maybe the cosmos and wine had muddied her mind. If she didn't recall how she ended up in bed, perhaps she didn't remember what had gone down, or hadn't gone down, in the family room. Some things were better left unsaid. Perhaps she'd get over whatever bee had landed in her bonnet while he went to the hospital to check on Lexi.

Flowers would help, he thought as he walked past the hospital's gift shop toward the Information Desk.

"Alexandra Moore. Her room number. Please. Maybe under Lexi Moore."

He was right the first time. He should've known she wouldn't be listed under her nickname.

"That way," the receptionist said, pointing the way he just came from. "Take a left at the end of the hallway. Elevators."

Chris perched himself in front of the cooler that occupied the entire right side of the gift shop. So many flowers to choose from. And so many colors. He knew Kassie loved gerbera daisies, but he didn't know what Lexi's favorite flower was. Roses? Nope. That would send the wrong message to Lexi and upset the apple cart even further with Kassie if she found out he gave her roses.

He scanned the cooler for something that was bright, cheery, and safe from misinterpretation. Some flowers were single stemmed, others arranged in vases. The vases shaped as booties caught his eye. Some were pink and white. Others blue and white. Clearly targeting visitors heading for the maternity ward. Clearly not yet appropriate for his purpose.

He shook out his thoughts and touched his chest as his heart fluttered at the thought of things to come. Then his toes curled inside his Sperry Top-Siders.

His eyes locked onto a medium-sized arrangement—not too big, not too small—with pink, blue, and white carnations clustered together in a ball. The vase was just as simple as the flowers. Plain clear glass. Taken together, there was no chance his gesture would be mistaken as anything but *Thinking of you. Get well soon.* Which is what he wrote on the little card the shopkeeper affixed with a white ribbon to one stem.

To squash a potential allergy attack, Chris held the vase at arm's length. He located the elevator and went up to Lexi's floor; the signage pointing him toward her room. As he neared, he saw her door was slightly ajar. He heard voices. Familiar voices.

Oh no, don't tell me.

He came all this way and promised Lexi he'd stop by in the morning. He couldn't just reverse course and hotfoot it back to the car. What would he do with the flowers? Give them to Kassie? Pink and blue carnations? That would never work; she really deserved long-stemmed red roses.

Chris considered walking around the floor until he figured out either a solution for the flowers or Lexi's company departed. The door swung wide open as a nurse emerged. His eyes locked on Sarah's.

"Here's Christopher now! Come on in, darling! Don't just stand there."

He bowed his head, wishing he'd either arrived earlier or later. Sarah and Charlie were supposed to be on a flight back to Chicago. Not at Boston Clinic making nice with Lexi.

Like a good son, he leaned down and gave his mother a polite peck on the cheek. He rested the vase on the rolling table in front of Lexi. "Here, these are for you. Hope carnations are okay."

Lexi's smile was so bright it could've provided more than sufficient energy to light up Fenway Park. Her leg was wrapped up, strapped to some type of cord, and lifted off the bed.

Charlie offered him his outstretched hand. "After dinner last night, we decided to extend our stay. We're even moving our things to the Lock and Key."

"For how long?" Chris surveyed his parents, waiting for an answer.

"Who knows? It's up to your mother," Charlie said.

"You don't think we would leave without getting to know the mother of our future grandchildren, do you?" Sarah beamed.

Chris swallowed the response he wanted to give. *You could've asked me if it was alright to come to the hospital.* Instead, he asked Lexi how she was feeling. She said she felt better than she expected she would after surgery, and thankfully, the excruciating pain in her leg was gone.

He wanted to find out if the babies had also made it through the surgery without out-and-out asking Lexi. Except, he rationalized, if there were a problem, he would've heard about it before he walked in the room.

His eyes followed the wires from the various monitors to Lexi, attempting to identify those that tracked the babies.

"There," Lexi said. "Those two are the fetal monitors."

Chris smiled and reached for her hand. "They're fine, then?"

"Yup. Just as Dr. Alexander said. I didn't lose them. They must be strong, like their father."

He looked at Charlie, who appeared to have one foot out the door.

"I hear there's an above-average café on the premises. Shall we, Sarah?"

"Good idea, Charlie. Let's leave the relieved mom and dad alone for a while. We'll be back in a bit. I have a few calls to make."

Chris pulled his fingers through his hair. "Give me a minute," he said to Lexi as he followed his parents into the hallway.

"I thought you had to get back to Chicago? What about the Great Art Hunt?"

"Come on, Christopher. You know I can handle my business anywhere in the world. Haven't you heard of Zoom meetings?"

"Of course."

"And anyway, the museums are right here in town and my partners in this quest are closer to me here than if I were in Chicago. I'm sure they'd be amenable to coming to Boston for a meeting or two. Who doesn't love to visit Boston?"

"But how long are *you* planning to visit? We can't entertain you."

"We? Who's *we*?"

They formed a triangle. Charlie between them, not saying a word.

"*We* means Kassie and me. We'll be busy for the foreseeable future, finding temporary accommodations for Lexi and moving her out of here. Not sure there'll be a lot of time for you to spend with either Lexi or with us."

Charlie put his hand on Sarah's arm, giving her a slight nudge. "Let's—" Whatever he started to say would have to wait.

"Speaking of Kassie, I'm not surprised she's not here. She's probably taking our little chat last night seriously. I knew she was one smart cookie. Just not the one you should be taking a bite out of."

Chris stepped closer to Sarah. "What the fuck?"

"Watch your language, young man. That's your mother."

Chris felt pressure on his lower back and spun around.

"You talking about me again?" Karen said, as if right on cue.

30

Hover Craft

Out of character, yet somehow instinctively, Chris gave Karen a bear hug. He held on for more than a beat and whispered in her ear, "Thank goodness you're here." The smirk she sent Sarah's way was indescribably delicious and not missed by any of them.

"What are you doing here, Karen?" Sarah said. "Quite a habit you're making. Showing up where you're not invited."

"Actually, Sarah, if you remember last night, Karen told us she'd be stopping by to see Lexi today," Charlie said. Apparently, coming to Karen's aid was fast becoming Charlie's and Chris's raison d'être, whether it was protecting her from free falling off an escalator or defending her from Sarah's prickly remarks. Perhaps there was some truth after all to *Like father, like son.*

Chris slapped Charlie on the back. "Thanks, Dad."

"No problem, son. Come on, Sarah. I need some coffee."

Sarah grumbled, saying she'd be back later.

Chris waited until Charlie and Sarah walked down the hallway and disappeared from view. Karen veered toward Lexi's room. He touched her arm. "Wait. Can we talk a minute?"

Karen's eyebrows merged as she squinted. "Can we sit? I need to catch my breath."

"Me too."

"Thank you, Chris. That was brave of you."

"I must say, of Charlie too. I'm beginning to see another side of my mother." Chris stopped, his eyes widened, expecting a tongue-lashing from Karen.

"That's okay. It's gotten really confusing, hasn't it?"

He noticed she touched the pink pendant as she continued. "I know I'm your real mother, and you know it too. That's all that matters to me now."

Sensing good vibes from Karen, Chris nodded, encouraging her to continue.

"Of course, I'm thrilled Kassie and Lexi recognize me as your mother as well. Knowing one's lineage is a good thing, especially if any health issues come up in the future—with you or those babies." She chuckled, shaking both hands in the air.

"You are right about that," he said. "But where are you going with this?" He had a favor to ask her and wanted to get back to Lexi.

"Simply, just call me Karen from now on."

Chris's eyes shifted from side to side. "Okay. That's what I call you now."

"True. What I think I mean is this. Don't get your knickers in a twitter about how you and Kassie and now Lexi refer to me. Everyone should call me Karen and call Sarah, your mother."

He straightened his back, growing six inches from where he sat on the hallway bench.

"You'd be cool with that?"

"I just said it, didn't I?" She laughed. "I'll still call you my son, not Sarah's. If that's okay with you? I lost you once. I refuse to do so again."

"That's quite a surprise, Karen. Very big of you. You kind of made my day. Thanks."

"Now, what did you want to talk about, son?"

He leaned into her as if he was about to tell her a deep, dark secret.

"By any chance did you hear what my mother …" He paused, letting himself get used to the new rules. "Did you hear what she said about Kassie just as you arrived?"

"The cookie part? Or the little chat part?"

"Oh, good. The cookie part pisses me off, but I really am curious by what she meant by their *little chat.*"

"Me too. Did Kassie mention it to you?"

Chris bowed his head, trying to remember the topics they discussed. Staring at the floor, he ticked them off on his fingers.

"We talked about going to a concert. About you crashing the dinner party."

"About that," Karen said. "Your father kind of invited me. But don't tell him or Sarah I said so. It wouldn't take much for her to knock him down a peg or two."

Chris raised his eyebrows, concurring with her. "Funny thing. I think Kassie's beginning to like you."

"Same here. But what gives you that idea?"

"She said you two talked about our being a modern family."

"We did, though, by the sounds of it, I'm not sure Sarah would include Kassie in the family."

Chris raised his chin and sighed. "I just remembered something. Before you arrived at the hotel last night, the four of us had cocktails in the lobby bar."

"That explains the spirited conversation at dinner."

"That and the mix of personalities. Anyway, when they told us our table was ready, Kassie and my mother hurried off to the ladies' room."

"You think that's when the little chat occurred?"

"Yes. It had to be. The only time they were alone."

Karen suggested he simply ask Kassie what she and Sarah talked about in the ladies' room.

"I could. But we're at sixes and sevens right now."

Karen looked up the hall. "Lexi?"

"I think she's jealous of Lexi. That she's pregnant."

"Maybe I should talk to Kassie."

"Thanks, Karen, but I think that's my job. There's someone else I want you to talk to."

Chris explained how he'd just learned his mother and father were planning to stay in Boston for some undetermined amount of time.

"Sarah's starting a new project involving some local museums and art experts. There's no need for her to be in Chicago, at least not for the foreseeable future."

"No pets?"

"No pets. Her philanthropy is her pet."

"And Charlie." Karen laughed louder than one should in a hospital.

Chris couldn't help but wonder if Karen relished the news that Charlie would be sticking around. Not so long ago, the image of his father rolling in the hay with Karen made him crazy. Now, that was the least of his concerns. He had bigger problems to solve. And perhaps he could capitalize on their relationship to get Sarah to stand down where Lexi was concerned before things spiraled out of control—more than they already had.

"You still talk with Charlie, I assume?"

Karen's eyes twinkled, as if she were a teenager caught in some nefarious deed by her parents.

"You want me to talk to Charlie? About what Sarah said to Kassie?"

"No, not really. I'll find that out some other way."

"Then what can I do for you?"

Chris rose and paced in front of Karen. "You know, since I arrived this morning, I've been focused on the three of you, when I should be with Lexi now—making sure she's comfortable and finding out what's next for her recuperation. I don't know how long she'll be here. How long it'll be before she can fly back to San Francisco. While she's here, I need to find a place for her to live that doesn't have stairs."

"Or a cat."

"There is that."

"So, what can I do?"

"Talk to Charlie. See if he can get my mother to stay out of my business. Meaning, lay off Kassie and give me time to get Lexi settled somewhere before she starts hovering."

"Does that go for me too? Am I hovering?"

"You always hover." They shared a laugh. "If you hadn't hung around Mike's life all those years, we probably wouldn't be sitting together here today."

"Would you tell Lexi I'll be by later? I'll see what I can do."

Karen jumped up, placed her palm on his heart, and headed for the elevators.

Chris's phone pinged. He expected to see Kassie's text reminding him to get Lexi's keys, but he was wrong.

Call me after 1. In a mtg til then.

OK, Annie. Talk later.

31

Surprise!

Peace at last. Chris exited the men's room and headed for Lexi. All he wanted to do was sit quietly next to her and get a real sense of how she was doing the morning after surgery—without interruption from his father or either of his mothers.

Nice of Karen to stop pressuring me to call her 'mother'. It'll make my life less difficult.

A life he privately acknowledged he'd royally fucked up.

If he hadn't split with Kassie after they first thought Mike was his father. If he hadn't crawled back into Lexi's bed on a trip back to San Francisco. If he hadn't accompanied her to Greece.

Maybe she wouldn't have gotten pregnant.

If he'd convinced Kassie they belonged together, that it didn't matter he was Mike's son, especially since it turned out he wasn't. If he'd been honest with Lexi, instead of taking advantage of what felt comfortable, and somehow safe.

If he'd used a fucking condom.

Lots of what-ifs. All of them within his control, all of them his responsibility. *All, plus the two growing inside Lexi's belly.*

Chris probably should've knocked on Lexi's door. Been polite. What if she was indisposed? Not ready for prime time, for visitors? More visitors. But he forgot his manners. It shouldn't matter. He'd seen Lexi in all stages of dress and undress over the years. She'd be surprised if he had knocked.

Lexi sat slightly upright. Her eyes were closed, hands folded just below her breast, which was larger than he ever remembered. Of course, there was a reason for that. Something else attributed to him.

For someone out of surgery fifteen hours ago, Lexi looked remarkably fresh and serene. Her hair was combed and her lips shiny and pink. He had to admit, no matter what bed Lexi was in, she graced it.

Like a church mouse, he crept past the foot of the bed to the far corner of the room, picked up a metal chair, and carried it to the side of the bed opposite all the monitors. The intravenous had been removed, which he figured meant Lexi was making progress.

He winced as the chair scraped the linoleum floor when he sat. Lexi peeked with one eye, her lips curled in a half smile. So much for not wanting to disturb her rest.

"I'm so glad it's you. Where have you been?" she murmured.

Chris apologized for coming and then going. "Family drama."

"I better get used to it, eh?"

He let her remark pass, not in any mood to get into a discussion about Sarah and Kassie, especially because he didn't know what had gone down between them. He opted to share some good news for a change.

"Listen to this. Amazingly, Karen just made things easier for me, for us. For everyone, for that matter. She's surrendered the moniker *mother* to Sarah. From now on, we can simply call her Karen. How about that?"

"One problem solved. At least for the time being." Lexi tilted her head toward the ceiling. "Let's carry that out into the future …" Lexi said, patting her middle. "That would mean these guys will call Sarah *grandmother*."

Chris was all ears, not sure where Lexi was going.

"But Karen is actually their grandmother by blood, right?" Lexi said. "So, what will they call her? Simply Karen? Or Grandma Karen?"

"Crap. I didn't think about that. I bet she didn't either. There's time to figure that out."

"Where is she, by the way?"

"Who?"

"Karen. Who else are we talking about?" She giggled.

Chris described how he ran into her in the hallway on her way to see Lexi. "She'll be back later. I thought you'd want to minimize visitors today as much as possible. You need to rest, I assume." He placed his hand on the bed next to her. She covered it with hers.

"Thanks. I appreciate that. I do hope she comes by, though. If she doesn't mind, I'm going to impose on her good nature and ask if she'd go shopping. Get me a proper robe and a few new nightgowns. This isn't very attractive." Lexi tugged at the front of the hospital gown.

As he could recall, no one had ever described Karen as being good-natured. But something had changed overnight. He hoped whatever altered Karen's behavior lasted more than a day.

"I'm sure she'll love to do that for you." *As long as I give her the money.*

"That'd be great. I didn't bring much with me from home. I never expected to land in the hospital." Lexi paused. "If my mother was here, I'd ask her. There really isn't anyone else here I'd feel comfortable asking."

SURPRISE!   175

Chris opened his mouth to offer.

"Oh, I wouldn't want to ask you. Better to let a woman."

"Thanks. Rather than getting lost among the pajamas and robes at Macy's, I prefer being here. I want us to have some time together. You and me," he said as he affixed his eyes to the fetal monitors. Lexi's eyes followed his.

Returning to her, he said, "How are you feeling? Can I get you anything?"

She rolled her head from side to side. "Get me a place to live!"

"Has the doctor said how long you'll be here?"

"Maybe until Monday or Tuesday. You know I can't go back to Kassie's."

He shook his head, reclaimed his hand, and interlocked his fingers as if in prayer.

"She wishes you could. She'd love to have you at the house. But with the stairs and Topher, she understands why it wouldn't work for you. She was full of alternatives yesterday. I guess it depends on how long you'll be in the cast," he said, waving his hand toward her leg.

Lexi chuckled. "Oh, that's not a cast. It's some sort of splint. Which is why I have to stay here until the swelling goes down so they can put on a cast. Then I can leave."

"Whoa. See how much I know."

"That's okay. This is all new to me too. It's gonna be hard for me to get around for a while. I'm hoping they give me crutches and not a wheelchair. No driving for a while."

"Speaking of …" Chris checked his phone. There it was. The text from Kassie reminding him to get Lexi's car keys. He missed the message. He responded, *Thanks. Got it.*

"Who you texting?"

"Your rental's blocking mine. I've been driving Kassie's car, making her housebound."

"Kind of what I'll be like soon."

He considered her remark. Her initial cheery attitude fading. He'd need to find ways to boost her spirits besides carnations.

"Do you have headphones with you? Maybe music will help pass the time."

"Yes, in my purse. In the front pocket." She pointed toward the cabinet. "With the car keys." She giggled. "Oh, just bring me my purse!"

He paused before opening the cabinet. An uncanny sense of déjà vu washed over him. He tried to shake it off, but no such luck. It lingered.

"I'll just return the car. You won't be driving it anywhere anytime soon," he said, racking his brain.

"Even if I could, there's no one here, except you, that I'd visit."

"Really?"

He moved alongside the bed to hand the purse to her.

"If you don't mind my asking, who's—"

"Aunt Venus! What are you doing here?"

32

Mission Accomplished

Chris gave Karen a mission, and she was delighted to accept it. The midmorning coffee rush was in full swing. The hospital cafeteria buzzed with healthcare workers in their various colored scrubs. Their masks and identification badges hung low around their necks. She positioned herself just inside the entryway, scanning the large room, looking for Mr. and Mrs. Gaines. She clutched her midsection, as the smell of bacon made her stomach gurgle.

At a table in a far corner opposite from her, she spotted Charlie reading a newspaper. It was hard to tell whether it was the *Boston Globe* or *The Wall Street Journal*, because he folded it like a book as she imagined subway riders did so they wouldn't infringe on their neighbor's space.

How am I gonna get his attention?

Karen watched Sarah jabbering away on her phone and sipping something from what looked like the largest disposable cup known to humanity. One would've thought with all her philanthropic bullshit she'd be more environmentally conscious and opt for a porcelain cup instead. But that was Sarah for you.

A bit of a hypocrite, if you ask me. And here I knighted her Mother.

Karen gazed around the cafeteria. More people seemed to be scrolling or tapping their phones rather than talking with a colleague sitting at their table. Shaking her head, amazed how unsocial society had become in the age of social media, she got out her phone and scrolled through her contacts.

Hey C. I can see you. Meet me in the hallway. Alone.

She shrugged her shoulders and grinned, proud she was finally getting the hang of this high-tech stuff. *If you can't beat 'em, join 'em.*

Without so much as a thought, she fingered her necklace. She hoped doing so would send strong vibrations through the airwaves to Charlie, and he'd get that eerie feeling that someone was watching him.

She spied him reaching in his pocket, checking out his phone, and then gazing around the cafeteria. He got her message. Karen did a mini fist pump for her eyes only. He said something to Sarah and headed in Karen's direction. She swooped out of the cafeteria and headed up the hallway, confident Charlie was close on her heels. She liked this mission. It felt like one of those challenges she heard the twentysomethings at the office talk about, though she didn't know if she'd succeed.

"Hey, you. Fancy meeting you here," Charlie said, cozying up as close to her as was appropriate in public. She thought he was going to lean down to kiss her, which she would've loved but knew better. She raised her palm, stopping him cold.

"Back at ya. Thought you and the missus were boarding a plane back to Chicago this morning?"

"That was the plan until Sarah decided she just had to meet Lexi. In person. You met her yesterday, so for sure she wouldn't let you be one up on her. After she gets off the phone, we'll head back up to see her. She's a pretty little gal." He glanced behind him, up the hallway, probably expecting to see Sarah barreling toward them. But they were safe. For the time being.

"About that pretty little gal. I haven't seen her yet this morning, but I did catch Chris outside of her room."

"Is everything okay? We were just there. She seemed dandy."

Karen touched his forearm ever so slightly, assuring him Lexi was indeed *dandy*.

"Let me ask you something. Did anything happen between Sarah and Kassie last night? Before I arrived?"

Charlie opened his mouth to answer.

Karen shook her head, stopping him. "On second thought. It's really none of my business," she said, remembering Chris mentioned he had it covered.

"So why the mysterious text and rendezvous? Not like our usual …"

Karen's knees almost buckled. His flirtations always made her weak. *Stay focused.*

"This might surprise you, but I'm carrying a message from your son—our son. So I'm just going to say it so there's no confusion. Whatever rift is bubbling up between your wife and Kassie, please ask Sarah to lay off of her. And, for that matter, don't hover over Lexi. This is not the time. Can you do that?"

"Of course. I'll try."

"Do more than try, Charlie. Chris has his hands full with Lexi. He feels totally responsible for everything. Everything. Her pregnancy and this surgery. And if she can't hop on a plane back to San Francisco when she's released, job number one for him will be to find a place for her to live temporarily."

A place for her to live … temporarily.

Karen's words echoed like a blast from the past. It wasn't long ago she had to find a place to live in Boston on a short-term basis.

"Gotta go." Karen bolted, leaving Charlie dazed and confused.

33

True Confession

Lexi choked, and then coughed, struggling to buy some much-needed time. Like the gentleman she knew Chris was, he immediately slid her purse next to her on the bed and rushed to her aid. He patted her back, but she kept right on hacking away.

He poured fresh ice water from the hospital's standard-issue stainless steel pitcher into a red Solo cup. As he handed it to her, she saw his eyes zero squarely in on hers. But he uttered nothing—not a single word, not even a grunt. She could tell he wanted to know who the hell was Aunt Venus?

She pulled her gaze away from Chris and stared at the cup. *This can't be happening. Maybe I'm still in surgery? Under the knife? Dreaming. Or the anesthesia is fogging my brain? Or what do they call it—post-surgery? No, no. I think maybe it's post-op. I really don't know or care what they call it. I call it—a fucking nightmare.*

Chris and her aunt stood with their mouths hanging open like newborn birds in their nests, just waiting.

Clearly, Chris waited for an explanation. In all the years Lexi had known him, she never mentioned having an aunt, especially not one living on the East Coast. And now with her aunt's grand entrance, rivaling those she'd seen Loretta Young make in reruns she watched with her mother, he'd know she lied to him when she said she had no relatives nearby. *He's going to hate me.*

Her aunt waited her turn to cross-examine. Lexi had to delay that from happening. She'd told her aunt about Chris. At least a fictionalized story. Lexi closed her eyes, reliving the conversation she had with her aunt before she stepped on a plane to fly to Boston. What details had she shared then? What had she texted her yesterday?

Her phone. That'd help.

Just as she did when she blamed the cat for her fall, Lexi had to think fast. Be on her toes, even though that was an impossibility at the moment. She picked up the red Solo cup and chose to make the water the issue, not Aunt Venus.

Spitting a mouthful of water back into the cup, Lexi wiped her face with the back of her hand. "I can't drink this. It tastes like someone marinated copper pennies in it." For a moment, she considered slinging it across the room but assumed she'd gain her aunt's disapproval rather than additional time to figure out her next move. Instead, she let her eyes plead with Chris.

He read her loud and clear. "I'll be right back. Did Lexi say *Aunt* Venus?" he said, addressing the visitor as he headed for the door. "When I get back, I'd really like to make your acquaintance. Properly."

"Take your time," Lexi said, reaching into her purse to get her phone. *I really mean it. Take lots of time.*

With Chris out of the room, ostensibly to get fresh water, Lexi was forced to face her aunt and the dilemma she got herself in. She rustled through the interior of her purse. While the phone was near the top, everything else inside looked as though it had been stir-fried. Her mind flashed back to her fall the day before. Almost as if in slow motion, Lexi saw for the first time the contents of her purse scatter across the tile floor.

"Give me a minute," she said to her aunt. "Chris needs my car keys." She dug through her bag, further delaying the inevitable. She found them and set them next to the water pitcher.

Lexi scrolled through her text messages, hunting for what she texted her aunt the day before. Then it hit her, the fog of anesthesia fading. She hadn't texted her; she'd called her. What had she told Aunt Venus? *Come on brain. Don't fail me now.*

The cat. Surgery. Didn't tell her I was pregnant. Chris, my fiancé. Oh shit!

She looked daggers at Aunt Venus, who remained silent, still waiting for Lexi, since she swept into the room.

"What are you doing here?" *You're going to spoil everything.* "I said I'd call you."

"That you did, my dear. But you shouldn't be surprised by my presence here. I texted you last evening and said I was on my way." Her aunt started to place her bag on the bed, but Lexi's leg in a sling occupied most of the space. As an alternative, she kerplunked the oversized Kate Spade tote bag on a metal chair near the door.

"Is that Alice in Wonderland on your bag?" Lexi attempted not only to delay but also to distract. Lexi patted the bed, searching for her phone.

Aunt Venus rotated toward the tote bag. "Why, yes, it is. I can get you one at the store here in town if you like."

Lexi had no genuine interest in the bag. A bit tacky, in her opinion. She was more interested in her aunt's mystery message. "I … I … I didn't see it," she said, until she did. "Oh, here it is."

Getting on 95 now.

See you tomorrow.

She noticed the time of the message. "I must have been in surgery. Sorry."

"Oh, my poor dear. Just look at you all strung up like a side of beef in a meat-packaging company freezer." She snapped a photo with her iPhone. "Don't be surprised if your mother hops on the next flight out here once she gets a load of this."

Lexi really hoped her mother didn't surprise her. One relative poking around in her business was enough. She was a big girl, a mother-to-be. *I must solve this myself. All of this.*

"That handsome fellow who was here. That's Chris, I gather?"

"Yes, but …" How would she explain that she'd lied about their engagement, and that he was the father of her children, plural? Lying to both her aunt and to Chris was a dumb idea. If she had any prayer of winning Chris, she must start by telling the truth.

The door swung open.

"Where's the water?" Lexi asked Chris.

"I bumped into Karen. She's getting it."

"Who's Karen?" Aunt Venus asked.

Lexi grabbed the question and ran with it. Another distraction, for sure. Yet, also a way to get her aunt and Chris to listen closely to what she had to say.

She explained in as many words as humanly possible that Chris, who was adopted, had only recently discovered Karen was his biological mother. She moved to Boston from New Mexico a few years ago to be with him and Mike, the man everyone initially thought was his biological father.

Chris nodded, validating Lexi's account of Chris's history.

Her aunt rolled her eyes and swiped her forehead. "Perhaps this Karen might be able to fetch us some vodka? I feel a saga coming on."

But water was all Karen physically carried into the room. Four bottles. One for each of them. As Chris had requested.

"Thanks, Karen. Come on in," he said. "I think some introductions are in order."

Karen handed two bottles to Chris, walked up to the head of the bed and unscrewed one, placing it on the table next to the car keys. She held onto one for herself and gave Lexi a quick kiss on the cheek.

"How you doin', Mama?" Karen said as Lexi inhaled a big swig of cold bottled water.

Oh my God. Lexi spewed the water like a geyser across the rolling table and down herself. This time, her coughing wasn't an act.

"What's the matter now?" Chris asked. He bumped Karen aside, taking her place next to Lexi. "You okay?"

"I will be. Just give me a minute." She reached for his hand and smiled at Karen, who Lexi believed would be her savior, if need be. She gulped deeply. *No time like the present to come clean. Let the chips fall.*

Motioning toward her aunt, Lexi began, "Chris, this is my Aunt Venus from Rhode Island. She's my mother's twin sister. It's been years since we've seen each other."

"Nice of you to drive up here," Karen said.

Lexi continued. "Aunt Venus, you were right. This is Christopher." She pursed her lips. *Just say it.* "I may have told you a little white lie. Chris is not my fiancé, though—"

"You told her we were engaged? Why?"

Lexi licked her lips. Her shoulders drooped, and her head tilted toward the fetal monitors. "You have to ask?" Chris's head bobbled as if he accepted and understood her deception. She exhaled in relief.

"You're pregnant?" Aunt Venus asked as she stared at the beeping monitors.

"Yes, she is," Karen said, "and I'm Karen Copperman, their future grandmama. Nice to meet you, Venus. Great name, by the way."

"*Their* grandmama? As in more than one baby?"

"We're having twins," Chris said, more boastfully than Lexi ever imagined he'd sound. *Maybe honesty is the best policy after all.*

"Well, I'll be an orangutan's aunt. Twins, just like me and your mother. She didn't tell me."

Lexi scrunched the toes on her right foot unconsciously. Her dry lips moistened, her cheeks glistened from tears streaking down, forming a path on her face.

"She doesn't know yet about the twins. I didn't tell her because we didn't find out ourselves until yesterday morning when I came to the hospital. So, please don't tell her, Aunt Venus."

"That's our job," Chris said, smiling like the cat that ate the canary.

"And I told you I was engaged to Chris because I didn't want you to judge me when you found out I was pregnant." She paused and then fixed her eyes on Chris. "That goes for you too. Please don't hate me for not telling you about Aunt Venus. I would've told you if I hadn't landed here in this hospital. I thought I could get through all of this on my own. You have to believe me."

Chris lifted her hand and kissed the back of it.

"Now let me get this straight. You're not engaged and you're having twins. Any more surprises up that ghastly johnny coat you're wearing, young lady?"

Lexi shook her head as Sarah joined the room.

"Oh my God in heaven. As I live and breathe! Venus Bixby, what are you doing here?"

34

Word Salad

Not quite a badass, but Chris felt pretty good about himself when he walked out of the hospital. A smirk on his face and a noticeable bounce in his step offered clear evidence his spirits were measurably higher than when he arrived there earlier that day. What once seemed like an albatross hanging over him now felt more like a sparrow sitting on his shoulder. Together, Karen and Aunt Venus had solved the Lexi problem, for which he'd be eternally indebted. He assumed Kassie would share his gratitude.

After rearranging the cars in the driveway so he could return Lexi's rental the next day, he found Kassie at her desk in her home office. It was easy to find her. He followed her signature grapefruit scent—a welcome change from the antiseptic smell at Boston Clinic. He stopped in the doorway to admire her, waiting for her to notice him. She appeared gloriously happy in her element. Her eyes glued to her laptop, her fingers gliding the untethered mouse across a frayed and faded Red Sox mouse pad, Topher curled up next to her desk. Both were totally oblivious to the starting and stopping sounds the car engines must have made as he shifted them around.

Instead of clearing his throat or announcing his arrival with "Honey, I'm home," Chris simply asked, "Is that a new cat bed?"

Kassie caught Chris's eye and glanced down. "Oh, this old gray thing? I'd forgotten about it, but Topher didn't." She related how earlier in the day when she was settling down to make some calls, Topher had poked incessantly the space beneath the closet door until she gave in and opened it.

At the risk of disrupting her work, Chris approached her guardedly, leaned down and gave Kassie a sweet kiss, and suggested a glass of wine. He could bring it to her, and they could talk. He was encouraged when she closed her laptop, switched off the wrought iron lamp, and gave the *Nevertheless, she persisted* ornament hanging from it a quick flick with a snap of her index finger. Considering all the women in his life that day, he was at a loss as to whom he'd ascribe that saying. Perhaps all of them. Maybe Kassie sensed he had a story to tell.

Nevertheless, he stalled. Wine was definitely mandatory. As he led the way to the kitchen, Kassie and Topher were close behind. Wherever she went, so would Chris's namesake.

Though excited to give her the ultimate breaking news, he wasn't sure where to begin. He couldn't just blurt it all out without providing context, without describing the scene. Choosing to ease into it, he first asked her how her day had been. Her smile pleased him.

"I'm touched that you asked. That you even want to know. Mike rarely gave me that consideration. It was all about him, ya know?"

He grinned, happy for the brownie points he earned. His head snapped when she asked, "How's Lexi?" She turned the tables on him. Was she stalling too?

No problem, though. The answer to the "How's Lexi" question was simple and straightforward. Contrariwise, he expected answering any questions around the who, what, and where of Lexi would require some measure of diplomacy on his part.

Taking one step at a time, he retrieved a fresh bottle of pinot grigio from the refrigerator and uncorked it, while Kassie removed two wineglasses from the dishwasher.

"Sounds like the surgery was successful," he said, pouring wine into her glass and pausing for her reaction. When none came, he continued. "Her leg's in a sling. She'll get a cast next week, and then she can come home." As soon as he said home, he blinked; he'd inadvertently opened the floodgates.

"Home?" Kassie swirled the wine in her glass and jutted her chin toward the family room. "Let's talk in there."

In an unusual move, Kassie slid into the BarcaLounger but did not put up the footrest. Her tiptoes barely reached the floor. He sat opposite her on the couch, stretching his legs across the coffee table as usual.

Rather than focus on *home*, Chris started with something less controversial: *mother*. Kassie agreed with him that Karen's magnanimous gesture would go a long way to uncomplicate matters and de-escalate emotions for everyone concerned.

She asked, "What do you think Sarah's reaction will be?"

He said he thought she'd be happy about it once he got the chance to tell her. Even though she and Charlie were at Lexi's bedside when he arrived that morning, they were off having coffee when he and Karen spoke.

That his parents hadn't hopped a jet plane to Chicago that morning was, of course, news to Kassie. To Chris's surprise, she shrugged when he said they planned to stay in town for some unknown period of time.

Chris expected Sarah's theory that she could plan her upcoming Great Art Hunt anywhere there was internet would validate

Kassie's belief that she could oversee Ricci and Son comfortably from Paris. So he downplayed that aspect of his parents' intention to hang around Boston.

And though they were on the topic of Sarah, he also decided to forgo asking Kassie what she thought Sarah meant when she called Kassie a smart cookie. And, for that matter, he'd keep his mother's offhand remark about him not taking a bite out of Kassie also to himself. If he started asking about Sarah, the rest of the day's developments might need to be told at another time—as Episode Two. And he was itching to tell Kassie about the arrival of Aunt Venus and what happened as a result.

"Do you believe in six degrees of separation?"

Of course she did. Kassie's psychic passion included anything and everything spiritual in nature. She sipped more wine and raised her eyebrows. He had her attention.

Without further fanfare, Chris broke the news about Venus, Lexi's long-lost aunt, living right down the road in Rhode Island.

Kassie almost choked and recovered without needing the Heimlich maneuver or ice-cold water in a red Solo cup.

"I thought she told us she had no relatives out here? They're all back on the West Coast."

"You are correct."

"So she lied?"

"You are correct."

"Why'd she do that? Did you smack her alongside the head?"

Chris laughed. Kassie did not.

"Seriously, Chris. She placed all the responsibility of finding her a place to stay until she could travel squarely on your shoulders and on mine. Not fair."

"Agreed. But stay with me, Kassie. There's more."

On the ride home from the hospital, he debated if he should tell Kassie that Lexi told her aunt that she and Chris were engaged.

By the time he pulled into the driveway, he reasoned if he didn't tell Kassie, and she found out from someone else, it would be curtains for him.

"You may not like this, but she told her aunt we're engaged."

"Who's engaged? You and me? What's not to like about that?"

He paused. In defense of Lexi's behavior, he said, "Lexi was afraid her aunt would judge her unfairly if she discovered she was going to be an unmarried mother." He paused again to let that sink in. "Having a child out of wedlock."

"Give me a break, Chris. I know what unmarried mother means."

He gulped. "You're right. I'm sorry."

"So, you're saying Lexi told her aunt the two of *you* are engaged?"

"She did, but she apologized and took it all back," he said in one breath.

Unsure whether that was good enough to satisfy Kassie, Chris got up and went into the kitchen to grab the rest of the bottle of wine and give her time to think.

She held up her glass for a refill. "Poor Lexi. Could her trip out here get any worse?"

Somewhat relieved at Kassie's taking Lexi's side and eager to move off that topic, he grimaced and said, "You've hardly heard the half of it."

"Oh my God, Chris. What else happened?"

"Sarah walked in."

"So, what's the big deal about that?"

Chris tried to draw a verbal picture. "All eyes were on Lexi, confessing her sins to me, Karen, and her aunt, when Sarah returned from the cafeteria."

"Sarah and Charlie?"

"No. Just Sarah. Charlie left to check out of the hotel and move their things to the Lock and Key."

Kassie snickered. "The popularity of that place astounds me. The thought of men behind bars freaks me out. I bet some of them died there. Wonder if their ghosts deliver room service in the dark of night?"

Topher, who was stretched out near her toes, rolled onto his back, lifted his paws into the air and purred as if someone were giving him a tummy rub. Kassie stretched her foot underneath him, flipping him over. She bent down and swiped her hand across his back as if she were swatting a fly. "Go away, Mother."

Not wanting to digress from his story, Chris ignored Kassie and their resident ghost he assumed was taunting Topher and haunting them. One O'Callaghan was plenty for him to deal with at the moment.

"Anyway," Chris said, "come to find out, the art expert from Rhode Island who Sarah mentioned she'd be collaborating with on the Great Art Hunt is none other than Lexi's aunt."

"You're shittin' me!"

"I'm not."

"What did you say her last name was?"

"I didn't. It's Bixby. Venus Bixby."

"Bixby? I've heard of her. She's well known in the museum circles. I bet Annie knows her."

"I think she's into fine art, like paintings, sculptures, not dinosaurs."

"Whatever. That's kind of cool. Maybe we can hit her up for free passes?"

"Is that all you can think of?" Kassie threw him a curve with that reaction. Recovering, he asked, "I was afraid you'd have a problem with the prospect of Lexi's aunt and my mother sharing day-to-day details about our lives. A little too cozy?"

"You're kidding, right? Your mother lives in Chicago, Venus in Rhode Island. I doubt Lexi will be top of their minds, especially when she's in San Francisco."

"About that." Chris bowed his head and rubbed his forehead. "She won't always be in San Francisco."

"Excuse me?"

"Not for a while, anyway." Chris cupped his mouth and ran his palm down his neck; then he blurted out, "She'll be staying in Charlestown."

Kassie sprung off the BarcaLounger and barreled out of the room without a word. He heard her clonking around the first floor. The bells on the front door clanged as she opened and shut it. Kitchen cabinets banged. The clothes dryer door slammed and hummed.

For someone who was supposed to be a communications expert, Chris realized he'd missed the mark in conveying the news to Kassie. He'd really blown it. He complicated something that should have been a slam dunk.

KISS, he thought. *Keep it simple, shithead.*

His phone pinged. Annie. He'd never called her like she asked. She'd have to wait.

Busy now. Call tomorrow.

He inhaled, waiting for a text response. None came, thankfully. He was in no mood for a back-and-forth text-à-text with Annie. Kassie was his priority.

She returned to the family room carrying a laundry basket heaped with clothes needing to be folded.

"Put that down and come over here and sit." Chris lifted the basket from her and placed it near the fireplace hearth, far enough away so she couldn't multitask. He grasped her hand and led her to the couch. "Sit down."

Holding her hands, he apologized for screwing up, not just how he told her about the day, but also with Lexi overall. Didn't matter how many times he'd have to say he was sorry, he would do it if that's what Kassie needed to be happy.

Unfortunately for him, she didn't readily embrace the idea of Lexi living in Charlestown, even temporarily, as he assumed she would. He failed miserably and suddenly feared if Charlestown created a problem for Kassie, the rest of the Karen/Venus plan could be in jeopardy.

Somehow, he had to get Kassie on the same page with him. So he started all over again. This time in as few words as possible. He'd feed it to her as if in bullet points.

Still holding her hands, he established the premise. "After everyone figured out who was who at the hospital, Karen, bless her heart, suggested we focus on Lexi. From Karen's point of view, two questions needed answers."

He kept his gaze on Kassie to be sure she tracked with him.

"First, could Lexi return to San Francisco when she's released from the hospital next week? The answer clearly *no*."

"Clearly," she said.

"Next. In that case, where could Lexi live temporarily, before she delivers?"

Kassie raised one eyebrow. "Not here."

"Right. Not here. And that's when Karen offered a brilliant solution. She suggested Lexi move into my apartment in Charlestown. Since I'll be living here, my place would be vacant. The lease is flexible, so that's not a problem. And on top of all that, with Karen living right there in the building, she offered to help Lexi whenever she needs anything."

"No stairs there."

"Right again. There's an elevator, and no cat."

Raising himself upright, Topher stretched, let out a whine, and pranced out of the room. Kassie shook her head.

"But it's rather small, isn't it? One bedroom. Hardly enough room for two cribs and all the kiddie paraphernalia—swings, high chairs, changing tables, diaper bags … "

Listening to Kassie rattle off as she did only reinforced why he wanted and needed Lexi and his children in close proximity to him. Not just so he could more easily fulfill his financial obligation to them, but for his own emotional well-being. His children must grow up knowing who their father was, and he needed them in his life on a more regular basis than San Francisco would provide.

Kassie's buy-in was critical. Following her lead about the limitations of the apartment in Charlestown, Chris reminded her it was a temporary solution.

"So, at some point, she'll pack up and head back to San Francisco? She's got more family there and her job, right?"

Gulp. Not the path he wanted to her to take. He took a large swig of his wine and put the glass down. On second thought, he picked it back up, drained it, and poured another.

To make the next crucial point, he got to his feet. "That's where Aunt Venus comes in."

"How so?"

"Apparently, she lives in a big house near Newport. Sounds like a mini-mansion." His arms stretched out and then up toward the ceiling, emphasizing the size of the house. "In a few months, she's heading to Asia on that art adventure."

Kassie stared into her wine.

"Don't you get it, Kassie? Her *huge* house will be empty."

Kassie lowered her head, sighed, and then peered up at Chris. "So, you're telling me she offered the house to Lexi? Let me get this straight. Instead of her living clear across the country, she'll be living in the next state?"

It may have taken Kassie a minute, but she'd made it easy on him. All he had to say was "Yes."

Chris's relief lasted less than a minute.

"You're okay with that, Chris? I can understand Charlestown until she delivers. It would be difficult for Lexi to travel in a cast *and* pregnant. But Rhode Island sounds a little more permanent to me. Doesn't it to you?"

He stepped toward the fireplace, then circled to face her. "If you're asking if I think Lexi living in Rhode Island is forever, how the hell do I know?"

He wasn't born yesterday. He knew damn well what she was asking, or implying.

"What sounds too cozy to me, Chris, is having Lexi and your children living close to us. I've been trying to picture you having two kids three thousand miles away and imagining how we were going to handle the responsibilities of you being a long-distance father. If they're only what, fifty or seventy-five miles away, I'm more concerned about Lexi being involved and interfering with our new life together than about any meddling by Sarah or this aunt of hers."

Chris collapsed onto the couch and slouched into the cushions. All the parties involved with Lexi had left the hospital satisfied and pleased with their creative problem-solving skills and ultimate agreement. All the parties involved, except Kassie. He was so caught up in the moment, he hadn't given any thought to how she'd react. He reached to massage her back.

"I get it. I should've discussed all of this with you first."

She swiped her fingers across her pursed lips.

"Sounds like you're okay with the near-term Charlestown arrangement, right?" he asked.

She tilted her head, acknowledging that.

"Okay. Good. We have time to figure out what comes later. Let's table Rhode Island for the time being."

"Sounds like a plan," she said.

He sighed. Half a victory was better than none. "Now tell me, how did your day go?" Unlike Chris, whose description of his day was a train wreck, Kassie summed up her day in a nutshell. "Paris."

35

The Changing Tide

"Paris is waiting." That's what Chris whispered to Kassie as they lingered near security at Logan Airport the Friday evening before Labor Day. Though a national holiday in the U.S., Monday was a workday in Paris, and the office there was expecting her.

Chris said his goodbye matter-of-factly. No encouraging lilt to his voice. No added cheer like, "Go get 'em, girl."

Underwhelmed and honestly disappointed by his dispassionate send-off, Kassie buried her head in his chest, gulping back a sob she felt bubbling up from her stomach. If she cried in front of him, he might interpret that to mean she had second thoughts about leaving. And since she didn't, her tears would have to wait.

How silly of her to expect he'd cheerfully let her go. He made his objections known on more than one occasion since the day after Lexi's surgery when Kassie made her decision crystal clear. She'd go to Paris for nine months—September through May. When she returned, she'd resign from Calibri Marketing with a successful merger notched on her belt. An accomplishment she could crow about to all the Boston marketing elite at industry dinners and conferences for years to come. Then, she'd proudly take the reins at Ricci and Son, and she and Chris would get married.

Happily ever after was less than a year away.

That was her plan all along, ever since Mimi Couture, managing director of Calibri-Paris, made her an offer she couldn't refuse and Mike left her the company in his will. Why would she ever let an annoying itch like Lexi upend a dream she worked her entire life to achieve?

But Chris had other ideas. For at least a week after the hospital released Lexi and he moved her luggage to his Charlestown apartment, along with the five—count them, five—new nightgowns Karen bought her, Chris pleaded with Kassie to stay, not to go to Paris. He and Ricci and Son needed her in Boston. He'd miss her so.

Then, for no apparent reason other than her steadfastness, he seemed to give up on the prospect of changing her mind, for which she was grateful in one respect. She was insanely busy planning and packing. Going over ground they already covered was unproductive and certainly not on her to-do list. To her, Paris was a done deal.

Except for one thing. She and Chris were transitioning from the joys of a newly engaged, happy couple into a pitiful pattern of squabbling almost daily, significantly more than they ever had before Lexi arrived in town. And almost always, the point of contention was about something totally insignificant: laundry, trash, what was for dinner. Kassie feared they were becoming an old married couple even before they said "I do."

Hoping to turn the tide, she raised again the prospect of getting married before she left for Paris, and if not then, how about

Christmas? Neither proposal suited Chris. She couldn't help but wonder if Sarah had been whispering in his ear. If she wasn't able to get Kassie to break off the engagement, perhaps she could persuade Chris to at least delay their marriage.

No matter what, he always had a reason why it wasn't a good idea for them to change their original plan, and the excuse always revolved around Lexi and the birth of "their children." At some point, Chris switched from referring to the twins as "his kids" to calling them "their children." And he didn't mean his and Kassie's. She put an imaginary pin in that detail.

To add insult to injury, it flummoxed Kassie when at dinner one night at Tryst in Arlington the week before her departure, Chris brought up the topic of her taking his name when they tied the knot. The topic arose as she placed her Amex card on the table to pay the bill.

"I've got this," Chris said, sliding her card back toward her. Then he stopped, picked it up, and read it: "Kassandra O'Callaghan."

"That's me. Thank you very much," she said, reaching for her card.

"You're a short-timer."

Kassie stared toward the card, not sure what he meant. *Short-timer* meaning she'd be leaving for Paris soon? *Short-timer* meaning her card was about to expire?

"You'll only be using this card for a short period of time."

She grabbed it in a panic. Shaking her head, she said, "What the …? It's not expiring."

"I never said it was. Once we're married, you'll be Kassandra Gaines. You'll need to change your last name to Gaines on your cards, driver's license. A whole bunch of things."

"You're joking." *That'll never happen.*

One thing they didn't argue incessantly about was moving all of Chris's things to Kassie's house and Lexi into the Charlestown apartment. That decision was quick and a win-win for everybody. Especially for Lexi. She could easily maneuver around the flat on crutches, and she had Chris and Karen jumping through hoops for her. If they couldn't get to the grocery store on her behalf to buy whatever her latest craving was, they helped her order online from Market Basket, and then one of them would stop by to put everything away once it was delivered.

Chris told her Lexi was ecstatic when she discovered there was a Whole Foods Market in the neighborhood as well. Good for her; not so good for Chris, who was pretty much footing her bills. She'd taken a temporary leave of absence from her job in San Francisco, her manager agreeing to reevaluate her employment after the babies were born. After all, Lexi wasn't certain where she'd be calling home come January, and she wanted to leave her options open.

Lexi's circle of benefactors—Chris, Sarah, Aunt Venus, and Karen—blamed Kassie for Lexi's life being in limbo. If only Kassie would stop being so "stubborn, selfish, obstinate, pigheaded," Lexi could focus on delivering two healthy babies rather than worrying about where they would live after they were born. "What's wrong with Newport?" the four of them nagged Kassie constantly.

"Nothing," she'd say simply to three of them. They had no designs on her; she owed them no further explanation. However, to Chris, she voiced in more graphic detail her displeasure at the prospect of having the Moore family, especially Lexi, living almost in her backyard.

"I know you. You'll want to be part of their daily lives. Feed them, bathe them, be there for their first steps." The pain of some other woman giving Chris what she could not prevented her from willingly and generously sharing her husband-to-be.

"I can't compete with all of that. I'm not as charitable as your mother or Lexi's aunt."

And so on the ride to Logan that evening when Chris said, "What's wrong with Newport?" all she could say was "Let's give it some time, Chris. Life seems to have a way of working itself out." He seemed satisfied with that. At least for the time being.

They also didn't argue about who'd watch Topher. Chris offered to take care of him while Kassie was abroad, and she considered it but only briefly. She observed Topher shying away from Chris the very day Lexi stumbled down the stairs. He became more aloof, she thought, than cats normally were. He stopped greeting Chris when he arrived home from work and showed no interest in rubbing up against him. When Chris offered Topher his favorite treats, he sat on his haunches and waited for Chris to place the goodies in front of him on the floor. Chris shrugged it off, attributing the change in Topher's behavior as proof he'd somehow gotten under Lexi's feet, causing her to fall.

Ridiculous.

Nevertheless, time was of the essence and Kassie had precious little of it to spend figuring out why Topher's mood toward Chris had changed. Her housekeeper, Teresa, suggested she enlist the help of a cat whisperer. A friend of a friend told her they worked wonders with kitties who suddenly exhibit strange behaviors, like pooping outside of their litter boxes or giving their owners the cold shoulder.

"Mr. Chris is a good guy. The cat whisperer will tell Topher that Mr. Chris will take good care of him," Teresa said. Kassie thanked her, adding she'd take it under advisement.

Which she did. She brought Teresa's crazy idea to her favorite counselor, Annie, who came into Boston proper for lunch the next day. Of course, Annie had a field day with the idea of a cat whisperer. "I'm surprised you're not going for it with all of your voodoo and séance crap."

"You're exaggerating, and you know it. When have I ever gone to a séance?"

"Oh, ye of short-term memory," Annie said. "Remember the voodoo doll you bought at the carnival years ago in Lake George, after you had your palm read?"

"Not my palm. My cards, silly." Kassie had forgotten all about the voodoo doll but always remembered the fortune-teller saying she'd meet a younger man who'd change her life. And people say it's all hooey. She hadn't seen the doll in a while. Perhaps with Lexi in the picture, now would be a good time to drag out some of the boxes stored in the attic. Kassie sensed she needed all the help she could get to keep that younger man in her life.

"I'll take him," Annie said, with a mouthful of chicken salad. "What are friends for if not to foster your cat while you jet-set off to Europe?"

Kassie jumped at Annie's offer but wouldn't let her off easily. "I'm not jet-setting anywhere. I'm going to Paris on assignment."

Unlike Chris, who gave up on trying to convince Kassie to stay put in Boston, Annie gave it one more good old college try over dessert. From her perspective, Chris had turned to Lexi for comfort once before; he could easily do it again. This time she'd be in Charlestown, not clear across the country.

"What if you succeed with this merger but lose Chris in the process? Have you thought of that?"

Admittedly, Kassie had thought about the risk she was taking. "Sometimes, Annie, you just have to play the cards you're dealt."

"I thought the cards dealt you Chris."

"That was a long time ago. Now there's a new deck. I believe in my heart of hearts they're showing Paris." Kassie tapped her chest with her fist.

Annie continued to press Kassie. "What will going to Paris prove that staying in Boston and being CEO of Ricci and Son would not? You're at the top of your career no matter where you lay your head at night."

"It's about finding me, defining me," Kassie said. "I feel as though the real me has been lost all my life. You know I've been doing right by everyone forever. My mother, Mike, and even Chris when we split after I thought he was Mike's son. That wasn't about me. That was so he could build a relationship with Mike without me around to muck up the works."

"And when he died, Mike handed you, not Chris, Ricci and Son."

"Right. He gave it to me either for legal reasons or out of guilt. I earned Paris on my own." Kassie reached for the check and got up.

In a bit more than a stage whisper, Annie said, "Whatever. I hope you find what you're looking for over there."

36

Warning Sign

"Paris, here I come." Kassie cheered herself on even if Chris failed to do so. She gathered her shoes and her carry-on luggage after successfully navigating the security checkpoint without enduring a pat down like she had when she left Charles de Gaulle airport in July. *Thank God for small favors.*

Now that was done, she pivoted toward where she left Chris on the other side of the PreCheck line, expecting to give him a salute, a wave, or exchange air-borne kisses. A last farewell. But she couldn't see him. *Chris, where are you? I'm waiting.*

It wasn't as if they'd planned to do this; she just thought maybe he'd want one last look as much as she did.

While she didn't expect him to be in especially good humor, his farewell barb about Paris waiting unnerved her. If he followed that up with something like "And I'll be waiting right here when you get back," at least she'd have been a tiny bit more optimistic that he, in fact, would be there for her after Paris. She began to wonder.

As she said her goodbyes, Kassie clung to Chris longer than she ever clung to anyone in her life. She needed to soak up enough of his love and good vibrations that could last at least until December when she'd be back for the holidays.

He dropped his arms first. Was that a little push she felt from him?

Now, as she conceded Chris would not be blowing her a kiss, an eerie feeling engulfed her. And the tears she refused to let him see flowed.

Planning her departure from Boston had been fairly inconsequential thanks to the Boston and Paris teams. Despite having to throw cold water on her face in the ladies' room to wipe away her tears, the boarding process for the overnight nonstop flight to Charles de Gaulle went without a hitch. All the legal documents supporting a one-way ticket were apparently in order and accepted with merely a grunt by the gate attendant.

Under normal circumstances, it could've taken three months to get the work permit approved, enabling her to manage the merger between Calibri-Paris and E. Z. Media in London. But Mimi, who was heading for maternity leave, had connections. Or let's say her husband had friends in high places. The application was submitted and approved in just thirty days.

Peering out the airplane window on takeoff was an exercise in futility. The window was clean; Kassie's eyes clouded with liquid sorrow. She pulled a tissue out of a small package she'd stowed in the seat pocket of her business class pod and dabbed her tears. Luckily, she anticipated that possibility and dispensed with wearing mascara that day, tossing the partially used tube in the bathroom trash can, knowing it would be more than three months until she'd be back to use it again.

Just stop with the tears. Not like you.

She had seven hours to plug up the waterworks. Kassie O'Callaghan, acting managing director extraordinaire, would not arrive in Paris a blubbering fool, for goodness' sake.

No matter how extraordinary she imagined she was, Kassie grasped the reality that she was flying solo on this venture. Whether she succeeded was up to her.

Any internal pangs of anxiety she felt about managing a corporate merger on her own were not what made her cry buckets. The culprit was the pit in her stomach caused by leaving behind all those she loved—Chris, Annie, Topher—and those she assumed she'd love in time—Lexi and the twins. Maybe if she dedicated an hour to thinking about each of them, she'd shed all her tears by the time the plane landed.

As the jet sped across the Atlantic, Kassie's thoughts wandered. She resented having to defend herself or her decisions to anyone. She'd done enough of that when Mike was alive. No longer was he around to chip away at her confidence with his favorite saying, "Sometimes I think you leave your brain at the office." Yet, deep in her soul, she believed if Mike was still alive to witness her grabbing the gold ring and flying off with it to Paris, he'd readily admit her brain was good for something after all. Perhaps he'd even be more than a little bit proud of her.

Odd that she was thinking about him now. Mike had seldom been on her mind over the last five weeks which, in retrospect, zipped by. Every minute of every day was filled with preparation. Besides all the personal issues she needed to address and solve, managing a business in a foreign country came with its own perks and challenges.

Kudos to Vicki, her assistant, for booking her flight in business class. Kassie had always flown in coach, so this was a real treat she could easily get used to. "Rank has its privileges," Vicki said, handing her a printout of her travel arrangements.

She was always uneasy about flying over the Atlantic and was relieved the flight so far that night was as smooth as—. Kassie paused to fill in the blank. *As smooth as a silky piece of dacquoise.* Grinning at her ability to describe something, anything, in French, she recalled her tutor recommending she indulge in that dessert the first time she found it on a menu or on display at a corner patisserie. Kassie assured her tutor she'd do that if she could remember how to pronounce *dacquoise.*

"*C'est facile*, Kassie. Just say duck-was."

Kassie snickered, acknowledging it was easy for the tutor to say. Not so much for Kassie. Nevertheless, as an obedient student, she recorded *duck-was* on her phone, adding it to a long list of words and common sayings she had trouble memorizing. If all else failed, she could show the picture of the dessert, which she tagged for good measure.

After a week of personal tutoring and two hours a day laboring on the Babbel app, Kassie lost patience with herself. Frustrated, she swallowed her pride and emailed Mimi. Did she have any suggestions to help Kassie improve her French quickly?

Mimi reminded her she'd be there for only nine months to merge a British company with a French company. No one expected her to be fluent in French. And she shouldn't forget English was the British company's primary language, and most of the staff at the Paris office spoke English. Fluently.

If that didn't embarrass Kassie enough, Mimi said she already identified and assigned two staffers to be available as translators whenever Kassie felt she needed them. And if Kassie wanted some instruction while in France, she could enroll in an immersion class or hire a private tutor. "Whatever Kassie O'Callaghan wants, Kassie O'Callaghan gets," Mimi teased.

The flight attendant leaned over and asked her if she wanted another glass of wine. She'd slugged the glass she'd been given while they were waiting to take off in Boston. Her first inclination was to take a pass. But then what the hell? She wasn't flying the plane. And she wouldn't be driving once she landed.

Chris, not Mimi, offered to arrange an Uber pickup for Kassie when she arrived at Charles de Gaulle. Not wanting to add any more stress to their relationship, she bit her tongue and said she welcomed his help. Of course, she knew he'd want to contact Tanya, the luscious tall blond driver who was at their beck and call when she and Chris were in Paris in July. When she reached into her briefcase to get Tanya's information from her business-card holder so he could make the reservation, she blinked twice when he simultaneously pulled Tanya's card out of his wallet and said, "I've got it."

I just bet you do, Bad Kassie's voice answered inside her mind. But she let it go. No need to pick a fight over a taxi ride.

Now, however, with red eyes from the overnight flight, tears, and multiple glasses of wine, Kassie looked forward to seeing Tanya, a familiar face, on the other side of Customs and Immigration, holding a sign reading *O'Callaghan*.

Once the plane reached the gate in Paris, a man she hadn't noticed across the aisle offered to help her retrieve her carry-on luggage. He had a thick accent she couldn't place. She smiled, nodded, and attempted to swallow before taking him up on his offer, but her mouth felt like ten cotton balls had taken up residence. She riffled through her purse, grabbed three mini Altoids, and licked her lips. All she could muster was "*Merci beaucoup*." Who said she needed French lessons?

The man winked at her and said in perfect English, "Welcome to Paris. Enjoy your stay," and handed her his business card. She glanced at it. *Matthew somebody*. She slipped it into her pants pocket.

As she was about to deplane, a flight attendant asked Kassie to follow her, which of course, she did. Once she was inside the terminal, the flight attendant steered her in a different direction than the rest of the passengers. Before she knew it, someone piled Kassie's luggage onto a rolling cart, and she was whisked through Customs and Immigration without even asking "How long will you be staying in Paris?" At first she thought she was getting business-class treatment. Then she realized it must have been the Mimi Couture touch.

Before heading out the door to the new arrivals area, Kassie stopped in the ladies' room to freshen up. She wanted to greet Tanya and Paris with her best face forward.

The arrivals hall was a buzz of confusion, with travelers uniting with friends and families, and with a multitude of drivers holding placards with the names of their clients written in bold letters. She scanned their faces; most were men, so it should have been easy to pick out a tall blond among the throng of black suits.

Confused by the mayhem, she switched to eyeing the names on the cards.

And then she spotted Tanya. Now a redhead. Waving a sign that read *Gaines*.

37

Eyeball Yoga

To put it bluntly, jet lag sucks no matter how exciting the desti-
nation. Kassie sensed a mind fog creeping over her soon after
settling in Tanya's car. She chalked it up to the time difference, a
lack of restorative sleep, and the three glasses of wine she had on
the flight. Whatever the reason, she calculated on her fingers that
she lost at least seven hours of sleep she wouldn't regain until she
flew back in December.

As Tanya pulled away from the airport, Kassie gazed out the
window and powered up her phone, which automatically adjusted
to Paris time. *How quickly it knows where I am when I'm not sure
where I am.* It was half past seven, which meant if she were still at
home with Chris, they'd be shutting out the bedroom lights after a
more than satisfying romp. Sadly though, she had to admit they'd
gotten it on less often lately as her departure date neared.

*So why not Paris? Sometimes couples need a mini-break to right
the ship, right?*

In all the hustle and bustle to get to Paris, she forgot she'd need a day or two or three to adjust to that side of the Atlantic. She only allowed about forty-eight hours to sleep off Chris, Lexi, and all their various relatives and to be awake, alive, and enthusiastic when she strutted into Calibri-Paris on Monday morning.

Kassie slid on her sunglasses not only to protect her eyes from Paris's bright daybreak but also to prevent Tanya from seeing an exercise she did with her eyes in order to wake up or stay awake. She perfected it years ago as a result of being in dull and boring management meetings at the ungodly hour of eight in the morning. She'd hide her face by either bowing her head or casually placing an open palm face down on her forehead. Raising her eyelids as high as she could muster, she'd count to five, look side to side, and then relax for ten seconds or so. Then she'd do it again. Better than yawning uncontrollably. Kind of like yoga for the eyeballs.

"How long will it take?" Kassie asked, looking forward to crawling into bed for a few hours.

"Not long. Saturday morning, you know. Less traffic than when you and Christopher were here in July."

There. That was Kassie's opening.

"Speaking of Chris. About the sign you were holding back there. It said *Gaines*. That's not my name. That's his. *O'Callaghan*. My name's O'Callaghan." Her ears popped when she swallowed, probably from the flight, or not.

Tanya apologized, writing it off as her mistake. Chris had emailed her to make the reservation, and she'd forgotten they weren't married yet. The clash between him and Kassie about whether she'd take his name after they wed flashed through Kassie's mind. Had Chris inadvertently left her maiden name off his request? Or did he purposely do it to make a point? She'd never know. *At least I've corrected the faux pas. See, I'm thinking in French already.*

Tanya lifted her right hand and wiggled her fingers. "I see you're wearing your beautiful Cartier ring. Engaged, but not married, eh? Have you set a date?"

Kassie realized Tanya wouldn't really know why she'd returned to Paris. Just that she was picking her up and taking her to an apartment downtown. So, in the few minutes they had, she brought Tanya up to speed with all that an Uber driver needed to know. After all, it was conceivable she'd use Tanya's services on more than one occasion while in the city.

All the talk about wedding dates and the mission energized Kassie a bit. As they drove toward the Latin Quarter, Tanya pointed out the most famous tourist attractions within walking distance of where Kassie would be living. The Louvre, of course, and Notre-Dame. And the Eiffel Tower.

"Been there," Kassie said, recalling that fateful night when her pomegranate rash invaded her body, disrupting Chris's passionate, yet abbreviated, proposal on the Pont Neuf. She bet Tanya would remember driving them to the Tower.

"You have my card?" Tanya asked as they pulled up in front of a charming four-story building. "Your office is not an easy walk from here."

Kassie groaned slightly at the thought of schlepping to work each day. She was more than a little impressed Tanya remembered she'd driven Kassie to the office back in July and even recalled the location. Then she realized Uber drivers kept records. So there was that.

"I can drive you to the office Monday, if you like?"

While the company picked up the tab for the ride from the airport, Kassie expected any future Uber rides to the office would be on her. A luxury, for sure. Shrugging that notion aside, she decided to splurge at least on the first day and until she discovered the cheapest means of transportation.

"Can we schedule that now? Say seven thirty pickup?" Kassie asked.

Standing face-to-face as Tanya opened the car door for her, Kassie couldn't avoid seeing her smirk.

"This is Paris," Tanya said. "I'll see you at eight thirty. No one will expect you before nine at the earliest, especially on your first day. Actually, not on any day." Tanya laughed.

"*Oui*. Okay." *I think I can get used to this custom real fast.*

Together, Kassie and Tanya unloaded her luggage from the trunk and the back seat. When she packed back home, she worried she wasn't bringing enough. Now, as she struggled with two large rolling bags, one midsized suitcase, a gym bag, a small carry-on, plus her briefcase and purse, she wondered what the hell she'd been thinking.

Whatever I need, I'll be able to find right here in Paris.

Between forgetting about jet lag and overpacking, Kassie began to doubt her planning skills. Perhaps Mike was partially right about her leaving her brain at the office.

Nah. I'm Kassie O'Callaghan, acting managing director extraordinaire.

"Are you Mademoiselle O'Callaghan?" Kassie lifted her head as a man with two empty hands and Popeye-looking arms seemed to appear out of nowhere.

"Here we go again," she mumbled. She was just about to tell him she's madame when she realized that was no longer the case. With Mike dying, rightfully she could be called mademoiselle, couldn't she?

Note to self. Check out this custom as well. Soon. Before I step in it.

Kassie, relieved to see someone besides Tanya coming to her rescue, let it slide. Instead, in her best American vernacular, she said, "Yup, that's me!" So much for her French lessons.

Gerard introduced himself as the caretaker of the apartment building, doing sort of a bow and wave, guiding her and Tanya toward the entrance to a courtyard. "Right this way," he said, taking all the non-rolling luggage, except for Kassie's purse, of course. "We've been expecting you."

How is it the French can speak perfect English, and Americans have no patience to learn their language? Must be a flaw in our DNA.

With Gerard in control of most of her belongings, Kassie's eyes followed vines that snaked their way up the entire structure. *Four floors. No way there's an elevator. This is Paris.* With her luck, her apartment would be at the top.

Though the bag she tugged behind her had wheels, she knew it was heavy. She packed it, after all. Her heart pounded at the prospect of climbing multiple flights of stairs, the suitcase clip-clopping behind her. What if she let go, and it fell down a flight, and the lock let loose? Was this the case with all her intimate apparel? *Gross.*

Not knowing which of the four doors to enter, she and Tanya waited until Gerard caught up with them in the courtyard. Once there, he gently placed all that he carried in front of a potted tree to the left of a set of French doors. He fiddled in his pocket, and with a click, the doors swung outward into the courtyard.

"Home," he said. And following Gerard's quick head tilt, Kassie walked into the entryway to the first-floor apartment she'd be living in until the end of May. Stopping herself from kissing Gerard, she said, *"Oui. Oui. Alors c'est la maison."*

38

Blissful Thinking

What is bliss?

Is it that first waking moment when all the problems of the world seem easily solved? Is it rolling onto the cooler side of the pillow and settling in for just five more minutes? Or is it discovering the bed you'll be lying in for the next nine months is comfier than the waterbed back in Boston? Even without the warm, naked body of the man in your life.

Kassie lifted her head off the feather pillow, opened her eyes, stretched out her legs, and wiggled her toes between the fine bed linens. *Gotta get me some of these for* la maison. *Home.*

"There's no place like home," she uttered to the stone walls and the dark wood ceiling beams in the bedroom when she awoke from her nap. But she quickly qualified her remark, if only to herself. Home wasn't Boston, at least not for the foreseeable future. And unlike Dorothy, Kassie wasn't quite ready to mourn all that she'd left behind less than twenty-four hours ago.

So, she switched things up a bit with a new mantra: "There's no place like my Paris home." *That should work.* "And there'll be no heel clicking here either. Not yet, anyway."

Also, unlike Dorothy, she hadn't run away. Or had she? If so, from what?

Shaking out of her mind questions she wasn't prepared to answer, she got up and used the toilet in a petite room, separate from the sink and the one-person shower. She wandered into the alley kitchen in search of a glass for water, opening the pine cabinets above the sink. There she discovered biscuits, crackers, cereal, tea bags, tiny bags of sugar, and a jar of what she assumed was strawberry jelly by the image on the label, among other staples. Maybe this part of living in Paris was like home, just labeled differently.

Kassie let her fingers do the walking through the other cabinets and drawers and found they contained the usual dishes, glasses, and silverware. However, there seemed to be an unusual number of wineglasses and goblets. Some were plain, some had some pretty etchings on them, and easily a half dozen bore the imprint of a winery. More than likely, previous guests had gifted them to the apartment rather than risk having them break in their luggage. She lifted one and then another, admiring the artwork and reading the names. She didn't recognize any of wineries.

Clearly, she'd need to go on a wine tour or at least a tasting soon. In the meantime, she'd need to buy some wine. Shouldn't be difficult.

She turned her attention to the refrigerator in the opposite corner. Not a mini fridge like you'd keep in a playroom or garage, and not the side-by-side monster she and Mike bought years ago, but about five feet tall, almost her height. Expecting it to be empty, she felt her mouth drop open, surprised to find a small bottle of milk, butter, two bottles of water—one flat, one with bubbles—three packages of cheese, and one bottle of chardonnay. Not her favorite, but she vowed to broaden her palette now that she was living in the best place in the world to do that.

Her stomach sent her a message. *Feed me!* Not ready for wine—gosh, she really hadn't had breakfast or lunch yet for that matter—she opened the bottle of flat water, arranged some crackers with several slices of cheese on a smallish plate, and began to explore the rest of the apartment.

Tanya had disappeared once she safely delivered Kassie and her luggage, reminding her she'd pick her up Monday morning at eight thirty sharp. Kassie confirmed with two thumbs up. Gerard spent about two minutes giving her a walk-through, handing her the keys, and then he disappearing too.

Seemingly, they both diagnosed the big dark circles under her eyes as evidence she wouldn't be going sightseeing anytime soon. Sleep was what this American required. They were right. There'd be plenty of time to pick up where she and Chris had left off when they attempted to explore the city two months ago. So, she crashed, kind of like Sleeping Beauty, or maybe it was Goldilocks. Whichever, waking up as she did after just four hours of sleep, Kassie felt like a princess thanks to the tender loving care she received from Tanya, Gerard, and the team at Calibri-Paris who made her arrangements.

She ventured into a small but inviting living room she only peeked into during Gerard's tour. It was tastefully decorated with a royal blue couch the size of a double love seat and a matching chair and ottoman. Kassie easily pictured herself cozying up there with a good mystery after a long day at the office. All she needed was a comfy throw to wrap around her. A great reason to go shopping, but then who needs a reason in Paris?

Hmm. How had she missed the bouquet of periwinkle irises and a bottle of Bordeaux on the low glass coffee table? Assuming they were from Chris, she skipped the card. Instead, another set of double doors piqued her curiosity. She put down her glass and plate, deciding to check out whatever was on the other side.

Gently, she pulled back the white dotted curtain a tad, expecting to see an alleyway or a trash receptacle. Her eyes widened in disbelief. After fiddling with the lock until it gave, Kassie stepped out onto her own private courtyard with a wrought-iron table and two chairs. Curious still, she went over to the hedgerow that provided a natural three-foot-high patio border to have a look-see.

How incredibly marvelous! She had a view of the River Seine.

Wait until Chris and Annie got a load of this. She went inside for her phone. Starting with the courtyard entrance, then each room of the apartment, and ending with a selfie of her with the river in the background, she'd show them rather than try to describe her new digs. *A picture's worth a thousand words.*

It was just after two in the afternoon there, so in Boston it was eight in the morning. Surely, they'd both be up and about.

To her BFF, she wrote:

I'm here. See I'm fine. Miss u already. How's kitty?

To Chris, she wrote:

Hey sweetie. Made it safely. Here's my apt. Thanks 4 flowers. ♥

Not knowing how quickly texts flew across the Atlantic, she downed the water and cheese and decided to unpack her essentials. She slipped her pack of toilet articles next to the glass vessel sink in the bathroom, promising to organize them later. She opened both roller bags, easily finding her black suit and light-blue shell she packed on top for easy access. As she hung them up, she gave herself kudos for maintaining her packing superpower.

With her energy returning, she decided to take a much-needed shower and then venture out among the living. She removed all her jewelry—earrings, rings, and the white-gold chain that held her cherished gondola and Eiffel Tower pendants—and placed it all safely in the top drawer of the bureau in the bedroom. Out of habit, before slipping off her slacks, she checked her pockets. Almost always a tissue, sometimes a stray paperclip. This time, she was surprised to find a business card. Suddenly, she remembered the gentleman on the plane who'd helped her with her carry-on luggage. Instead of tossing it in the trash, she decided to keep it as her first souvenir of this adventure. As she placed it on top of the bureau, her eyes caught his first name. *Matthias.* Not Matthew, like her father. But close.

Just as she was about to head out to check on the pub and bakery Gerard had recommended, her phone chimed. Twice.

Annie said:

Lookin' good! Topher's lost without you. Me too.

Chris said:

Nice. What flowers?

If they weren't from Chris, who sent her flowers and wine? Kassie snatched the card that accompanied the gifts. But, of course—the office. Not Boston. Paris. She wasn't sure Boston ever sent gifts to anyone. She'd have to change that first chance she got.

"Flowers to welcome you. Wine to set the mood for Monday."

It was signed *Patricia Bisset*—the lovely receptionist whom she met on her first visit there in July. Patricia coordinated Kassie's living arrangements and served as an intermediary between her and Mimi. Kassie reckoned it was she who should send something special to Patricia, not the other way around. She'd definitely take care of that.

39

Flower Power

The weather in Boston that Labor Day weekend was quite similar to the weather in Paris—low 70s and clear. Yet if you pointed out the similarities to Chris, he would've said he didn't have a clue about what was going on outside the Commonwealth of Massachusetts.

He'd freely admit feeling the buzz around town. Heading into September, the Red Sox were playing their way into another post-season. Too bad he dropped off their number one fan at Logan the night before. Too bad she'd have to figure out the best way to follow the games online and in the middle of the night Paris time. Not his problem. Kassie was resourceful enough to figure it out on her own. Just as she figured out how to put their relationship on the back burner until she decided to heat things up once more.

Damn it. It was déjà vu all over again. She pushed him aside, or so it felt to him that she did, when she thought Mike was his father. He had to hop a plane to Venice to convince her it didn't matter. All that should matter was that he loved her. Now, if she thought he'd follow her like a puppy dog to Paris and beg her to come home, she was sorely mistaken.

He wished he didn't have such a bad taste in his mouth, but he did. For weeks, he tried to reset her priorities. Being CEO of Ricci and Son could be her own personal grand slam, if she would just embrace it.

But Kassie insisted Paris was calling to her. She couldn't explain why. When he asked if her dead mother was encouraging her to go, she guffawed and told him it didn't work that way. It? Whatever *it* was—he humored her for years about her spiritual proclivities. He thought they were cute, endearing. Over time, they annoyed him.

For the first Saturday morning in almost two months, Chris woke up relaxed. The cause for his most recent anxiety was three thousand miles away. Now, he could head over to Charlestown to visit Lexi and make sure she was doing okay without feeling guilty. And he wouldn't have to explain again to Kassie that Saturday mornings were the best time for him to make this weekly visit. Of course, what she didn't know wouldn't hurt her.

He also brought lunch over to Lexi on Tuesdays and Thursdays when he knew Kassie was immersed in a classroom learning French. He could've told her it was a lost cause. It's hard to learn a foreign language as you get older. A you-can't-teach-an-old-dog-new-tricks kind of thing. But he kept that opinion to himself. He'd learned with Kassie he had to pick his battles. Challenging her on her ability, or inability, to learn something new was not a clash he was confident he'd win.

So instead, he went where he was welcomed. Each week since they released Lexi from the hospital, he sent her a bouquet. She always placed the flowers on a table in the farthest corner of the living room, away from his nose.

He arranged with a nearby Charlestown florist to deliver whatever their special of the week was for about seventy-five dollars, give or take ten, on Mondays. Perfect timing. He always received a gratifying smile and kiss on the cheek when he arrived with lunch the next day.

On this sunny Saturday and in an equally sunny mood, Chris decided to mix things up a bit. He swung by Whole Foods in Charlestown and bought a dozen pink roses and a tall glass vase, not taking a chance any of the vases from the prior flower deliveries would suffice. He also bought fresh strawberries, which he knew Lexi loved, and chocolate croissants. Before checking out, he threw a bag of the store-brand S'mores Granola made with chocolate chunks and marshmallows into the small basket. His favorite breakfast. He'd leave it at Lexi's. Just in case.

Getting into his car to head over to Lexi's, he heard a message pop up on his phone. A text from Kassie, he figured. He secured both the brown paper grocery bag and the long white box containing the roses on the floor in the back so they wouldn't shift and be damaged if he had to stop suddenly.

Once behind the wheel, he checked the message. He was right. Kassie.

Hey sweetie. Made it safely. Here's my apt. Thanks 4 flowers. ♥

Chris put his sunglasses on top of his head, scrolled through the pictures she'd sent. He placed the phone upside down on his left thigh, wiped the sweat off his hand on his right thigh, and looked around the parking lot. He gulped and read her message three times before responding:

Nice. What flowers?

WTF? Maybe she's psychic, after all.

40

Voices in Her Head

"Monday, Monday." Kassie pulled back the covers and swung her legs over the side of the bed. Monday was her favorite day of the week. Who knew what adventures the following weekdays would bring?

"*Lundi, lundi*," she sang out, mimicking Mama Cass, as she stretched her arms to the ceiling and scrunched her toes on the thin fabric disguised as carpet. At least she came away from her French lessons knowing the days of the week.

She rubbed sleep out of her eyes with her knuckles and gazed around the room, still getting her bearings. Though each room in her quaint apartment had windows, little sunlight shone in since it was on the first floor of the building and the entryway was off the courtyard. On her way to the loo, she spotted light peeking around the curtains on the French doors in the living room.

That's odd. It shouldn't be sunny this early.

Postponing the trip to the bathroom, Kassie searched for her phone on the small pine table next to the bed. Not there. She patted the bed covers. Nothing. She lifted the pillow. Her heart sank.

WTF! Seven thirty-five! This can't be happening.

"Damn jet lag!" she shouted and stamped her feet like a two-year-old.

Her mind shifted into overdrive. She had fifty-five minutes, not even an hour, to get ready for what she expected would be one of the most important and consequential days of her career—of her life.

As she made the bed, Kassie contemplated delaying Tanya. *That would be rude and unprofessional.* Like Kassie, Tanya was a businesswoman. Surely, she had regular clients, a schedule to keep. Parisians and tourists depended on her. Kassie shrugged her shoulders, acknowledging she was neither a Parisian nor a tourist.

What did that make her? *Late. That's what.*

She jumped in the shower. Luckily, when she finally awoke the day before around noon, she unpacked and organized the bathroom. So all her toiletries sat at the ready, right where they needed to be.

Just move your ass, sweetie.

Those words slipped through her mind as her fingers slid the conditioner through her hair. Pausing for as much time as she allowed, she thought of her mother. Had she accompanied Kassie to Paris, and if so, for what purpose?

Toweling dry and wiping a circle of steam off the mirror, she shook her head and wrapped a smaller towel around her hair.

She waved a finger at her image. "No, Kassie O'Callaghan. This is your gig. You're on your own. Now, get a move on."

Fearing how a wardrobe malfunction could screw up her day and make her late, Kassie brought her long-established practice of laying out her lingerie and clothes the night before with her to

Paris. Little did she expect that she'd cause a malfunction by turning off her phone. With Topher as a built-in alarm clock, Kassie rarely overslept back home.

Determined to overcome this self-imposed challenge, Kassie began dressing almost on autopilot. Underwear first, then her knee-high stockings and her black slacks. In the time that took, the steam in the bathroom had abated. She applied her makeup first, keeping it light, but taking pains to be sure any residual dark circles were covered. No need to telegraph to her new staff that she was significantly sleep deprived.

She unwrapped the wet towel around her hair and slung it over the edge of the bathroom door to dry. Hustling to check out how much time she had left, she slammed her little toe on the bed frame. *Fuck. You better not swell.*

Eight thirteen. Not enough time to fully dry her thick blond hair she'd allowed to grow almost to her shoulders. Back in the bathroom, she plugged in the hairdryer that came with the apartment. One of those small hairdryers hotels stock as a courtesy but were pretty much useless. Unless you only have three minutes to change your hair from soaking to damp. Which is what she did. She had no choice. No way she could wear her hair down, so she wrapped it around her hand into a somewhat stylish low bun.

Making tracks back into the bedroom, careful to avoid the bed frame this time, she slipped on the light-blue shell and struggled to insert one of her favorite silver hoop earrings. She let out a sigh, thankful the other earring didn't put up a fuss.

Almost finished, Kassie grabbed the suit jacket and wrapped a Jerry Garcia silk scarf around her neck, adding vibrant reds, oranges, yellows, purples, and blue accents to her otherwise understated corporate attire. Retrieving her low black heels from the closet, she looked behind the door for a full-length mirror. *Rien. Nada.* Nothing in any language.

She gazed down, checking to make sure at least she zipped her pants. She had. At least something had gone right that morning.

Eight twenty eight. Somehow she made it. She applied mauve lip gloss and grabbed her purse and briefcase which, of course, she organized the night before. On the chance she wouldn't be able to buy a new notebook on Sunday, she packed a new Moleskin, lined of course. Purple, of course. And a half dozen purple ball-point pens. From experience, she refrained from buying felt-tip pens ahead of time, knowing the pressure inside the plane could make them explode.

Clutching the keys off the kitchen counter, Kassie headed out the door, through the courtyard to Tanya, who was waiting awake, alive, and enthusiastic.

Despite her enthusiastic *"Bonjour, Mademoiselle O'Callaghan,"* Tanya was unusually quiet as they began the ride to Calibri-Paris. Kassie *bonjoured* her back, glad Tanya got her last name right this time. Beyond that, she stayed silent as well.

Once settled in Tanya's car, she took a deep cleansing breath, willing it to instill fresh new oxygen and energy from the top of her head to the tips of her toes. The little one on her left foot talked back to her. She wiggled it and demanded it behave.

She stared out the window, for the first time witnessing Paris come alive at the start of a new workweek. All the men and women hustling off to who knows where seemed happy, or at least engaged with someone. Most had their phones glued to their ears even as they crossed the crowded thoroughfares.

Scratching the spot just above her lips in thought, Kassie looked at her right hand. Then her left. Her wrists. And then she touched her throat just below her neck where her pendants normally rested. She closed her eyes, collecting herself. *Don't panic.*

How could she have left for the office on such an important day without all her jewelry? Almost all. She touched her ears. The earrings were there, at least.

She closed her eyes, retracing her morning routine. Even though it was abbreviated, she should've remembered to put on her engagement ring, if nothing else. Touching her ring and pendants throughout the day always made her feel close to Chris. Now her talisman sat, like her and Chris, at a distance. Accepting her fate, she began mindful breathing again.

Don't be so hard on yourself. You can do this.

Patricia Bisset surprised Kassie as she stepped off the elevator, greeting her with double-cheek air kisses. Had the security guard in the lobby alerted Patricia the new gal had arrived and was on her way up?

"We'll get you a permanent identification card, Kassie, so you can breeze through the lobby, okay?"

Kassie said, *"Merci beaucoup,"* which launched her into one *merci* after another for all Patricia had done for her. Business class was *"très magnifique,"* and the quaint apartment was *"très agréable."* She'd fulfilled Kassie's wish to spend her time in Paris living more like a local than as an expatriate, housed in one of the city's new modern high rises with shiny stainless steel appliances, floor-to-ceiling windows, and concierges knowing her every move. Not that she'd do anything she couldn't write home about.

She smiled inwardly. So far, the office looked just as she remembered. Bright, modern, shimmering. On the handful of calls she had over the past month, either with Mimi or Patricia, it never occurred to her to ask where her office would be located. On her previous visit, she'd only seen the lobby, walked through the hallways, visited the ladies' room, and met with Mimi in her to-die-for office. She'd settle in wherever they put her. After all, it was only nine months.

As Patricia led her through the hallway, she recalled the large conference room with seating for twelve and the glass panels with a smoky tint and three-inch Eiffel Towers etched conspicuously about four feet from the floor, most likely to prevent head-on collisions and nose bleeds. Today, she noticed platters of pastries displayed on a side credenza. Perhaps for a morning meeting. Didn't matter what side of the Atlantic, coffee and Danish were a required staple for morning meetings, especially on Monday.

Kassie's mouth watered, reminding her she missed breakfast. Last time she'd make that mistake. Not only was her toe talking to her, so was her stomach. Would it be rude for her to ask Patricia if she could steal a croissant and a cup of tea? She decided to find out.

"Setting up for an important meeting this morning? I wouldn't guess you bring in pastries every day."

"*Oui!* A very important meeting. Your welcome."

Kassie blinked. Did Patricia thank her for asking about the meeting, as in "You're welcome"? Or did she say the pastries were there to welcome her? Trying to navigate French was bad enough, but if she couldn't decipher her own language, she'd be in a mess of trouble.

"To welcome you to Calibri-Paris," Patricia promptly added, perhaps reading Kassie's confused expression.

What Patricia couldn't read was Bad Kassie, who in a most unusual manner silently warned Kassie: *Eat your words, not a pastry. Don't let the staff label you an ugly American before they meet and get to know you. After that, all bets are off.*

"Great," Kassie said to both Patricia and her self-deprecating alter ego.

Firmly under Patricia's guidance, Kassie followed her up the spiral staircase she recalled led to Mimi's office. Halfway up the stairs, she felt a pain shoot from her toe up her leg. She paused ever so briefly before moving on, fearing if she stopped for long and complained, Patricia would think she didn't have the energy to climb a flight of stairs.

At the top of the landing, Patricia opened the door to Mimi's office, stepped aside, and with a slight wave of her hand, instructed Kassie to enter.

"What's this?" Kassie walked into the massive corner office with the white desk large enough to land a small airplane, or perhaps a drone.

"This is your office while Mimi is away." Patricia smiled as Kassie stepped inside. "Mimi said, and I quote, 'If Kassie is acting managing director, she must start by acting like a managing director.'"

Before Kassie was alone to soak it all in, Patricia pointed out the essentials: the private *salle de bain* adjoining the office, the sparkling new seventeen-inch Apple laptop bought especially for her, and the adjoining seating area with a couch, two chairs, and a glass coffee table.

"What's this?" Kassie imagined her eyes rolling as she pointed to the seating area. Seemed that was her go-to expression that morning.

"I thought you might want some tea and a bite before the ten o'clock meet-and-greet with the staff. *Oui?*"

"*Oui*. Gra—" She caught herself from saying *grazie*. Her limitations showed.

"As you and Mimi planned, two managers from E. Z. Media flew in from London last night and will join the meeting as well this morning."

"And after that?" Kassie asked.

"Lunch with the full merger team."

No rest for the weary, or the jet-lagged. She'd be forever grateful to Mimi for suggesting they establish the Calibri team before Kassie arrived. One fewer task on her list. Mimi recommended two women—Louise Blanchet to lead the financial side of the transaction and Simone Allard to spearhead all technology integration. Kassie agreed. Mimi knew best. And after a virtual meeting with them both two weeks before Kassie departed Boston, she was confident in Mimi's choices and looked forward to working with the women.

"And there is a client meeting midafternoon that you might like to be part of."

"Why is that?"

"One of our largest clients, Vin Pour Toujours, is taking on a new investor. A new partner, if you will. They are all coming in to share their vision for the winery going forward. Of course, they're relying on Calibri-Paris to be part of their future success."

The foreign language side of Kassie's brain sparked into action. Vin Pour Toujours? She paused, hoping not to open her mouth and insert her foot. She took a chance. "Wine Forever. The name of the winery. Am I right?"

Patricia indicated she was. Kassie did a mini-fist pump. *Oui!* The message on the card she received on Saturday suddenly made sense.

"Ah. I think I will be in the mood for such a critical meeting. *Merci.*"

You go, girl. And indeed, as soon as Patricia left her alone, Kassie did go—straight for the almond croissants.

41

Day One

As was her custom, Kassie sat in a chair in the middle of the conference table rather than at either end. A power move she learned years before at one of the annual Women in Business conferences she attended in Boston. She also left her notebook, pen, and phone in her office, signaling this was a meet-and-greet in the truest sense.

Kassie made a mental count of heads. There were sixteen people in the conference room, which meant there was standing room only. Take away her and the two managers from London, that left thirteen members of Calibri-Paris. *Thirteen. Is it a sign? I think so!*

Her positivity must've been contagious, as the staff was in good humor, it seemed. Or perhaps it was just for show. For her benefit. And for the two managers from abroad. Not sure it mattered, as long as the good vibes lasted more than the hour they were together.

Before Kassie made her own comments, everyone introduced themselves. Of course, she'd already met Louise and Simone via Zoom. One by one the Calibri employees said their names while pointing to the tag they were wearing, reinforcing their French names for the benefit of the Anglos among them. Kassie was grateful for that. She knew it would take her a couple of days to be able to identify each person without a prompt.

However, she made particular attention to greet Owen Zelly and Phoebe Clark, the thirtysomethings from London. *Nice of E. Z. Media to send a man* and *a woman*. Remembering how she was treated when she'd accompanied her male counterparts to meetings, especially early in her career, Kassie surmised Ms. Clark was a token. Owen, after all, carried the surname of the owner of the firm. But she was wrong.

When Kassie acknowledged the two of them sitting diagonally to her left and asked if they would share some history of their firm, it was Phoebe who sat up straight, placed her intertwined fingers on the table in front of her, and waxed poetic and proudly about their client list for three minutes. A minute too long in Kassie's opinion.

Impressive list. But so is Calibri's.

Phoebe deferred to Owen to expound upon how his father, Ernest Zelly, had started in the advertising business, serving London's most prestigious newspaper. "Over time," Owen said, "the advertisers approached my father for marketing advice. And *voilà*, that side of the firm was born."

"And so was Owen," Phoebe added, her twinkling eyes looked up to the ceiling. A muffled titter swept around the room. Owen shrugged, seeming not to mind.

Boom. Kassie tried to read the room. Or, to be more precise, she tried to read these two characters she was to integrate into her firm. Did Phoebe just throw shade on Owen in front of everyone? Was this their shtick?

Whatever it was, the two teams barely hiccupped and instead launched into what initially sounded like a spirited getting-to-know-you tête-à-tête. Listening more closely, Kassie picked up a different vibe all together. *They're one-upping each other.* Who went to the better university? Who had the better pedigree? Whose client really was the client from hell?

As this was happening, Kassie seared the Londoners' names into her brain the best way she knew how. Starting with Phoebe Clark. *Hmm. PC. Not so Politically Correct. That'll work.*

She switched to Owen. *OZ.* Her brain started down a path. The wrong path. *Don't go there,* Bad Kassie warned. She couldn't help it. *Ozzie and Harriet? Dr. Oz? The Wizard?*

Kassie looked around to find Owen and couldn't help but sympathize with him. Growing up, he must have received more nicknames than even she could conjure. She watched as he refilled his coffee cup and chowed down on a pastry, a key indicator that he'd had enough of either meeting the Calibri team or deflecting Phoebe's bravado. She got that. Shame on her for not responding to Phoebe's comment with a show of support for him. She owed him one. *Simply Owen.* No trickery required.

Clearly, Kassie had her work cut out for her. Much more needed to be done to ensure these two separate companies from two separate countries would successfully merge as one.

Pushing her chair back, Kassie took the floor. She adjusted her scarf and straightened her back. She didn't need to clink a glass to get attention. All eyes were on her. Her make-or-break moment had arrived.

First, she apologized for not mastering the native language and begged their patience with her. "I understand two of you have drawn the short straws and will serve as my translators. *Merci beaucoup*, in advance. I'll try to make life *très facile* for you in the coming months."

Grins all around.

She continued giving the expected conventional remarks about how glad she was to be in Paris; how she was there to oversee the coming together of two great, storied firms, *not* to replace Mimi; and how she'd be arranging one-on-one meetings with each of them soon. She asked if anyone had questions.

Since no one did, she admitted she had one. "Where can I get a good bottle of wine around here?"

Everyone, including their guests from the other side of the Channel, chuckled and started sharing their sources. Nothing brings people together like good wine.

There was no wine served at lunch, thankfully. Kassie, still adjusting to local time, had more than a sneaking feeling wine would send her over the edge. The comfy couch in her comfy office would be way too inviting, and odds were great she'd sleep right through the afternoon client meeting.

Lunch for the five-member merger team—Phoebe, Owen, Louise, Simone, and Kassie—was set up in the conference room. Meaning Kassie had to make her second trip down the spiral staircase, and then another one back up. And then another one down, and another one up. Had no one ever thought to install an elevator or some sort of moving apparatus? This would never pass muster by the Occupational Safety and Health Administration (a.k.a. OSHA) in the U.S. Nevertheless, she grimaced through the endless throbbing in her shoe.

Apparently, having released their anxiety at the earlier meet-and-greet, the four merger managers now appeared more at ease with one another. Kassie sensed she was the only jittery one among them. She'd led teams before, especially marketing teams from large international commercial banks who were merging. But this was a merger of two companies. Bigger than a bread box, as it were. Be that as it may, she'd fake it until she made it. Always worked before.

As it happened, it did work again. Kassie led them on a discussion about how to organize the staffs across the companies and functionalities. Taking her lead, the four managers showed they came prepared. Charts. Lists. Owen, bless his heart, stepped up to the whiteboard and started a list of questions needing answers, and then he snapped a picture of it and emailed it to the team.

But when it came to assigning responsibilities across the two firms, the managers jockeyed for positions. Not surprised there'd be some conflict among them, Kassie said she'd take their recommendations under advisement and get back to everyone in the next day or so. That seemed satisfactory, and she adjourned the meeting. For a brief moment as the room emptied, Kassie considered calling Tom in Boston for advice.

Silly girl. You're the acting managing director. Now act like it.

She headed back to her office, taking one step at a time.

Whose idea was it to schedule a client meeting on my first day? Kassie held onto the handrail on her way back down to the conference room, trying to prevent a grand entrance with a face-plant for the ages. With her luck, they'd think she had conducted her own private wine tasting upstairs. Whatever. Kassie loved client meetings. She was in her element.

That was until she entered the conference room, and a man she thought she recognized rose up on the opposite side of the table to greet her. She blinked and her mouth watered. Her mind scrolled, like the photo app on her phone, praying she could place the face with a name before she embarrassed herself. She came up empty.

Uh-oh. He's coming toward me. Smile.

As Kassie lifted her right hand to shake his, he leaned toward her. She turned to give him her right cheek, expecting the air kisses she was getting used to receiving. He ignored her motion. Instead, he reached for her left hand and kissed the back of it.

"*Bonjour*, Madame O'Callaghan. We meet again."

Again? Still no brain connectivity.

"Matthias Gataki," he said, his deep-chestnut brown eyes locked on hers.

"Monsieur Gataki." She was buying time. And then it hit her like a Dustin Pedroia home run into the Monster seats at Fenway. She was back in the airplane. She envisioned a business card. *Matthew somebody.*

"Matthias," she said, repeating the name he'd said, as if trying it on for size. "As in Matt?"

"Some call me that. You can call me whatever you like and whenever you like," he said, still holding her hand.

Goosebumps.

42

Gotcha!

"Monday, Monday" in Boston was Labor Day. The museum was open, but Annie took the day off just for the hell of it. She figured Chris was off as well, because almost all corporate-type businesses, like Ricci and Son, closed on national holidays. He'd kept her at more than arm's length after she gave him an earful about how Sarah gave Kassie grief weeks before at their dinner at the Lock and Key Hotel.

"I don't believe it, Annie," he'd said. "Why would Sarah ever suggest Kassie break our engagement? And, if she did, why hasn't Kassie mentioned it to me?"

"Perhaps because, like you just said, you wouldn't believe it."

And that was that. Neither called the other to clear the air. When they needed to be in each other's presence as Kassie prepared to leave, they kept a safe distance from each other. Annie was surprised Kassie hadn't picked up on it. Her mind must have been elsewhere. She couldn't blame her. She had Paris in her sights.

The texts on Saturday were the last she heard from Kassie. Not that her BFF owed her daily reports, but Annie was eager to hear how her first day in the Paris office went. That was as good an excuse as any to break radio silence with Chris and give him a jingle. It was evening already in Paris. Surely, he'd have talked to her by now.

Topher followed Annie into the living room and jumped up on the couch, curling up beside her. He rested his cute little head with his little button nose on her thigh.

She scrolled through her phone and made the call. Chris's phone rang more times than she thought was possible without flipping over to voice mail. Was he ignoring her? Or maybe he blocked her number?

Just as she was about to hang up, a female voice answered.

"Oh hi, Annie."

"Who's this?" Annie gulped, knowing full well who it was but not wanting to give her the satisfaction.

"It's me. Lexi. How are you? Is everything okay with that cat?"

Annie gazed down at Topher and gave him extra loving to compensate for the animosity he may have sensed streaming through the air.

"He's fine. Let me talk to Chris."

"Impossible."

"Why's that?"

"Do I have to paint you a picture? He's busy right now." Lexi giggled.

Annie sensed the hair on the back of her neck getting hot, not sure what Lexi was implying. Whatever it was, Annie refused to play her game. Though she was curious, there was no way for her to know where Lexi and Chris were unless she asked. Were they at Lexi's or Kassie's house? While it mattered, Annie decided not to go there. Maybe she really didn't want to know. If Chris had brought Lexi to Kassie's house, it would be difficult for Annie to keep from telling Kassie. She decided to assume they were at Lexi's—the lesser of the two evils.

Should she hold? No way would she ask Lexi to have Chris call her back. So she simply said, "Whatever. I'll catch him later" and ended the call.

Annie never professed to have the supersize sixth sense Kassie did. She shouldn't jump to conclusions. Yet her bones ached, telling her something was rotten in Charlestown. The best way for her to calm her frayed nerves and overactive mind was to bake.

Of course, just as she was about to put her first batch of oatmeal chocolate chip cookies in the oven, her BFF called.

"Your timing sucks," Annie said, setting the sheet pan on top of the counter.

"That's a fine howdy doody."

"Sorry. Just about to shove cookies in the oven."

"Why are you baking? What happened?"

Annie stifled a sigh. After decades of friendship, Kassie recognized Annie's triggers, just as Annie recognized hers. They could almost finish each other's sentences.

"Happened? Why do you think anything happened? I'm off today and bored. You're not here to annoy me."

Kassie didn't respond, not right away anyway. Annie attributed the long pause to the international connection and considered it a gift, enabling her to shift the conversation.

"How'd your first day go, missy?"

Kassie suggested she get a glass of wine and put her cookie baking on the back burner for a while.

"Wine, eh? That bad a day? Or that good a day?"

"Depends."

"I've got all afternoon. Why don't you start at the beginning?"

Annie returned to the couch. So did Topher. Although she was usually bored by the goings-on at Kassie's office, it comforted her to hear her friend's voice. She grunted and ahemed at each of Kassie's pauses, assuring her the connection had not failed.

"So, Kassie, do you classify your meetings with the staff and the merger team the good part of your day or the bad?" Annie asked half joking, knowing full well how Kassie got off on such things.

"Kind of both. The staff seems great and open to having me here while Mimi is out."

"So, what's the problem?"

"The merger team. I sensed some underlying friction I'll need to define and defuse."

Annie chuckled. "Have no fear. Right up your alley."

"The good part of the day was discovering I might not have to do it alone."

"How's that? Is someone from the Boston office flying over to rescue you? That wouldn't be like you to ask for help."

Annie sipped her wine as Kassie filled her in on the rest of her day, beginning with how she stubbed her pinky toe.

"I hate when that happens," Annie said.

"Me too, especially when I had to go up and down the damn stairs all day. Frosted my ass. Until this afternoon."

"Pray tell. What happened this afternoon?"

"I met a man."

Annie stifled a gasp and jumped off the couch, almost stubbing her own toe on the coffee table. Topher scurried out of the living room, probably for safer environs.

"You did what? What kind of man?"

"A Greek man. He owns a winery in Greece. He's investing in a French winery that happens to be one of our most major clients. So now he's a client too."

Annie walked out to the kitchen with her phone. The cookies were untouched. Topher hadn't jumped on the counter and given them a good lick. She guessed he was upstairs, taking one of his many naps on the spare bed with Kassie's afghan. Both the cookies and Topher were safe. She wasn't sure about her friend.

"You think this Greek guy will help you with the obstreperous merger team? By doing what? Getting them drunk?" She refilled her wineglass and sat at the kitchen table.

"Kind of."

Annie stared out the kitchen window, watching two squirrels chasing each other up and around a tree. She listened to Kassie fill in the details. She hadn't heard Kassie this excited about anything since … well, let's just say, in a very long time.

"As I was about to get off the airplane, this gentleman helped me with my carry-ons and he gave me his business card, which I just tossed on top of the bureau."

"Why didn't you throw it away?"

"No reason. But now I think it was a sign."

"You would." Annie rolled her eyes, thankful Kassie couldn't see. "So, wait a minute. I get where this is going. I know you and coincidences. Don't tell me the guy on the plane is the Greek guy?"

"Uh-huh."

"So, explain to me how this fellow will help you with your merger woes?"

As Kassie continued her story, Annie tried to visualize Kassie and this fellow heading up the staircase to her office.

"Good thing he was one step behind me. I almost collapsed from the pain in my toe. He caught me before I did back flips down the stairs. Imagine what could've happened?"

"I can't. You've never done back flips." Annie went along with Kassie's saga, detecting a newfound joy in her voice.

"*You'd flip* if you saw this guy. He's gorgeous. But I digress."

"You sure do."

"Anyway, he helped me limp into my office. I took off my shoe, and he got down on one knee—"

"What? He proposed?"

"No, Annie. Come on, get serious. He asked permission to remove my stocking, and then he rubbed my foot. After we examined it carefully, we decided it wasn't broken."

"Oh, thank God. You'll live for another day."

"And good thing too. We sat for a while, in my office—with my shoe back on, for your information—talking about the merger. Of course, it's in his best interest that it goes smoothly. I told him about the conflict I sensed between the offices, and he had a suggestion."

"Spare me the anticipation."

"An offsite. Like we do in the States. Where we whisk people away from their normal environments and give them a problem to solve. Before you know it, they emerge stronger together."

Annie grunted. "Sounds like it has merit. Where will you go? Not back here to Boston, I gather? That would be totally weird."

"He owns a winery in Greece, Annie. Remember. I just told you that."

"You're going to take your team to a Greek island? When? You just got to Paris!"

"We haven't settled on a date yet. We will Thursday night."

"What's Thursday night?"

"He's taking me to dinner."

"A dinner date?"

"It's not a date."

"Does he know that?" Annie's eyes widened, and she straightened up. What a difference three days made. Chris was somewhere doing who knows what with Lexi. And Kassie was planning an offsite with …

"Does he have a name?"

"Matthias Gataki."

"That's a mouthful."

"I know. I thought so too."

"Wait. Isn't Matthias Greek for Matthew?"

"It is. Like my father. Weird, huh?"

For once, Annie suggested it may be a sign.

"I asked if people called him Matt for short. You know what he said?"

"No, but I'm sure you'll tell me."

"He said I could call him whatever and *whenever* I want."

Annie paused, thinking about her unsuccessful attempt to reach Chris, totally unsure of how to respond to Kassie's revelation. *Give it time. They're just behaving like teenagers, adjusting to being apart. Let it go.*

She tried, until Kassie said, "Now, why don't you tell me what your cookie baking is not telling me?"

43

Cinderella

Some things got settled over the next two days in Paris, some things did not.

On Tuesday, Kassie discovered the Calibri board in Boston had approved a sizable travel, entertainment, and conference budget for her personally and for the teams. As such, she secured Tanya's Uber services to get to and from the office each day. Granted, this meant she'd miss the experience of hustling to work among the Parisians, which should be part of this remarkable opportunity she'd been handed.

Tanya applauded Calibri for their generosity and assured Kassie she wouldn't miss a thing by riding comfortably to the office each day. After all, she'd have plenty of time on the weekends to explore the City of Lights and its surroundings.

A bottle of wine loomed large on the coffee table when she walked into her office that morning. She plunked her purse and briefcase on a chair and picked up the bottle and read the lovely floral label. Vin Pour Toujours. Chardonnay. She expected to find a card or a note on the floor. Nothing. She inhaled deeply and exhaled disappointedly. This was from the client, not the investor. Surely, Monsieur Gataki would've included a note. Wouldn't he?

"Oh well. *C'est la vie.*" She picked up her belongings and moved to her desk, where a map was spread wide open. A large Post-it note read in black Sharpie: *Where in Paris is Kassie O'Callaghan?* Little red flags pointed to all the crucial spots she should visit. Another Post-it note read: *So you don't get lost. Your Calibri Teams.*

"Hmm. Teams. Plural." A step in the right direction.

With the map and Tanya, who offered to give her private tours, she was confident she'd left her bad habit of working weekends behind. She ran her fingers across the map, stopping at Notre-Dame. She and Chris missed seeing it in July. Perhaps she'd ask Tanya to make it their first stop next weekend.

Who'd have ever thought Tanya would become my new best friend?

Her BFF back home in Boston never answered Kassie's question the night before about what had motivated her to bake cookies. Annie blew her off with "What else should I be doing when you're not here?" And when Kassie asked her if she'd talked to Chris, Annie changed the subject.

"You know who else misses you?" Annie asked.

Kassie missed Topher too and told Annie to give him an extra tummy rub for her. With that, their first long, long-distance call was *fini*.

That wasn't the end, though, of Kassie's musing about why Annie didn't answer her question about Chris. If she'd talked to Chris, Annie would've said so. If she hadn't, there'd have been no reason for Annie not to say she hadn't.

She's not telling me something.

Kassie sat at her desk, fired up her computer, and retrieved her phone from her purse. Nine fifteen in Paris. Six-hour difference. She counted backwards on her fingers. Quarter after three in the morning was way too early to either call or text Chris.

Beyond the flower confusion on Saturday, they only exchanged a few superficial texts on Sunday about how her trip was, about the Red Sox, about the weather.

The weather? Had their interactions been reduced to talking about the weather? Neither had typed *I love you* or *I miss you* or sent a kiss emoji. And why had neither of them suggested they talk by phone, one-on-one, like big people? Had Chris experienced the same eerie feeling she had when they said goodbye at the airport?

Whatever. At least she knew they'd connect when they had their first Ricci and Son biweekly management call on Thursday afternoon.

Kassie's first appointment of the day knocked at her door. With back-to-back getting-to-know-you meetings with the staff scheduled for most of the day, fretting about Chris would have to wait until she got home that evening. *Home. Where the blank is.* She'd have to fill in that saying with something appropriate for her circumstances. Maybe it was the word *home* that was giving her heartburn.

Mostly, Kassie was pleased with all her meetings that day. The message she tried to convey the day before—that she was not there to replace Mimi, but to focus on the merger—seemed to resonate with everyone.

Each of the men on the staff was smart, an expert in their field, and super willing not only to pull their weight in Mimi's absence but also to assist *wherever and whenever* Kassie needed it. Where had she heard those words before? Oh yes. Maybe Monsieur Gataki didn't really mean what he said when he said it. Maybe it was just a common European expression she needed to get used to without assigning any importance to it.

Each of the women on the staff dazzled. They were intelligent, multilingual, and professed to miss their fearless leader, Mimi. They were also gorgeous. Their hair either was long and swayed when they swayed or was cropped exquisitely, emphasizing their expert eye makeup or fashionable eyewear, or both.

Kassie felt frumpish among them. On Monday, she'd worn her best black pantsuit. That day, she wore her best navy pantsuit. On tap for Wednesday was her gray pinstripe pantsuit.

The Calibri-Paris women and Phoebe from E. Z. Media were fetching. Not a pantsuit among them. Dresses and two-piece suits with just-below-the-knee skirts and modest slits up the side were the order of the day. No dull corporate colors anywhere. The women donned bright reds, greens, and even Kassie's favorite color purple—all radiating confidence. As she walked through the office that morning, she could hear them complimenting each other's outfits, almost as if they planned their wardrobes together. But, of course, they didn't. This was Paris. Fashion capital of the world.

Get with the program, Kassie. At first she was unsure whose voice it was, settling on Bad Kassie. Her mother would care little about her attire.

She pulled her leather business-card case out of her briefcase and flipped until she found her salvation. She called the only department store she knew, La Maison de Paris, and scheduled an appointment for Wednesday afternoon with the only personal shopper she ever had. Gabriella saved the day for Kassie in July; she just had to do an encore.

On Wednesday, Tanya picked up Kassie at the office promptly at two, or fourteen hundred hours. Just as she was determined to shed her American attire and become like the women at the office, at least in appearance, Kassie vowed to learn and adopt military time. She believed anything she could do to encourage the Calibri-Paris staff to accept her would help pave the way to a successful merger.

Whatcha see and *whatcha hear is whatcha get.* Acknowledging she'd changed the lyrics to suit her purpose, Kassie hummed the seventies hit by the Dramatics as Tanya pulled up to La Maison de Paris.

"Been here, done this," Kassie said, unbuckling.

"*Bon* shopping."

"*Merci*, Tanya. Can I call when I'm ready?" Of course she could. When she made the appointment with the store, Kassie had planned to spend only an hour there. Not wanting to be absent from the office too long.

As she had in July, Gabriella greeted her in front of the fountain at the entrance to this magnificent store. At that moment, Kassie couldn't help but recall Hemingway's love for France and his advice on how simple it was to make Parisians happy. He wrote in *The Sun Also Rises*, if you want people to like you in France, "you have only to spend a little money."

"*Bienvenue.* So happy to see you again, Madame Kassie," Gabriella welcomed her.

Kassie extended her hand, convinced she was about to make Gabriella one very happy personal shopper. "*Merci*, Gabriella. But this time it's mademoiselle, I think. I'm not sure. It's a long story." The thumb on her left hand reached across her palm to rub her engagement ring. *Crap.* She'd forgotten it again that day. In fact, she hadn't worn it since she put it in the bureau at the apartment on Saturday afternoon.

If Tanya had noticed, she didn't call her on it.

And Gabriella wouldn't notice because Chris hadn't proposed until after Kassie met her in July. In fact, a lot had happened since

Kassie's first shopping spree at La Maison de Paris. She used the short ride on the elevator up to the dressing room to explain why she returned to Paris and the store.

"Remember, I bought two dresses? One for a business meeting, and one for dinner here with Chris?"

"*Oui*. Monsieur Chris. Handsome. Is he with you here in Paris?"

"Handsome? *Oui*. Here? No."

Kassie also said no to the offer of champagne and gave Gabriella an abbreviated version of how she came to be standing in her underwear with a familiar pink silk knee-length robe tied around her once again. Starting with the main event—why a return to Paris? Her company's board of directors tapped her to manage a merger between the Paris office and a British company.

"*Felicitations!*"

"*Merci*. I know that means congratulations!" Kassie admitted she was trying to learn the language, but she had a long way to go.

She moved on to how she and handsome Chris had to cut their last trip short and rush back to the States. "My husband had a heart attack."

Gabriella gasped.

"Oh. It's okay. He died."

Gabriella fanned a card she was holding in front of her face.

"Good news, though. Chris asked me to marry him."

Kassie followed Gabriella's eyes, searching for a ring that wasn't there. She lifted her left hand. "I forgot to put it on this morning. What's on the card?" Kassie changed the subject.

Gabriella pointed to Kassie O'Callaghan printed across the top. Her measurements listed below that. On the reverse side, she could see a list of her prior purchases, including the two dresses and all the intimate apparel Gabriella had previously and astutely insisted she purchase.

Kind of creepy. Roll with it, Kassie.

"How can I help you today?"

Kassie shifted her gaze to the pantsuit. "Dress me like a Paris businesswoman," she begged. Shocked at how she blurted that out, she considered asking for that flute of champagne after all but thought better of it. Instead, she explained how she brought all the wrong clothes with her from Boston.

"I need to fit in. Not stand out during the day at the office, or at night during business dinners."

Gabriella barked orders at her assistants and handed them the card with all of Kassie's body data.

A half hour and a half dozen stunning outfits later, Kassie got a shock.

"You're thinner. Have you lost weight?"

She hadn't noticed. Not really. Her pants fit well. But now that Gabriella mentioned it, the waistbands were not at all snug these days. She shrugged her shoulders. "I guess that's what happens when your husband dies and you move to Paris," she said without any snark this time. Had the impact of either her engagement or Lexi's pregnancy caused her sudden weight loss? Odd. But too much information to share with Gabriella.

"A week. Everything will be ready next *mercredi.*"

"*Mercredi,*" Kassie repeated, the wheels of translation turning. "Wednesday! Why?"

Gabriella explained that all the skirts needed some alterations in both the waist and length.

"*Mais non.* I wanted a new outfit for tomorrow night."

Gabriella shook her head and frowned.

Kassie lapsed into an explanation about having an important client dinner the next evening. "Do you know Vin Pour Toujours?" she asked, as she grabbed her slacks to get dressed.

"*Mais oui. Très bon vin*," Gabriella said, adding the chef's kiss sign.

"They're the client I'm having dinner with. Well, not actually," Kassie said, blabbering. "Matthias Gataki. That's who I'm having dinner with. He's a Greek business owner who has an interest in the winery."

"Monsieur Gataki?"

"You know him?"

Gabriella helped her with her suit jacket. "Matthias Gataki? Oh, *oui*. How you say, rich and famous? He's one of the most eligible men in Europe. *Ooh la la*."

Kassie laughed and tried to shrug off Gabriella's tease. "No *ooh la la* about it. It's not a date. It's just dinner on a weeknight."

"Don't be so sure, Madame Kassie. Do you have with you the dresses you last purchased here? The midnight-blue tulip-shaped dress is here in Paris? *Oui*?"

"*Oui.*"

"Wear it. Every night is date night in Paris."

"But I'm engaged."

Gabriella lifted her ringless left hand. "Engaged? Not married."

44

Thursday

Departing for the office each morning at half past eight was fast becoming a welcome routine. So was getting up at the respectable hour of seven. But she knew herself. To be sure she had enough time to shave, do her hair, and allow for any unanticipated event—like stubbing her toe or oversleeping—Kassie had set her phone alarm for both five forty-five and six a.m.

Lucky for her, Mimi's private *salle de bain* at the office meant she could easily freshen up and change right there before heading out for dinner with Matthias Gataki.

So, rather than wait until Thursday morning when anything could go wrong, Kassie took the time the night before to plan and pull together what she would need the next evening. With one of her favorite playlists and sounds of Nat King Cole keeping her company, she started by searching for the spare makeup kit she brought with her from her Boston office. After opening and closing every drawer in the bedroom, combing the closet floor, and triple-checking the bathroom cabinet, she found the kit tucked inside the pocket of one of her roller bags.

"There you are," she said, relieved. She had no desire to either take the time or spend the money to replace the contents of that kit.

She flipped through the clothes hanging in the closet and located *the* dress. Carefully, she slid it out of the cleaner's plastic bag, gave it a good shake, and hung it on a hook she found in the living room. She grabbed the smallest carry-on and placed the makeup and lingerie inside. Holding two pairs of shoes, she looked at her left foot and wiggled her toes. It'd been nearly three days since she'd crashed into the bedframe. Her toe was still sore, but it screamed much less than it had earlier in the week. She wrapped one pair of heels with tissue and put the shoes in the carry-on. She'd wear the lower heels to the office as a backup. As with everything, Kassie believed in choice.

Nearly finished, Kassie went to the bureau, where she'd put three jewelry pouches. She dumped them on the duvet cover and sorted through them, pulling out a sparkling rhinestone necklace and matching drop earrings that were once her mother's. Those found their way into the carry-on as well.

Lastly, she located her engagement ring in the bureau drawer. She was about to place it in a small glass bowl on top for safety when she sat on the bed instead. Sliding it on her finger, she thought back to the night two months ago when Chris tried to propose on the Pont Neuf.

Kassie massaged her feet. "What's with you guys, anyway? You always seem to insert yourself at the most inopportune times," she said, recalling how the pomegranate rash on her feet had interfered with Chris's proposal.

"However." She paused, letting the thought hang out there naked. On Monday, there was that interaction, that moment, with

Monsieur Gataki and her injured toe. Perhaps no stubbed toe, no date with a rich and famous Greek vintner?

Date? It's not a date.

She put the ring in the bowl and fired up her laptop. "Bring it on, Google."

Thursday morning went without a hitch. Mostly. Kassie tried, but failed, to haul everything to Tanya's car at once. Two trips were necessary before she slid herself into the backseat along with her purse, briefcase, carry-on, and the midnight-blue tulip-shaped dress stored safely back in the plastic bag.

As Tanya was about to close the door, Kassie stopped her. "Hold it. I forgot something." Once back in the car, she slid on the ring and said, "Sorry about that." She could've easily been saying that to Chris as to Tanya. In any case, both were covered. She waved her left hand so Tanya could see the ring in her review mirror.

"Finally, you remembered."

That she did. For two reasons: the Zoom call with Chris and Bill coming up that afternoon and dinner that night with Monsieur Gataki. For the former, if she wasn't wearing the ring, Chris might think he'd caught her with her pants down. For the latter, she didn't want Matthias to think she wanted to get caught with her pants down.

As they drove past throngs of people heading for work, Kassie stared absently out the window, trading the clear blue skies of Paris for her clouded and confused inner thoughts.

Crazy girl. Who thinks like this? She twirled the ring around her finger. As if the ring provided her with superpower, some renewed positive energy, connecting her with Chris despite the distance between them. Or could the ring shield and protect her from surrendering to a sudden restlessness she felt brewing inside?

It's a ring. Not body armor.

And on that note, Kassie looked up to see Tanya opening the car door for her.

"Wherever you were, we are here now."

Kassie stepped onto the pavement without explanation.

"And where are you going with all this?" Tanya offered to help Kassie into the lobby.

"Dinner tonight with a client."

Tanya grabbed the carry-on and lifted the dress briefly so the sun bounced off the plastic sheen. Her eyebrows lifted.

"Dinner? You sure it's not a date?"

"Not a date. It's Thursday." Kassie said, blinking and suddenly recalling back in the States that Thursday was, in fact, called date night. Since Tanya was from the U.S., Kassie expected she knew this too but hoped she'd forgotten.

So much for that assumption.

"My dear Kassie. Whether you're in Boston or Paris, Thursday is date night. And in Paris, every night is date night."

Inside the lobby, Kassie assessed the challenge of maneuvering everything up to her office. She slung the strap of her briefcase across her body, draped the dress across her left arm, and balanced the other two bags with each hand. She got this. "Every night is date night," she mumbled. "We'll see about that."

She tilted her chin toward Tanya, who was about to leave. "I'll call you if I need you."

Almost at the lobby exit, Tanya wheeled around, gave Kassie a twinkly-eyed smile, and a mini-wave. *"Amusez-vous."*

"I've amused her?" Kassie murmured as she headed for the elevators.

"No, she told you to have a good time."

Kassie turned to the voice of the security guard.

"May I see your badge?" he asked.

Kassie's morning flew by. With back-to-back meetings with the Calibri-Paris staff and the merger team, she applied few brain cells to prepare for the afternoon and evening events. That was just how she liked it.

Except, as she picked through her lunch salad, moving ingredients she didn't like or couldn't identify to the side, Kassie realized she hadn't heard from Matthias Gataki since Monday. Part of her envisioned receiving flowers from him that morning with a note revealing the time and place of their rendezvous.

Since that foolish fantasy failed to play out, she reran their conversation in her mind, recalling that he said he'd be in touch.

When?

She scrolled through her business emails, searching for one from him she may have missed. No such luck. No voice mail messages either. Was she going to be stood up in Paris?

It's not a date. People cancel or reschedule business dinners all the time. They're not stood up.

She walked to the full-length windows, admiring the immense Paris landscape spread out before her. She surveyed the activity below and stepped back. *You won't find him among the pedestrians. Anyway, he's not lost. Just late.*

Fifteen minutes before the Ricci and Son management meeting with Chris and Bill, Kassie freshened up and brushed her hair. To appear awake, alive, and enthusiastic, she pinched her cheeks and applied fresh lip gloss.

She hadn't seen Chris in almost a week, and there still had been no texts since Sunday. Her excuse for not calling him was that she knew they'd be connecting that day. What was his excuse for not calling her, or even suggesting a call? She sighed. They were both guilty of neglect. She believed that was about to change at fourteen hundred hours. Or at eight a.m. depending on the continent.

Kassie logged into Zoom with two minutes to spare, allowing for technology to make any cross-Atlantic adjustments.

Precisely at eight o'clock Boston time, the host—Ricci and Son—let her into the room. While they could see Kassie and her background, which was Paris's crystal-blue sky, she could see three people gathered in the largest conference room. She only expected Bill and Chris, so she leaned in for a closer look.

Clearly, Bill sat at the head of the table. He obviously had never learned the power play she had. To her left, his right, was a female who was waving at her.

"Oh it's you, Cecilia. Good morning! Ça va?"

"*Bonjour*, Kassie!"

Fearing Cecilia would interpret Kassie's question as permission to launch their conversation in French, she checked out the person sitting to Bill's left. It was Leo, Bill's son, of course. Rumor had it Cecilia and Leo were inseparable since they met and began their internships at the firm. Strange, though, that they'd be in the management meeting.

"Hello, Leo! So glad to see you. When do classes start?"

Leo did a little wave and said his classes started in two weeks and that he planned to continue working at the company as much as he could.

"Are we paying you and Cecilia well?"

They both gave her a thumbs-up. Kassie made a note to verify they were being paid equally and to see what she could do to sweeten Karen's deal as well.

Bill held up a piece of paper and said something that sounded like he was setting an agenda for the meeting.

Not so fast.

"Aren't we missing someone?" Kassie said.

Despite being on Zoom, she easily picked up their side glances and body language. Leo's tapping his fingers on the table and Cecilia's taking a swig of her Starbucks coffee were clear indicators that somebody was hiding something. Kassie didn't know if it was one of them or the person who was noticeably absent.

She allowed the distance between them to provide sufficient pause before asking more pointedly, "Where's Christopher?"

Using his full name got everyone's attention, even hers, after she said it. She really wanted to know where he was.

"Getting coffee?" she asked.

"No," Bill said, "he'll be in later. I think Lexi had a doctor's appointment this morning."

Kassie swallowed hard before she or Bad Kassie spoke. "Obstetrician or orthopedist?"

"Not sure. He sends his apologies," Bill said, shuffling papers in a folder in front of him. "I hope you don't mind Leo and Cecilia sitting in. I've had them shadowing me each day, and Chris when he's here."

If Bill meant for his last comment about Chris to land with a bang, he succeeded. She filed it away.

"Of course I don't mind," she said. "That's a great way to learn the business. So let's get started, shall we?"

Since this was the first of the biweekly meetings they agreed to have while Kassie did double duty, and there'd only been two business days since she left the States, it took less than fifteen minutes for Bill to brief her on new client business and the firm's financial status.

With that, Kassie said, "Thank you, Bill. Sounds like it's going well so far."

"Not to worry, Kassie. I've got everything under control."

They said their goodbyes, and she left the meeting. With her elbows on her desk, she rested her forehead on the top of the triangle her hands had formed.

Bill thinks he has everything under control. We'll see about that.

She thought about putting an alert on her phone to remind her to call Chris on Friday and have a little conversation with him. An alert wouldn't be necessary. She'd remember.

Kassie opened a Word doc and made some notes about what she learned from Bill. She sent it to her Ricci and Son email. She'd review it and the financial documents she received before she spoke with Chris. For a split second, she considered texting or emailing him. There was always the chance he'd try to reach her when she was out that night, and it was a chance she didn't want to take.

If I'm even out tonight?

There was a light knock on her door. "Is your meeting *fini?*" Patricia inquired as she walked in.

A lot more than my meeting may be fini.

Patricia's arrival with a package distracted Kassie from expending any more gray matter on that thought.

"Put it over there," Kassie said, pointing to the coffee table.

"Another gift for you."

"From the staff again, you think?"

Patricia shrugged and backed out of the office.

Kassie eyed the package with suspicion. It was bigger than a shoe box but smaller than a carton of Xerox paper. The box was wrapped in navy-blue paper with pictures depicting scenes of Paris, and a large, pure-white ribbon tied it all together with a giant bow on the top.

Again, she searched for a card. This time, she knew nothing had escaped onto the floor. She would've seen it fly away when Patricia placed it on the table.

Should I call security? Are packages screened before they're delivered? She made a note to inquire about that important little detail.

Kassie opted on the side of believing the package was safe for her to unwrap. In a way, it felt like Christmas morning. She tugged at the bow. It magically untied in one fell swoop, and the ribbon around the box floated to the sides. She found a flap on the right and tore the paper, beginning there and all the way to the left.

"What the heck? Is this some kind of joke?"

The box was a deep-green-grass green, with a large white cross on the top. Inside was a pouch, a rather large deep-green-grass green pouch, that fit snuggly in the box. She found a handle on it and lifted it out and set it on the table, shoving the outer packaging and wrappings to the floor.

The pouch displayed another large white cross, and First Aid was printed above the cross. She assumed the words *Trousse de Premiers Soins* underneath were the French equivalent.

Still clueless as to the sender, Kassie swiped her hand underneath the pouch's flap, releasing the Velcro closure. Not one but two white cards were taped to the top of the contents.

She opened one. The handwritten message read: *To the rescue.*

Her eyes squinted as she shook her head, trying to figure out what that meant.

She opened the second card. *Be outside at 1800. Matt.* Her fingers counted to six.

45

Not a Date

Kassie blew off her meetings for the rest of the day, apologizing and rescheduling for Friday.

"Do I need rescuing?" She waved the cards over the contents of the pouch she'd started to sort through. A man had never sent her a first aid kit or offered to come to her rescue before. Flowers, yes. Stuffed animals, yes. But not aspirin and Ace bandages. And why?

Then it dawned on her. Of course, her pinky toe!

Did he expect her to collapse in his arms? *Not a date.*

He commanded her to be ready at six. "Not a date," she whispered.

He'd signed the card, Matt. "Not a date." She stamped her right foot. *Then what was it?*

At the appointed hour, Kassie strode through the lobby. Her knees shook ever so slightly, not so anyone but she would notice. Her left foot quivered, sending her a message. *Take one step at a time.*

Out on the sidewalk, she counted five cars. Four vehicles had a chauffeur standing guard, waiting to open the back door for their client. At the far end of the line, two men were situated beside a gunmetal-gray sedan. Perhaps a Peugeot. She wasn't sure.

The taller of the two said something to the other, pointed to Kassie, and stepped in her direction. She looked away, tilting her head down slightly. She didn't want him to see her grinning. She could've walked toward him, met him halfway, but she froze in place.

Let him come to you.

Enjoying the cool September evening air, Kassie gazed his way, seeing Matthias Gataki as if for the first time. With each of his long strides, she consumed him totally from bottom to top. Black penny loafers. Well shined. Gray slacks. Just as relaxed as he seemed to be. His crisp white shirt, tieless and opened at the collar, made a statement of its own. He ran the fingers of his left hand through his dark, elegantly damp hair. As he neared, he leisurely removed his aviator sunglasses, tucking them inside his tailored black blazer. His face reminded her of a Greek god, but softer.

"You're a vision," he said. He leaned in and air kissed both cheeks. "Madame, shall we?" He offered her his arm.

She stepped forward. Her ankle swerved. Her heart swelled as if she'd been resuscitated.

Still determined to maintain some semblance of a business dinner, Kassie played tourist as they drove through the streets of Paris to his restaurant of choice. He complied as best he could, reminding her that Greece was his home. He was, in fact, as much a visitor to Paris as she was.

She mentioned she planned to visit Notre-Dame on Saturday, half wishing he'd suggest tagging along.

"I'm flying home tomorrow."

Not a date. Keep telling yourself.

They arrived at Boisclair de Paris just in time, saving her from the embarrassment of trying to explain her reference to Saturday. Whatever line she could've come up with would've been a lie.

The hostess greeted Monsieur Gataki as if they were old friends, showing them to his "usual table" in a quiet corner, away from the flow of servers and food carts. As they sat side by side, he explained the menu was fixed. Was that okay with her? Though she wasn't quite sure what a fixed menu was, she went with the flow.

"That's good. Otherwise, I'll call my driver, and we'll go someplace else more to your liking. Now, for the wine."

"White," she said, after learning she'd be having crab as an appetizer, lamb with some kind of cheese concoction for the main course, and dacquoise for dessert.

He ordered a Bordeaux *blanc* from a winery she'd never heard of.

"Not from Vin Pour Toujours? Or your winery, Monsieur Gataki?"

"I thought we decided you'd call me Matt. *Oui*? If I can call you Kassie, you can call me Matt."

"About that …" Kassie grabbed the opportunity to solve the *mademoiselle* and *madame* dilemma. "My husband died a few months ago, so I don't know if I'm a mademoiselle or madame."

Matt said he was sorry for her loss, shifted in his seat, and smiled delicately. He explained the history of the two courtesies and how *madame* had evolved as the more commonly used title.

"Unless you want to be a *mademoiselle*?" He winked, his thin lips curving upward.

Realizing she'd gotten it all wrong for so long, Kassie shifted in her seat, her bottom bumping into his. Neither of them moved.

Over the crab with lime appetizer—the size of which would be scoffed at back in the States, especially Boston or even Baltimore, where a crab dish is served more on a platter than a six-inch piece of delicate china—Kassie focused the conversation on the merger.

Matt reiterated his offer of an offsite at his winery in Greece. "Soon. You should come soon. We'll be harvesting our grapes. You can help."

How did early October sound? She noticed him close both fists and give them one sharp shake as he said, "Perfect."

Over the main course—consisting of one lamb chop the size of which could fit in the palm of a baby's hand and a half dozen haricot verts that were added more for their green color than sustenance—Matt informed her the cheese in the dish was *mizithra*, a Greek cheese made from sheep's milk. He said it brought harmony to the meal. Kassie took a taste and said, "Perfect."

She turned the conversation to his business ventures—Vin Pour Toujours and Gataki Winery—as the server uncorked a second bottle of wine. Her Google search the night before provided a Wikipedia summary of Matthias Gataki. He'd inherited the family winery when he was thirty-five. Over the twenty-five years or so, he'd grown it to be one of the premier, award-winning brands in Greece. Though she knew this much and more, she wanted to listen to him tell the story.

His deep, throaty tone and the raspy expression in his voice mesmerized her. Obviously, multilingual, he often spoke fast, slowing down at times, perhaps in search of the right English word. She couldn't put her finger on it. Was it Italian mixed with Spanish? Whatever it was, his accent was yummy.

Kassie picked at the dessert.

"You don't like the dessert?" he asked.

"Oh, this is my first duck-was," she said proudly. "I want to savor it." Actually, she was trying to drag out the dinner as long as possible.

Matt appeared to be in a rush. He waved a high sign to the server and signed the bill, while simultaneously giving her a bulleted synopsis of his family's history that mirrored what she'd read online.

"I'll tell you the rest of the story when you come to Katakolon. In fact, for you, Kassie, a private tour."

He rose to his feet, lifted her hand. "Now, how do you Americans say it? Let's blow this joint."

Kassie didn't know how he did it, but the car and chauffeur were already waiting out front. He hadn't asked for her address, so she figured he'd take her back to the office. After all, it was a "school night" for her, and he was heading home the next day. And it was not a date.

"Oh, Matt. I should've thanked you sooner for your very thoughtful gift." She realized neither of them had mentioned the first aid kit.

"How is that toe of yours?"

She laughed, not really wanting to go there, and was saved as the car stopped and the chauffeur and Matt got out. Kassie peered out the window, not recognizing anything. They certainly weren't in the business district of town. It looked more like a cozy neighborhood.

Matt opened her door, leaned in, reached for her hand. "Time for one more?"

He ushered her into a small bar that reminded her of the pubs in Venice. Chris's face flashed through her mind; she pushed it aside. This was Paris. A side of Paris that was new to her. In fact, everything she experienced that evening was new, and she didn't want it to end.

And this was Matt.

Inside the dimly lit bar, there were four individual highboy tables, each with two chairs. The first two tables were taken with couples easily twenty years younger than they were. As she followed him to the last one, Kassie saw him slip the proprietor what looked to be a fifty euro note. Promptly, the third table was moved to the side, and its two chairs were whisked away to parts unknown. On his own, Matt shifted what would be their table an additional three feet away from the other couples.

Kassie stared at the chair. *How in God's name will I get up there?*

"Let me help," Matt said, to the rescue.

They sat across from each other and sipped Grand Marnier for the next two magical hours, their faces nearly touching. His tender-looking mouth gave her X-rated ideas, and his slightly crooked nose suggested an underlying story she looked forward to hearing about sometime in the future, if there was a next time.

He asked about her late husband. She asked about his late wife. Through the low lights, her eyes traced strands of dark and slightly gray hair that swept across his forehead. His eyes were mournful as he spoke of the decades he'd been happily married and then brightened as he told her about his son and daughter.

"They're minding the winery while I'm here having an unforgettable evening with an unforgettable woman."

She rolled her eyes but embraced the compliment.

Kassie mentioned she too had competent staff managing the business she inherited from her husband, but she didn't expound on it.

"Children. Do you have children?"

"No," she whispered.

He touched her cheek. "You're warm."

"Grand Marnier." She sensed she was blushing. *Blushing! Fuck! I haven't blushed since—? Don't go there, Kassie.*

Instead, she talked about her father, the policeman, who died way too young. But whom she loved very much. And of her mother, who'd died after too long of an illness and who continued to haunt her. She ran her fingers over the necklace and tugged her right earlobe.

"I'm waiting for her to arrive here in Paris. Do they give visas to ghosts?"

They laughed so loud, the couple nearest them stopped their tête-à-tête and looked their way. Matt said he always thought Gataki Winery had its own resident ghosts. "You can hunt for them when you visit. We'll do it together. How's that?"

He asked about her career and how she came to land the Paris assignment? She told him how she'd climbed the corporate ladder and how Mimi's pregnancy was the pot of gold at the end of the rainbow.

"Don't be so sure."

"What's that supposed to mean?"

"It may not be the end."

What it was, though, was the end of a truly lovely evening. Almost the end, anyway. She gave him her address, which he conveyed to the driver. The silence in the back seat said it all. They looked at each other, then turned away and gazed out the window.

He rested his palm on her left hand. She didn't pull away.

She fumbled through her purse for her keys as they walked through the courtyard. Her fingers jarred her phone to life. She could see a message was waiting. *Let him wait.*

At the door, Matt lifted her left hand and kissed the back of her palm. He paused.

She waved her engagement ring; tears formed.

"Engaged?"

"*Oui.* But not married."

46

Girl Talk

Kassie pulled the largest tumbler out of the kitchen cabinet and filled it with ice-cold water. Once she wiggled out of her dress, she folded it and placed it on a chair in the living room. There must be a dry cleaner nearby. She stripped and put on her comfiest Red Sox oversized T-shirt, which doubled as a nightgown.

She peered into the bathroom mirror. Closely. She opened her eyes as wide as possible, willing the booze to relocate itself. Preferably outside of her body. As she brushed her teeth, she figured it was close to midnight, which meant Chris should be getting home from the office right about then. Before calling him, she'd listen to his message. Hear what he had to say about not attending the management meeting earlier that day.

Sitting cross-legged on the living room floor, she found the incoming message. Not from Chris. She frowned. From Annie, saying she was just checking in. She washed down her disappointment with a large gulp of water. How had everything with Chris gotten so goddam complicated?

Hi Annie, you home?

Yup. Just feeding your cat.

Up for a Zoom session?

Who? Me or Topher?

Both.

Cool. Give me five.

That gave Kassie time to refill her water glass and curl up under the covers with her computer balanced on her lap.

There was a pause between the time Kassie saw Annie on the screen and their mutual hellos, reminding her of how far away they were.

"Say hi to mama," Annie said, tilting her screen to include Topher.

"Hey baby, I miss you."

He lifted his head and inched his whiskers closer to the screen.

"What's that humming? Is that him purring?"

Annie confirmed and shifted a bit, so she was now centered. "Isn't it late over there? You could've just texted."

"We need to talk."

"We? Or you?"

"Me. To you, asshole."

"What's up?"

"He stood me up."

"Who stood you up? That guy you met? What's his name? You can't trust those Greek sex gods. I could've told you that."

"No, not him. Chris. We had a Ricci and Son management meeting scheduled for today, and he was AWL."

"AWL? Absent without leave? Come on, Kassie, he's not in the military."

"How about absent with Lexi?"

Kassie could see Annie lift a wineglass.

"And you know that how?"

Kassie reiterated her conversation with Bill, Cecilia, and Leo. "The gang was all there *sans un.*"

Annie begged her to keep her exceptional grasp of the French language to a minimum. "I thought Karen had volunteered to shuttle Lexi around?"

"Me too. What's worse is that I had to hear it from Bill. Chris didn't have the decency either on a personal or professional level to let me know he wouldn't be there. And, Annie, we haven't touched base with each other since Sunday."

"I think you could use a cookie." Annie displayed one Kassie assumed came from the batch she baked on Monday.

"I need more than a cookie. This is way more complicated than I ever thought it could be."

"How so?"

Kassie grunted. "Don't play games. You, of all people, have shared this roller-coaster ride with me."

"Enlighten me."

"Really, Annie? You knew my initial affair with Chris was a much-needed distraction from my highly dysfunctional marriage to Mike."

Annie said she thought she was getting a bit dramatic, especially because she eventually fell in love with Chris.

"Dramatic? How about when I suddenly became Chris's stepmother? And then you cooked up that scheme for him to show up in Venice, whisk me away here to Paris, so he could ask me to marry him?"

Annie licked her index finger and crooked it, making the number one sign.

"No one's winning here. I'm losing. I've been losing fucking forever."

"I'm sorry, Kassie. I know it's not funny, but you are engaged. There is that."

Kassie snorted. "And how long did that happily ever after last? A week or two until we discovered Chris needed a lesson in birth control? He's in his forties, for God's sake."

Annie placed her fist over her mouth, giving Kassie more air space to continue on her rant.

"I don't think I can do this, Annie. I can't be his wife, step-mother to his kids, and his boss all at the same time."

"Did you stop to consider all this from Chris's perspective?"

"I'm beginning to. I've only been away a week, and I think it's over between us."

"How can you be so sure?"

Kassie slid the engagement ring off her finger and held it in front of the camera. "See this? It's a sign of all signs. Today was the first day I've worn it all week. And you know why I put it on today?"

"Do tell."

"So Chris would see it during the Zoom meeting and think we were all good."

"A cover-up?"

"Precisely. And I kind of did the same thing tonight. I didn't want to give Matt any idea I was free and available."

"Matt, eh? And how did that go?"

"It *was* a date, Annie."

Kassie recounted the day and the evening. The first aid kit. The chauffeured car. The strange fixed-menu dinner where it was all business. And then how her world shifted off its axis in a tiny, dark neighborhood bar as they dropped their masks and shared their inner selves.

"He wanted to know all about me, Annie. Me. Who I am. My upbringing. Why I'm here. He even called me a *vision* and said I'm *unforgettable*."

"Did you sleep with him?"

"Christ, Annie, no! If I did, I wouldn't be sitting here in my Red Sox shirt talking to you. Anyway, I'm still engaged."

"Did you tell *him* that?"

Kassie nodded. "But speaking of sleep. I've gotta get six hours to be awake, alive, and enthusiastic in the morning. Later, gator." She blew Annie a kiss and scrolled toward the red Leave button.

"Looks like your mama found what she was looking for."

"I heard that."

47

Listicle

I do declare! If there are fifty ways to leave your lover, I may be about to make it fifty-one.

Kassie watched the Paris landscape fall away as the plane climbed toward its cruising altitude. She never imagined she'd return to Boston just two weeks after she left. But she had a job to do, a message to deliver, and face-to-face was her only option.

Sitting in coach, since this trip was on her dime, she found her purple Moleskin notebook and pen in her bag and started the most important list of her life.

Think before you speak. *She vowed to keep Bad Kassie under wraps.*

Honesty, decency, the right thing. *Anger had driven her to tell Mike she wanted a divorce. This was not anger.*

It's not you, it's me. *Scratch that. If not for Lexi, would their relationship have deteriorated?*

Kassie glanced up, put her pen down, and reached for the tea the flight attendant delivered. As the tea cooled, she gazed out the window. They were above the clouds now. She needed to remain grounded in the reality that everything changed with Lexi. Too much happened after she arrived for either Kassie or Chris to grasp what it all meant.

Yet, her time in Paris, however short, broadened her perspective.

For one thing, Mimi delivered her twins. The morning after Kassie's dinner with Matt, pink and blue balloons arrived at the office. A few minutes later, Mimi's husband swooped in with news that mother and children were doing fine. He showed pictures of his new little son and daughter that Patricia immediately tacked to a bulletin board in the break room for everyone to check out at their leisure. If that weren't enough hoopla, small groups gathered round as he scrolled through his phone for even more evidence that his children were the most beautiful newborns the world had ever seen.

Being the new kid on the block, Kassie hung back and watched as it all played out. A spectator, perhaps, but an interested party just the same as she viewed the scene as coming attractions. She imagined Chris proudly introducing his twins to the Ricci and Son's staff. What color would his balloons be? Where would she be when he held his and Lexi's babies for the first time? Home alone?

Three's a crowd. Five is impossible.

Put yourself in his position, Annie had said.

She started by calling him that Friday night, the day after he was AWL. He sounded off-balance when he answered, though she wasn't sure if it was surprise or a guilty conscience. They danced around one another for a while until she asked him point blank why he wasn't at the meeting.

"You are a senior manager, and that meeting had been scheduled for weeks. The least you could've done …" She stopped there, unsure whether it was Kassie, the spurned boss, or Kassie the jealous fiancée scolding him. So she backed off on the inquisition.

Conflicting roles: fiancée, boss, stepmother.

He apologized but said there was good news. "Lexi's cast comes off early next week. Then physical therapy for a time." And yes, Karen would help with those visits until Lexi could drive.

But he had bad news too. "All bets are off with Aunt Venus. Lexi and the kids won't be moving into her house, even while she's gone on the Great Art Hunt."

Kassie's heart sank to her knees. "How come?"

"Sonny and Cher."

"Excuse me?"

"They're her precious cats. She refuses to board them. Even for Lexi."

Kassie prepared for Chris to drop the other shoe, which of course, he did, without giving her an opportunity to respond to the weird cat names.

"Lexi's decided to stay around Boston. She's been in touch with her company. They're setting her up to work remotely. Computer, printer, Wi-Fi, the whole bit. Brilliant concept, eh?"

"The wave of the future," Kassie said. "Where will she live? She'll need two bedrooms soon."

"Shouldn't be a problem. Karen and I have already started helping her search for places."

"And you're okay with that?" Kassie at least expected a momentary pause as he interpreted the full meaning of her question. It never came.

"I'm thrilled."

He deserves to be happy.

When it was her turn, Kassie mentioned her bruised toe and the funny first aid kit. She had little else to share with him. He didn't seem interested in how things were going with the merger, in her team, or in her.

"Tanya and I are good buddies now. We're off to Notre-Dame tomorrow." She thought at least the mention of his good pal Tanya would pique his interest.

"Have a great time," he said. "*Au revoir.*"

"Goodbye," she said.

I deserve to be happy.

The Monday after their conversation, she'd received a wrapped package at the office. A book. *Haunted Wineries of Europe.* The card read: *Casper, to the rescue.* Her right eye twitched, but she paid no mind to it.

Soon after she arrived at the apartment after work on Tuesday, a courier knocked at her door, carrying a dozen red roses. The card read simply: *Unforgettable.* Before slipping under the covers that night, she booked a flight to Logan for Friday morning.

Aspects of the merger consumed Kassie on Wednesday and Thursday. She'd assigned Patricia the task of organizing the offsite with Monsieur Gataki's daughter with the promise that Patricia would be part of it. They zeroed in on the first weekend in October. Still fine weather, fewer tourists.

That gave her just over two weeks after her trip to Boston to decide what she wanted her personal agenda to be when she met Matt in Greece on his home turf. That she fell asleep each night since their dinner fantasizing what it would be like to make love to him was a huge clue that breaking up with Chris was as much about her as it was about him.

Before she left the office Thursday evening, a small package arrived. This time, she didn't have to look for a card. She told Matt she was flying back to Boston for a long weekend but didn't explain why.

The small, elongated blue box with a white bow, clearly from Tiffany's, contained an owl pendant and chain. The card inside described it as an Athenian Coin Gold Necklace. Matt's message read, "*Because you can see what others cannot.*" She debated wearing it back home but decided to keep Matt's gift safely in the box in her carry-on. His words etched in her mind were enough to keep her focused on her mission.

"What did you tell Chris?" Annie asked as they pulled out of Logan Airport's parking lot. "Did you tell him about *Miss-your* Gataki?"

"No, I did not." Kassie shook her head. "There's nothing to tell."

"Yet."

"Okay, not yet. Maybe never. I don't know! I just told Chris I needed to see him."

"He must figure something's up."

Kassie nodded. She brought Annie up to speed about Lexi's cast and Sonny and Cher, Aunt Venus's cats.

"I bet there's a story behind those names," Annie said.

"Whatever. The story is that Lexi's not moving back to San Francisco. She's gonna make a home for her and the kids somewhere around here. To be near their father."

"Why am I not surprised? You're doing the right thing, you know."

On the way to Kassie's house, they stopped at Whole Foods so she could pick up some prepared meals. Cooking dinner for her and Chris after a long flight was not on her agenda. While she poked around, she lost Annie to the wine aisle.

"You better buy some."

"Ya think?" Kassie veered toward the French wine. She chose two bottles, then moved to the section labeled *Greece*. Together, her eyes and fingers grazed the top shelf, all the way to the bottom. She spotted what she was looking for and handed Annie two bottles to add to the cart.

Annie read the label. "You really gonna do this?"

48

Lost and Found

The house was empty. Kassie struggled between relief and disappointment that Chris wasn't there with open arms. Perhaps another sign it was time for them to move on.

It seemed strange to Kassie to be there again. She'd programmed her mind to a temporary life in Paris and had little time to settle there. She hugged Annie goodbye and promised to call her, after. Then she unloaded the groceries, put the wine in the fridge, and walked through the house.

Everything looked spic and span. Teresa's expert touch showed. Must be easier for her with Topher living with Annie.

Kassie's Spidey-sense kicked in. She wasn't sure what she was looking for. She'd know it when she found it.

She hauled her carry-on up to the bedroom. Nothing unusual there. She showered, covered herself with the white terry robe Chris had given her, and then texted him that she was home. Dinner was on her, compliments of Whole Foods, of course.

When can I expect you?

Four-ish.

That gave her three hours to do what? Not enough time to drive up to the Newburyport cemetery to visit her mother and Mike. She really didn't need to do that. They were right there with her in spirit. Of that, she was confident.

Perhaps she'd bury herself in a book from the to-be-read pile she'd left behind.

She scanned the bookshelves in both the family and living rooms. Nothing caught her eye. Surely, the bookcase in her office would have something to occupy her mind until Chris came home. She flipped on the overhead light and started toward the bookcase. The light flickered. Out of the corner of her eye, she spotted a picture frame in the middle of the desk blotter. Upside down.

Topher.

If thoughts could kill. She hung onto her favorite photo of him and searched for a murder mystery. Perhaps something by Agatha Christie.

Kassie jumped. *The Body in the Library* tumbled to the floor.

"It's just me, KO. I'm home."

Chris's fingers loosened her belt.

"Oh, hi. I didn't hear you come in." She sat up and tightened the belt. "I must've fallen asleep. Long day. It must be twenty-two hundred hours."

"Come on now. Don't give me that crap. You're not in Paris." Chris sneered and walked away.

She followed him into the kitchen, determined not to argue. "You hungry? I'm starved. Past my dinnertime."

Chris said he'd eaten an early lunch so he could go for something.

"You grab the plates, I'll get the food."

Standing in front of the microwave exchanging a carton of chicken marsala for a carton of green beans, she felt Chris approach her and nuzzle her neck. She turned, kissed him quickly, and handed him a bowl of scalloped potatoes.

"Wine?" he asked.

"In the fridge. I bought two kinds."

He pulled out one bottle and held it up to the light. "Vin Pour Toujours. Something you and Tanya discovered?"

"Nope. A client." Kassie was about to tell Chris it was the first Calibri-Paris client she met when he retrieved the other bottle she bought.

He held it at arm's length. She watched his eyes blink.

"What? You don't like Greek wine?" she asked.

"I do. It's not that. I think I've had this before. Gataki Winery. Hmm." He scratched his head, slid it back in the refrigerator, and uncorked the Vin Pour Toujours.

While they ate, Chris asked if she'd been following the Red Sox. She said she had, but with the time difference, it was difficult to catch the games online in real time. Had he gone to any games while she was gone? He said no, that with Mike gone and her in Paris, managing the office was more than a day job for him and Bill. Chris opened the door for a discussion about the business, but she elected not to walk through it as the warm-up act for the main event.

"Why are you here?" Chris said as he cleared the table. "Obviously, it's not cause you miss me. You barely kissed me." He slammed the dishwasher door so hard it locked.

Kassie jumped up. "I'll be right back." She returned with Topher's picture.

"Oh my God, did Topher die? Why didn't Annie call me?"

Think fast. This was not in the plan. Where's my list? Fuck. Upstairs in the bedroom.

Out of her sight. Out of her mind. Kassie was flying solo. List-less.

"Why don't we go sit on the porch?" Kassie said, pushing past him toward the family room and through the French doors.

Chris emptied the remaining wine between them and followed close behind. He handed her a glass as they both settled down on the porch swing.

"I've been here before," she said. It was as good an opening as any. "Mike and I got stoned out here the night I served him divorce papers."

"You want to get stoned? You flew here from Paris to get stoned?"

She reached for his hand. How was it he focused on the first part of that remark and not the second?

"No, I flew here to tell you I want a divorce."

"But, we're not …"

Kassie raised her eyebrows.

"Oh, I see."

"I'm sorry, Chris. Being away in Paris, away from you and this insane predicament we've found ourselves in, made me realize I can't do this. I can't be your wife, a stepmother, and your boss. Please, please understand."

He downed his drink and refilled his glass. "Is this because of what my mother said?"

"No, Sarah has nothing to do with this. Wait? How did you find out? Did Annie tell you?"

"Yes. You should know I had words with Sarah. I warned her to butt out of our affairs."

Kassie grunted. "Affairs. Good word choice. Maybe we were better for each other before we decided to get married. That happens to some couples, ya know?"

Chris gazed across the backyard. She wasn't sure he bought her thesis.

"I know it seems weird at my age," she said, "but I'm just beginning to discover who I am, what I want. I spent most of my life focused on either caring for my mother or Mike. Doing what they wanted. Always changing my goals so I could be who they wanted me to be."

Chris lifted his eyes. "I wanted to marry you, not change you."

"But don't you see? Being your wife would change me. I'd also be stepmother to your children. It's not the change I'm looking for."

"You always wanted kids."

"My kids. Not Lexi's."

She let that sink in.

"She's been here while I've been away, hasn't she? Topher's picture? I found it face down in the middle of my desk."

"You don't know Lexi did that. It could've been—"

Kassie shot him a you're-shittin'-me look. She wouldn't let him bring her mother into this. "No one else would've done that, and you know it."

"That's not a crime."

"To me it is. She's sending me a message. There was a time, a brief time, when I thought Lexi and I could mend fences. Now, I'm not so sure we can, or that we should."

"She was here only once. She was cooped up in that apartment day after day. We came here for dinner. We ordered in. Nothing happened."

"No need to explain. You should be free to do whatever you want without thinking you're hiding from me or anyone else."

He inhaled and let out an enormous sigh.

She got off the swing, tightened her robe, and paced back and forth. She told him that Mimi had her twins and about how her husband pranced around the office like a peacock.

"I love you so much. I want you to have a moment like that. You deserve to buy dozens of balloons," she said as she flung her hands in the air. She bent down, lifted his chin. "And fill your phone with first steps, first teeth, first smiles."

Tears filled their eyes.

"And if I'm around when all of those once-in-a-lifetime events happen for you and for Lexi, I won't survive. I'll die inside. And so would our marriage. One photo. One tooth. One smile at a time."

Kassie slumped onto the swing and leaned into him. She welcomed his arms around her, the arms she'd forever crave. Should she open her robe to him one last time?

His phone pinged. "It's Lexi."

Chris carried his phone into the house. Kassie lingered on the swing, wondering if that's all there was. Moments later, he returned with fresh glasses, a corkscrew, and the Gataki wine. He placed them on a side table.

"I remember now. Lexi and I had this wine the last night we were in Santorini."

"The night she got pregnant?"

"Could be."

"Maybe it's a magical potion?"

He reached for Kassie's hands, lifting her to her feet. He hugged her, then pushed her up against the siding, pinning his body to hers.

"You sure you're not up for breakup sex?" he whispered.

"Go. Go to Lexi. She'll be lost without you."

Once more they kissed as new lovers kiss, and he left.

Alone with her thoughts, she detected a little laugh bubbling up from inside her pounding chest. When her pulse settled down, she brought everything inside, setting both bottles of Gataki wine on the kitchen counter next to her car keys.

Kassandra O'Callaghan changed and then called her BFF.

"Hi, Annie. Can I come over? There's someone I want you to meet."

Epilogue

During the year after the Boston Red Sox became World Series champions again, Kassie found what was missing in her life: Kassandra O'Callaghan.

But the journey to find herself was filled with highs as glorious as Mount Olympus and with lows as grave as the catacombs under Notre-Dame.

Merger became her watchword. When someone asked, "How's the merger going?" Kassie had to stop and consider the question in the context of who was asking.

In October, far, far away from Fenway Park, in a Greek seaside town named Katakolon, the Calibri-Paris and E. Z. Media offsite unified the teams and solidified their mission just as she had predicted they would. Kassie had engaged an executive development consultant with over twenty years' experience with mergers. With team-building exercises held one morning at ancient Olympia (where the Olympic Games began in 776 B.C.), an afternoon sail on the Ionian Sea, and an evening tour of Gataki Winery (including dinner and music under the trees), the two teams emerged as one. How could they not? They had Greek gods on their side. Pleased by Kassie's success, the Calibri board in Boston checked that merger off their to-do list and moved on. Apparently.

At about the same time, Lexi settled into a two-bedroom flat in a newly renovated building across from the apartment in Charlestown. Wouldn't you know, her obstetrician ordered bed-rest? Not uncommon with twins. Catering to her needs, Chris missed more than one biweekly Zoom meeting with Bill and Kassie, for which she gave him more than a little slack. She hoped after the twins were born in January, he'd switch gears and dedicate as much time to Ricci and Son as he did to his own sons. But as it turned out, fatherhood consumed most of his time, further vali-dating Kassie's decision to break things off with him.

In late March, she received a text message from Karen, of all people.

FaceTime me at six tonight. My time.

As she clutched her pink necklace, Karen thanked Kassie for promoting her to junior account executive, and then she dropped a bombshell. Cecilia had overheard a conversation between Bill and his son, Leo. Not knowing who else to turn to with Chris in absen-tia (Cecilia's word, not Karen's) much of the time, Cecilia confided in Karen. With the European merger in the books, Calibri turned their attention to gobbling up smaller domestic firms. Ricci and Son being their latest target. Bill Mahoney, their inside man.

Nothing like a little palace intrigue to bring Chris and Kassie back together. Not romantically. But for the good of the firm; for the legacy of one Michael Ricci.

A few days later, Chris picked Kassie up at Logan and swung by Charlestown before heading to her house to strategize. She wanted to see his sons. To hold them. Lexi beamed as she showed Kassie the Meander necklace Chris had given her after the twins were born. "See, we'll always have Greece in common," Lexi said. Kassie graciously agreed, wishing mother and father the best. With a tear in her eye, she gave Lexi an honest-to-goodness warm squeeze.

Closure number one accomplished.

The next morning, Kassie and Chris pulled into the Ricci and Son parking lot at the uncivilized hour of seven thirty. The only car there was Bill's. Chris had said they needed to talk. Wasn't a lie. But the *they* was him and Kassie. She could've said, "You're fired," but this was no joke, no reality show. Instead, she handed Bill a nice-sized check and told him there would soon be an opening at Calibri Marketing Group he might want to look into.

Closure number two accomplished.

Kassie drove alone across the bridge from Cambridge to downtown Boston, marched into her manager's office at Calibri and said, "*Au revoir. Sayonara.* So long, farewell. You know what you can do with this job." She conferred with Mimi ahead of time. With no questions asked, Mimi agreed to cut her maternity leave short. She was excited to get back in the saddle again at the expanded Calibri-Paris.

Closure number three accomplished.

Before leaving Boston, Kassie and Chris announced the name of the firm would not change. Ricci and Son would endure with Kassie the majority owner and Chris as president. He committed to managing the company's day-to-day affairs as long as she wanted to stay abroad.

Kassie arrived back in Paris on April 14. Though it wasn't needed, Tanya's sign was correct this time. They became such close friends touring Paris, Kassie had no qualms filling her in on her adventures back home. Whether Chris had asked Lexi to marry him yet seemed to be Tanya's most pressing question.

"You really like him, don't you?" Kassie said.

"Yuppers."

"So do I." She exhaled. "By the way, there's no ring on her finger. Not yet, anyway."

The next afternoon, after catching up on some much-needed shut-eye, Kassie packed her company laptop and phone and rode the *métro* to Calibri-Paris. Patricia helped pack up her belongings, including her cherished first aid kit, and marked the boxes to be delivered to her apartment. Kassie addressed the staff for the last time, thanking them for a job well done. Just after eighteen hundred hours, she waved to the security guard and exited the building for the last time.

Kassie paused on the sidewalk and closed her eyes. She paid homage to the people who altered her life. *Mimi, Patricia, Tanya.* Screaming sirens interrupted her adding Matt to the list. Parisians rushed past her through the streets toward the Île de la Cité. She pushed her way into a corner café mobbed with people all trying to find out what the commotion was about. They could see it on the television screen, but everyone emptied into the street crying, praying. Notre-Dame was on fire. No words, French or English, could ever describe the horror of the orange flame and smoke billowing into the evening sky. Later that night, President Emmanuel Macron pledged to rebuild, saying, "Notre-Dame is our history, our literature, our imagination … the epicenter of our life."

Kassie waited until she made it back to the apartment to check her phone, which buzzed non-stop. Her entire contact list had either texted or called. Her hands shook as she scrolled through the texts and read the message from the one person most central to her life.

Pack up. I'll be there tomorrow.

In the six months since the offsite in October, Matt and Kassie alternated visits between Paris and Katakolon. When in Paris, they played tourist, with occasional wine tours of competitors close to the city. When in Katakolon, she and Matt strolled the grounds among the sweet, sensual jasmine and oleander, as he tutored her personally about the one-hundred-and-twenty-five-year history of the winery. His son taught her about harvesting grapes and the wine-making process. His daughter steadied ladders so Kassie could pick olives. In the evening, the entire family gathered on the stone patio to make plans to renovate their modest hotel so they could offer more corporate meetings like the offsite.

Kassie's big contribution to the plan was to restructure the entrance to include a library stocked with books in many languages. She knew publishers who would be more than delighted to help them fill their bookshelves.

Once, Matt suggested a weekend in Venice, but she couldn't go there. Not just yet, anyway. Perhaps in a year or so. Too many memories of Chris. So, they sailed around the Greek islands on his private yacht, which he'd renamed *Casper*. She smiled with contentment. A childhood memory of her father finally connected the dots.

Kassie had never quite spent a whole springtime in Paris, but she wouldn't trade Katakolon or Matthias Gataki for the world. She'd found the true meaning of bliss.

After she settled in his home on the Gataki estate, Kassie agreed with Chris it was time to offload the house back in Boston. If she'd make arrangements with a real estate agent, he'd take care of selling the furniture and storing anything personal until she was ready to handle it.

"Where will you go?" she asked with a surprise lump in her throat.

He assured her he'd find a place near the boys. He and Lexi were still a big question mark.

Even though she was neither engaged nor married now, Kassie never raised either option with Matt. Their future together was as solid as the ivy-covered stone chapel that stood opposite the winery's main building. She often wandered in there to cool off on days when temperatures hovered between ninety and a hundred. To protect her from splinters, Matt had a thick foam pad cut to fit one of the wood benches and had it covered in a light-purple fabric.

One afternoon as she sat there fanning herself with a FedEx envelope containing real estate documents and the latest Ricci and Son financial statements, she took measure of her life. Her career ambitions may have taken an unexpected path, but she was happier than she ever imagined she could be. The entire Gataki family had welcomed her as part of theirs. Who knew Matthias Gataki, a Greek man with her father's name, would complete her? But he did. Almost.

Swinging the handles of a water bottle and a plain brown shopping bag, Matt came in and sat close beside her. "What are you thinking about, my dear?"

"My old home," she said, "and my new old home." She laughed. "Wine?" She tilted her chin toward the bottle.

"No, water."

She reached for it.

"It's not for you. But this is." He tugged a multicolored afghan out of the bag.

"Where did you get that? I left it in Boston."

Matt looped the afghan over his arm and carried the water bottle. He offered her his free hand. "Come with me."

A small van had parked in the courtyard, rather than the designated parking lot for deliveries. Underneath the Greek she couldn't read were the words she did recognize: *Special Delivery*. The driver stood at the back door, fiddling with something.

"Kassandra O'Callaghan?" he shouted toward her.

"That's me." Curious, she stepped to the rear of the van.

All that Kassie had clung to fell to the cobblestone.

Topher leaped into her arms.

Where the hell have you been?

What's Not Lost Playlist
On Spotify.com

https://spoti.fi/3wtaHQZ

Access songs depicting the story on the *What's Not Lost* Playlist on Spotify.com, which is free*!

"Audition (The Fools Who Dream)," *Emma Stone*
"We Don't Talk About Bruno," *Carolina Gaitan, Mauro Castillo*
"Shape of You," *Ed Sheeran*
"Daydream Believer," *The Monkees*
"Venus," *Frankie Avalon*
"Mack the Knife," *Bobby Darin*
"Livin' On A Prayer," *Bon Jovi*
"All In Love Is Fair," *Stevie Wonder*
"Need You Now," *Lady A*
"Love Bites," *Def Leppard*
"Monday, Monday," *The Mamas & The Papas*
"Whatcha See Is Whatcha Get," *The Dramatics*
"Unforgettable," *Nat King Cole*
"Till There Was You," *The Beatles*
"50 Ways to Leave Your Lover," *Paul Simon*
"There's A Place," *The Beatles*
"Audition (The Fools Who Dream)," *William Goldstein, Maksim Velichkin*

*Best browsers for Spotify's Web Player are Google Chrome, Firefox, Edge, and Opera.

Book Club Discussion Guide

1. What's not lost in *What's Not Lost*?

2. Early in the story, Kassie defines happily ever after as having both a successful career and the man she loves. What happens to make Kassie redefine happiness? Does she grow along the way?

3. Should Kassie stay in Boston? If so, how would the story change?

4. In all three books in the series, Kassie struggles with motherhood issues. Now, in *What's Not Lost*, it's Chris's turn to define what it means to be a father. How does he come to terms with his father and becoming a father?

5. Lexi and Sarah are significant obstacles for Kassie. Which one is her biggest nemesis? Do you agree with Kassie's thought process on how to solve Lexi's living arrangements? Would you tell Chris of Sarah's scheme?

6. Kassie's husband, Mike, died before discovering Chris was not his son after all. How would the story change had he lived?

7. Would Chris ever leave Kassie on his own?

8. Do you agree with Kassie that she can't be all things to Chris (wife, boss, stepmother to his children)? Would she give up on Chris if Matthias Gataki doesn't arrive on the scene?

9. Who is the heroine in this story? Kassie? Cecilia? Karen?

10. George Eliot wrote, "What do we live for, if it is not to make life less difficult for each other?" How does Kassie make life less difficult for others?

11. Relationships change throughout the story. Is there a scenario that surprised you?

12. What role does Annie play in the story?

13. Neither *What's Not Said* nor *What's Not True* includes a prologue or epilogue. What do you think of them as devices in telling this story?

14. Who says the last line in the Epilogue?

15. This book completes the trilogy. Are you satisfied with the final ending or should the story continue?

Acknowledgments

Little did I know when I wrote *What's Not Said* that I'd planted a kernel that would ultimately grow into a series. To be honest, all of this would've never happened without Ayse McCarthy, Lyn Englehartson, and Vicki Crumpacker. I'm eternally grateful to each of you for your faith in me and for motivating me to write the sequel, *What's Not True*, and then this, the final installment in the trilogy, *What's Not Lost*.

To my granddaughter, Cecilia—my not-so-silent collaborator in this journey—always know you are the reason I throw back my covers each morning to start my day. Your constant needling me about book titles, cover images and colors, and what your namesake is up to challenges me to think out-of-the-box. Watching you grow keeps me grounded and focused on what's important in life.

I'm especially indebted to Melanie Olson, a member of the Women's University Club of Seattle, Washington, book club. Your ideas influenced this story's path, and I thank you for sharing your creative thinking with me.

While the Gataki Winery in the story is fictional, the spectacularly beautiful Mercouri Estates winery in Katakolon, Greece, inspired me to conclude my trilogy there. Having visited the winery off a cruise in 2019, I enjoyed the superb Mercouri wines and stunning landscape first hand. The vineyard and its history are well worth visiting on your next trip to Greece. And when you're there, tell Dimitris Kanellakopoulos you learned about Mercouri Estates by reading *What's Not Lost*.

It is true that writing a novel is a solo endeavor. Yet once drafted, it takes a village to breathe life into the manuscript. I'm fortunate to have ongoing professional relationships with many talented and generous people and organizations. I'm continually grateful to Brooke Warner, She Writes Press; Meryl Moss, Meryl Moss Media; and Jim Alkon, BookTrib. I could not have produced and published *What's Not Lost* without Sara Walker, my editor; Tabitha Lahr, cover designer; Danna Mathias Steele, book designer; and Allen Tarasovic, logo designer. I'm privileged to be supported by and associated with many authors, influencers, and marketing gurus, including Suzy Leopold, Lauren Carr, Heather Skinner, Pia Ledina, Libby Jordan, and the entire She Writes Press community of award-winning authors.

To my friends and family, especially Lindsay and William, my daughter and son, thank you for your patience and encouragement as I pursue this second career. I must warn you. While the *What's Not* series has reached its conclusion, a new cozy mystery series is blossoming.

And, to you *dear readers*, I humbly thank you for taking the time to read my story and for all your support. Not sure what I'd be doing without you!

Author's Note

If you enjoyed *What's Not Lost*, please spread the word to your friends. Your honest review on sites such as BookBub, Goodreads, Barnes and Noble, and Amazon would be greatly appreciated.

You can reach me at: https://www.valerietaylorauthor.com. And follow me on social media at:

Facebook.com/valerietaylorauthor
Twitter @ValerieEMTaylor
Instagram @ValerieETaylor

Finally, I invite you to join me in my writer's journey by subscribing to my newsletter at: valerietaylorauthor.com/subscribe. I promise not to spam you!

About the Author

Author photo © *Lifetouch, Seattle, WA*

Valerie Taylor was born and raised in Stamford, Connecticut. She earned a B.S. Marketing degree and an MBA from Sacred Heart University, as well as a graduate certificate in health care administration from Simmons University (formerly Simmons College). She had a thirty-year career in the financial services industry as a marketer and writer. After her divorce, she spread her wings and relocated her career to Boston and then to Seattle. When she retired, she resettled in her home state to be near her two grown children and granddaughter. She's a member of the Westport Writer's Workshop, the Independent Book Publisher's Association, the Connecticut Authors and Publishers Association, and the Women's Fiction Writer's Association. She's a published book reviewer with BookTrib.com. She enjoys practicing tai chi and being an expert sports spectator. *What's Not Lost* completes the trilogy that began with *What's Not Said* (2020), followed by the sequel, *What's Not True* (2021). Next up? A cozy mystery series is in the works.

WWW.VALERIETAYLORAUTHOR.COM

valerietaylorauthor

@valerieemtaylor

ValerieETaylor